The emptiness expanded, blocking out stars, and continued to grow until it had reached the size of a planet's orbit—then it collapsed as suddenly as it had grown, to a tiny dark body, imperceptible except for its huge mass—a mass greater than the big sun, which had now begun to slide toward it.

Kalish recognized it as a burned-out star that would voraciously suck up anything that came too close to it. Horrified, he realized that their own suns could not withstand its pull and would eventually spiral into it. He joined hands with the crowd and cried out to the other priests in thousands of squares all over the planet, "The light modulators of Sol have stolen our suns— let us be avenged!"

The curse went out at many times the speed of light to the edges of the doomed galaxy and beyond. It was still being sent as the big sun died and as the smaller suns were devoured, until the last priest in the last square had frozen to death: *"Avenge us—avenge us—avenge us!"*

EARTH SHIP
AND STAR SONG

by

Ethan I. Shedley

FAWCETT POPULAR LIBRARY • NEW YORK

EARTH SHIP AND STAR SONG

This book contains the complete text of the original hardcover edition.

Published by Fawcett Popular Library, a unit of CBS Publications, the Consumer Publishing Division of CBS Inc., by arrangement with The Viking Press

ISBN: 0-445-04639-2

Printed in the United States of America

First Fawcett Popular Library printing: February 1981

10 9 8 7 6 5 4 3 2 1

To Mechel Beizer

I

Van Alkmeer

A rivulet of sweat started at the hollow between Grand Ecomeister Geret Van Alkmeer's shoulder blades and continued gathering drops as it trickled down his back. The smooth plastic of the bed pad on which he sat aggravated the heat, and the oily, stale air that dribbled out of the ventilator grille was a continual reminder of the machinery that struggled to maintain their lives. The lights were not yet on; last night he had again sat thinking for hours after they had been turned off.

Now he sat in the dark, contemplating the malignant situation, waiting for the lights. This day they came on schedule, after only two attempts. He rolled up the bed pad and slid it into its niche. He stood and crossed to the desk on the other side of the small room that served him as home and office. A slot in the wall on his right opened to reveal two unwrapped, tasteless biscuits and a cup of equally unappetizing protein soup

The annunciator chime sounded as he finished eating. Van Alkmeer keyed the answer switch. Wolfson's blurred, shifting image appeared on the opposite wall. "Yes, Modelmeister?" Van Alkmeer asked.

"We've just run the latest quality-of-life projections."

"And?"

"Not good. It's not good at all."

"How far out has the turning point receded this time?"

"There's no longer a turning point, Grand Ecomeister. Seven hundred years from now, on or about the year 2800, it will be all over."

"You are sure? I remember—was it five years ago?—you made some changes in the model—it predicted impending catastrophe then—and that turned out to be an error."

"I know, but this time it's different. We've had these projections for almost four months."

"Then why wasn't I told before now?"

"We had to validate the new model," Wolfson said. "The testing was finished only last night. These are the first official projections. On or about the year 2800 man will cease to exist. The quality-of-life index will go to zero. Not life as we know it, but no human life sustainable on the planet Earth."

"Has the Resourcemeister audited your results?"

"Yes. Bar Yarkon's team has been on it all along. He's satisfied that the projection is valid."

"There has always been hope in the past," Van Alkmeer said. "Now you tell me that even hope is gone. I'm not so willing to give up, though. There are probably more sacrifices to make—we can reduce the population—there are alternatives—there are always alternatives."

"This was the *optimistic* projection." Wolfson was exasperated with the old man. "The alternatives have been cranked into the equations, as have the sacrifices and the population cuts. The trend cannot be reversed. It is all over!"

"Well, it won't be over by tonight, anyway," the Ecomeister retorted. "I want you here for a meeting of the senior Meisters—at 7 p.m. And, Wolfson, I assume that you ran the projections yourself, as usual?"

"Certainly, Ecomeister."

"Good. See to it that the senior Meisters get a copy of your report—only the senior Meisters this time—and have one printed for me here." He signed off abruptly and then called his deputy, Karkii. The screen was still blurred and, worse, kept fading in and out. Karkii's image was punctured by random blips caused by the interference of the printer that was now spewing out Wolfson's report. Van Alkmeer could see that Karkii was talking, but the voice was so distorted that it could not be understood. When the printer finished, Karkii's image sharpened and his voice became intelligible.

"Did you get a copy of Wolfson's report?" Van Alkmeer asked.

"I'm reading it now." Karkii held up the page with the infamous data. "Is it another of his mistakes?"

"I don't think so. You might get hold of Bar Yarkon for the audit report."

"That's difficult. He's in Greenland on a survey."

"I want a meeting of the senior Meisters here, tonight."

"Pardon me, Grand Ecomeister, but that's probably not possible. The circuits are just not reliable enough for a conference."

"No, Karkii, I mean a face-to-face meeting. In person."

"I suppose that's possible, except for Bar Yarkon."

"Including Bar Yarkon!"

"But he's in Greenland!" Karkii repeated.

"Bring him here—it's only a few hours' trip."

"A few hours? By *jet*, you mean? But the fuel . . ." Karkii was nonplussed by the suggestion—by the profligate waste it implied. He, like everyone else, was accustomed to reckoning wasted energy as an equivalent reduction in human life-span. Bringing the Resourcemeister back from Greenland by jet was an energy debit of fifty life years—a child not to be born, or ten old men dead before their due time. He stared out of the screen, waiting for Van Alkmeer to rescind the order.

"I have faith in Wolfson's model," Van Alkmeer explained, "but it must be reviewed in detail. If there is no flaw in it, then we have some decisions to make that

9

cannot be put off It is important enough that it be done in person The communication system distorts too much We'll spend the fuel, it's no waste, considering the crisis Please have everyone here by 7 p m "

"How about Harrison?"

"Certainly! Or is he also on a trip?"

"No. He's here, but he does tend to be obstructive."

"That depends on one's point of view, Karkii. We will make decisions tonight that Harrison is to have a part in—and please see to it that he has a nontechnical summary of Wolfson's report. It's important that everyone understands it."

Karkii nodded agreement and signed off. Van Alkmeer returned to study the report. It was not the model that he distrusted, but the possibility that vital facts, however bizarre, might have been withheld from it. Much of the data on which the projections were based required human judgment—judgment that could be distorted by one or more individuals' wish to be rid of a painful and pointless existence. More than once they had seemed to be headed for oblivion, only to find a cherished, unquestionable belief that could be challenged, thereby once again averting the catastrophe.

The senior Meisters arrived at the appointed time and wordlessly sat on the floor in a circle. Techmeister Shimoza, Lifemeister Harrison, Recourcemeister Bar Yarkon, Deputy Ecomeister Karkii, and Modelmeister Wolfson were all shorter than Van Alkmeer—a fact that made him self-conscious of his height and weight and the excessive resource consumption that they represented. He was of the previous generation, born before the adoption of universal genetic selection. The face-to-face meeting intensified the difference—he was personally more comfortable using the communication system, despite its faults, but this was no time for psychic ease. He opened the meeting by recognizing Wolfson, who reviewed the quality-of-life model and briefly discussed some of the alternatives that had been used to attempt a reversal of the prediction. They all led to the same conclusion. Wolfson finished by saying, "The only assumptions that changed the trend are so exotic that they are better called miracles."

They could find no errors in the model, or evidence of the kind of thing Van Alkmeer had hoped for. Any new technological approach intended to prevent the impending ecological disaster would only increase the strain on their already precarious situation—a strain that would bring the collapse before the new technologies could have reversed the trend. It was the same with natural resources—they were abundant, but the effort required to exploit them would hasten rather than forestall their doom. "So!" Karkii said. "There are four alternatives left to us. We can continue as we are with life becoming more oppressive, more hopeless, and face death seven hundred years from now; we can remove all restrictions and go out in style by committing suicide in about twenty years or so; we can elect long-term cryosleep for a few; or we can emigrate."

"There is another alternative," Lifemeister Harrison interjected. "The Bacharan proposal!"

"The Bacharan proposal," Wolfson grumbled, "is an example of what I referred to earlier as a miracle."

"Perhaps," Van Alkmeer said, "but is it a viable option? The Lifemeister seems to think so. Conscience demands that we explore every approach, no matter how strange."

"At that rate," Shimoze objected, "we could be exploring from now until the collapse."

"Nevertheless," Van Alkmeer insisted, "few such propositions come from scientists of Bacharan's stature. I want the Techmeister to review it for us."

Shimoza was disgusted by the ineffectual old man with his vacillations and democratic ideals and, worse, with his encouragement of Lifemeister Harrison, whose responsibilities would be better handled if they were distributed to the various technical specialties—and anyhow, most of it concerned ephemeral concepts that

11

had little or nothing to do with the central issues of survival. Again, instead of making a decision, the old man had to waste hours and energy talking. It was time, Shimoza assessed, that the old man retired, and if not voluntarily and soon, then involuntarily—then there would be no more time wasted on Harrison and Bacharan and their precious idiocies.

He took the floor wearily. "Bacharan, as you know, is a theoretical physicist. His work, until a few years ago, was excellent; I cite his pioneering study of black holes as an example. More recently, though, he investigated energy along new lines. Our problem, at the root, is not a lack of energy but an excess of it in the unusable form of heat. Our ancestors' pollutants created a carbon dioxide layer in the atmosphere that now traps the sun's heat. This has raised the planet's temperature a few degrees—enough to upset the ecological balance of the oceans with a consequent reduction in free oxygen. We are in an ecological spiral that will eventually make the Earth as barren and hostile as Venus. To live we must consume more energy—for air, for food, for bearable temperatures—and the more energy we consume the worse the situation gets. What we need is a big ice cube. This is where Bacharan's theory comes in. He proved that energy could be created and, more important, destroyed. We could, if this is true, change the atmosphere, cool the oceans—in short, reverse the spiral."

"That certainly represents a hope, doesn't it?" Harrison asked.

"It does not!" Shimoza said. "Because of the methods by which he expects to achieve energy control. He claims—and this is where I begin to doubt his sanity—that all we have to do is to *stop* using energy, contemplate our navels, sing 'Hare Krishna,' pray to Allah, spin a prayer wheel, invoke the gods of Valhalla, and miraculously, in three weeks, the human race will control energy with its collective soul!"

"While in four weeks we'll be stinking in our own wastes," Karkii said.

"It does sound more like a religious cult than physics." Van Alkmeer had been only vaguely aware of the Bacharan proposal. He continued, "Wasn't the project terminated?"

"Yes," Shimoza said, "there was no point in prolonging it since it was clearly a dead end."

"I don't understand how such mysticism could have been supported. It was under your approval, Shimoza, wasn't it? Or is his theory not all that unfounded?"

"I did support it at first, because it did follow logically from classical physics and explained some things that had not been understood before. The theory is correct and productive to a point—the point at which his equations tell us to have faith and to trust the Universal Soul."

"Is that what the equations say," Van Alkmeer asked, "or is that just Bacharan's interpretation of them?"

"The interpretation is inevitable. I've checked the mathematics. If you believe his equations—the final ones, that is—then you would have to accept that interpretation. The conclusion is inescapable. It's quite clear." Shimoza's tone was apologetic over the weird turn that the research had taken.

Van Alkmeer turned to the Modelmeister. "How long could we last if we followed the Bacharan plan?"

"As Karkii said, three or four weeks," Wolfson replied.

"No. I mean—how long could we curtail our energy use without irreversible effects—could we try the plan for a few days or a few hours?"

"Every minute spent under the Bacharan proposal can be translated into several years less time for life on Earth!"

"I take it then, that the problem with Bacharan's proposal is that it forces us to take irreversible steps. If it fails, man is utterly doomed. But this is not a decision that we must make here and now—some other group of Meisters ten or twenty years from now could consider it again. By then they might be desperate

13

enough to try it, or to have better reason to believe in its success."

"That's not technically possible," Shimoza contradicted. "There's a critical mass effect. We *did* try the Bacharan proposal with an isolated group of volunteers last year. It didn't work. Nothing happened, except that they all died. Bacharan then refined the theory. He now claims that two things went wrong with the experiment—it could not work with less than a certain number of persons—a large number—and it had to be almost unanimous. Our population is now marginal, and at the present rate of decline it *will* be too small in just a few years. The choice, I'm sorry to say, is still ours."

"Does he really want us to pray?" Bar Yarkon asked.

"No. According to Bacharan," Shimoza explained, "prayer is merely one of several methods by which the proper kind of aura can be created. He says that any kind of contemplation, self-examination, and total—he emphasizes total—resignation to fate and faith that the proposal will work will do the trick."

"This is a waste of time!" Wolfson objected. "It isn't physics or even metaphysics. It's nonsense. It will turn out to be a mere curiosity— a trick problem for physics students. Our inability to discover the flaw in his garbage does not substantiate it. There's no point to continuing this discussion!"

Karkii disagreed. "You're wrong, Wolfson. There is very much of a point to continuing this discussion, but not for the reasons Harrison wants. Are you aware, Grand Ecomeister, of Bacharan's cult following?"

"It's that bad, is it?" Van Alkmeer asked.

"Right now it's a minor problem. It's still confined to free time, what little there is of it. But with the cutbacks we're going to have to institute today—I think that there's a dangerous number of persons out there who would rather be in a stupor, claiming to be a Bacharan follower, than doing their work. This proposal—this theory—is dangerous. It must be suppressed before

14

it does become a real cult." He glanced at Harrison. "The theory seems to have appeal in surprising places."

"We must face Death and welcome Him in order to be delivered from Him," Wolfson intoned.

"What was that?" Van Alkmeer asked.

"I was quoting Bacharan's latest pronouncement," Wolfson explained.

Van Alkmeer considered the proposal—the objections were emotional and cultural. There was no way of proving the validity of science—it was accepted because it worked. Technology and mysticism were both based on myths—on unquestioned and unquestionable beliefs—what worked was what mattered. Technicians such as Shimoza and Wolfson could never be convinced, no matter what the supporting evidence might be. They could never discard technology. Technology had saved them and would keep on saving them, if not on Earth, then on some other world. Yet it was that very technology that had destroyed the Earth, and it could destroy a new Earth also. He turned to Harrison. "Tell me, Lifemeister, do you believe in the Bacharan proposal?"

Harrison looked at his colleagues. How many were there in the world that could muster the faith that the proposal demanded? Would he himself, at the point of death, continue in pacific reflections, or would he, with tens of thousands of others, try to get the machines to work again? He reluctantly acknowledged that man, as presently constituted, could not carry out Bacharan's plan—even at the point of death. "I had hoped," he said at last, "that Bacharan's proposal offered dignity, that we might go out quietly and peacefully, or perhaps if it did work . . ."

"Dignity!" Karkii shouted. "It might be dignified for the first week. It will be less dignified when the temperature starts to rise. It will be least dignified in three weeks when the point of no return is reached and death is inevitable. How dignified will it be when discipline is gone? Rape? Murder? Drinking urine? People dropping in the corridors? Cannibalism? How dignified is that? Answer me, Harrison. Are you so tied up with life as you'd like it to be that you've lost all sense of human nature?"

"Are we agreed, then, that the Bacharan proposal is unworkable?" Van Alkmeer asked, breaking the prolonged silence that followed Karkii's outburst. He paused, waiting for Harrison's objection, but the Lifemeister had nothing to say. "The matter is closed then. Let's consider the other alternatives—"

"Not quite closed, Grand Ecomeister," Karkii interrupted. "There's still the cult thing. We can't afford the risk of a cult, nor the resources that would be consumed in who knows what kind of obscene rituals."

Van Alkmeer looked at the Lifemeister for a confirmation. "He's right," Harrison agreed. "The danger of resources being dissipated in a cult is real."

"Then what do you propose to do about it?" Wolfson challenged the Lifemeister.

He said nothing in response to Wolfson's demand, but stared upward, his face grim, and eventually announced quietly, "Bacharan will be recycled, his close collaborators reoriented if possible or recycled if not. Shimoza can cook up a refutation that's adequate for a layman. All references to Bacharan's theory will be suppressed and restricted to Meister level. Is that adequate?"

"Quite!" Karkii said. "Any technological objections, Shimoza?"

"None. Bacharan is of no further use. His theories cannot possibly have bearing on future technology."

"The matter is closed now," Van Alkmeer repeated, bringing them back to the main purpose of the meeting. "Let us now consider the other alternatives—a quick but glorious end, or the long slow decline—or rather, let us discuss where between these two alternatives we should go." He recognized Harrison.

"There are no morally justifiable intermediate routes. Either we elevate the quality of life for this and the next generation—with no third generation—or we maintain the status quo, following the long, slow road

16

of maximum conservation. The slow route retains a choice for future generations. With the quick route—there are no future generations. Any intermediate path curtails their freedom of choice. We have no right to do that. But neither is the quick way tenable; The population at large cannot conceive of a hedonistic life, never mind living one. That takes education and orientation. Have you ever read a poem, Karkii? Can any of you sing? Bar Yarkon, what would you do with food that you didn't need but could have just for the taste of it? The chances are that if we attempted it, while our material goods would increase, the psychic components of life quality would not improve. Other than technology, our culture exists mostly in the archives. Conservation is so totally ingrained in us that we would feel torment over any excess consumption. Instead of a glorious explosion of art, poetry, of song and happiness, we would have bitterness—a dismal end in its own way as ugly as that which Karkii postulated for the Bacharan proposal. It would take two, three, maybe more generations to change attitudes so that they could take advantage of a final dissipation of resources. I can't see this, not when it offers only death without hope."

"We've disposed of two alternatives, then," Van Alkmeer recapitulated. "I will dispose of a third. We cannot, must not, maintain the status quo. It is an avoidance of decision, not a decision. It is a hope for a miracle rather than a solution. If the only choice were between the status quo and the Bacharan proposal, I would opt for Bacharan, for there at least is a theoretical basis for a miracle."

"Then, Grand Ecomeister," Karkii observed, "your logic dictates that we rule out cryosleep also. What will cryosleep do for us but put a few thousand selected individuals into suspended animation for a million years? Will the ecology, unattended, heal itself in that time?"

"No," Wolfson anaswered, "not in a million years, but perhaps in five million—"

"Then what *does* cryosleep offer?" Harrison interrupted, siding with Karkii. "It extends the status quo—eases our consciences perhaps. Avoids the issue. And who will carry out the research to solve our problems while the selected few sleep? Or is there to be another miracle? And who will do the selection of those unlucky ones who wake, if they wake, a million years from now, cursing us? Better to stay as we are and try to solve the problem—try to find a solution that can be accepted and implemented while we still have the resources."

"By which you mean the Bacharan proposal again?" Shimoza insinuated.

"I don't know," Harrison confessed. "Perhaps energy control will be rediscovered in a more acceptable form. A form that's compatible with technological concepts rather than one that's antagonistic to them."

"We agree then," Van Alkmeer concluded, "that our only option is emigration?" The others murmured their assent. "How do we stand with the ships?" he asked the Techmeister.

"We can build the ships. We have the resources, as Bar Yarkon will confirm, to construct them in enough time and numbers—"

"How many is that?" Harrison interrupted.

"Five thousand ships, two and a half million individuals. Enough ships and time to leave—"

"And to find a suitable planet to colonize?" Van Alkmeer asked.

"Yes and no," Shimoza answered. "The problem is the drive. A reaction engine drive, even fusion powered, is too slow for interstellar distances. Many planets will have to be explored in a relatively short period of time. If we are to have any hope for survival, we must perfect the faster-than-light drive—the black hole drive."

"I thought that the drive existed," Harrison said. "You seem to imply the opposite."

"The equipment," Shimoza explained, "has been built and tested in part. We've not done the final testing because of the danger. It's a problem of control. The drive works by creating a black hole—"

18

"But they occur in nature," Harrison interrupted again. "How is that a danger?"

"Creating a large black hole," Shimoza continued patiently, "is easy. Unfortunately, it could absorb our entire solar system and take it to who knows where and in what condition. If the mass of the black hole does not exactly match that of the object being transported by it, large stresses are created, stresses that would probably destroy the object. A black hole as small as a space ship is small indeed compared to a star, which is the usual scale of such things in nature. The paradox of the experiment is that the only way we can measure the size of the hole the drive creates is to create one and to observe its effect on an object that t absorbs."

"I see," Harrison acknowledged, "but exactly how do you propose to perfect the drive?"

"We launch a reaction-engine-driven probeship to a nearby star—that'll be about six years' travel time—create a black hole and observe the perturbation to the star system's planets and sun. That will give us approximate values for the drive-equation solution. With that information it will be safe to experiment in our own solar system. We will then create holes that will absorb some of the outer planets. Eventually we can experiment with large asteroids and finally with ships. The experiments will start with the Alpha Centauri star system. The absorption of Alpha Centauri—"

"I want to raise a moral issue," Harrison interjected. "If I understand the plan, it will result in the destruction of that star system. Haven't we destroyed enough on our own planet? How can we adopt a course that may deny life to another intelligent race?"

"What do you want to do—experiment here on Earth?"

"No, not on Earth, but perhaps accept the risk and start with one of our outer planets rather than with another star system."

"I think," Shimoza said, "that sometimes you are more interested in speculative philosophy than technology. If, with our present state of ignorance, we try for a small one, we have no idea what would happen. The risk is simply not acceptable. You think we haven't agonized over the problem of destroying another world? We've been agonized for years—from the time the experiment was first proposed."

"By Bacharan, wasn't it?" Van Alkmeer asked.

"Yes," Shimoza said, "by Bacharan—always by Bacharan and his incredible alternatives. There is no other drive, and there is no other way to perfect it. And without the drive emigration is impossible."

"Yet," Harrison insisted, "we do not, not we here or all mankind, have the right to risk some other race's future for selfish reasons."

"I suppose," Shimoza conceded wearily, "that your comments deserve attention. But it won't matter, you know. We'll agree to emigration, experiment, risks moral issues, and all." He turned to Wolfson. "What's the probability of intelligent life in the Alpha Centauri system?"

Wolfson went to the Grand Ecomeister's desk. He used the keyboard to enter the question. He had the answer in a few seconds: "The computer gives us a probability of 0.2; four-to-one odds against intelligent life."

"Not encouraging odds," Harrison said. "Not good enough to go ahead with."

"Not so," Shimoza retorted. "Those are raw odds. We've been monitoring the electromagnetic spectrum of all nearby stars, and we've been beaming them messages for years. Any race as advanced as ours, or even a hundred years behind us technologically, could have responded by now. How about taking that into account? Let's rephrase the question to include the fact that there has never been a response to our signals."

Wolfson worked the keyboard again. He explained what he had done while waiting for the computer. "I posed a more complete question—taking into account not only the lack of electromagnetic response, but requiring the investigation of any signal that could be interpreted as a response, no matter how strange. Furthermore, possible nuclear emissions, gravitational anomalies, infrared activity—in fact, anything we can measure or detect—are being considered. If there is life on Alpha Centauri's planets, intelligent life in any way like ours, that has started to use fossil fuel, it should show up. In addition, I've asked the computer for the most pessimistic projection it can make consistent with known facts—more than this we can't do."

"What do you mean by pessimistic, Wolfson?" Harrison asked. "Is it pessimistic if there is life out there, or is that optimistic?"

"I would call the detection of life in the Alpha Centauri system a pessimistic result since it would mean that we could not conduct the experiment."

"I understand." Harrison nodded wryly.

They waited in silence as the computer searched records, made correlations, and investigated new possibilities. At length it displayed an output, which Wolfson read to the group. "The probability of life, intelligent life, on any planet of Alpha Centauri is less than 10^{-27}. I think that even Harrison will accept those odds."

"There is a fallacy in our thinking and in your model," Harrison continued to object. "It's all based on the assumption that an intelligent race must follow the same path that we have—replacement of animal power by fossil fuels, discovery of electricity, nuclear energy, an interest in life on other worlds, and so on. It's an egocentric point of view. It's the kind of assumption the Western cultures made to rationalize their destruction of the Indians, the Hawaiians, and the Eskimo. It's the same attitude that has brought about the present situation. 'Our way is the only way.' Any other way is not 'civilized' or not 'cultured' or not 'intelligent.' Wolfson can enter new data into his computer all day or, for that matter, for the next ten years, and he'll come up with the same answers. The models are biased, as are the data, the analysis, and the very instrument used to do the calculations. The moral issue remains.

If we do this experiment we may kill—not just a few thousand or millions, but we are knowingly contemplating genocide. Our mythology tells of the mark of Cain..." He let the sentence go unfinished.

They did not speak in response. They let his words take root and struggled with the question that only he had been willing to voice. Shimoza broke the silence. "Most stars have planets that can sustain life. I, for one, have no objections to destroying a bunch of dinosaurs if that's the price of our survival. Evolution works on a galactic scale also—every dominant race succeeds by being more aggressive than its neighbors. Why should survival of the fittest stop at planetary boundaries? Yes, we run a risk, but it's a twofold risk of destroying another race but also of being destroyed in retaliation. Yet no one has raised *that* possibility. I can't see trading our only hope for the dubious satisfaction of not harming a race whose very improbable existence has not been demonstrated."

The argument continued with everyone but Van Alkmeer opposed to Harrison. In the end he too agreed that there was no alternative. Nevertheless, they were all touched by Harrison's point—what had at first been a technical issue had become a moral one as well, and they were uncomfortable with it. Bar Yarkon attempted to assuage the gloom by exclaiming with a touch of irony, "Let us agree to feel hypothetical guilt for the improbable genocide of the conjectured other race!"

They left Van Alkmeer alone, sitting in the middle of the floor. He felt old. He had had three decisions to make that day: emigration, retiring, and choosing a successor. The decision to emigrate, in his mind, implied his retirement and, therefore, the need for a successor. Now he had one decision left—to choose the new Grand Ecomeister. Deputy Ecomeister Karkii was the obvious choice. He was best trained and the most decisive. He had the respect of the entire council and of the population as a whole. Yet Van Alkmeer doubted the obvious. What are the ideal qualifications for an

Ecomeister? he asked himself It was not merely tech
nical knowledge It was not administrative talent, if
not for Karkii's support he himself could not have func
tioned Similarly, he dismissed leadership and the ability to compromise—they were desirable traits but insufficient. In the end it was vision that counted—a
broadness of view that allowed the holder of the office
to see beyond technology, beyond facts. The ability to
see the whole, whatever disciplines it encompassed.

Wolfson and Bar Yarkon, for all their excellence,
were too narrow—too engrossed in their specialties to
see the totality. Wolfson would follow his models and
question their validity only under pressure or in the
face of disaster—when it was too late; a computer would
do no worse a job. Bar Yarkon would be a miserly dispenser of resources—conserving them at all costs,
never willing to take a real risk—perhaps to the point
of disaster also. Neither of them would do.

The new policy of emigration would require major
changes in man's life. For one thing, because it was no
longer necessary to continue to a bitter end on Earth,
the quality of life could and should be temporarily
raised. Earth would be left no later than 2200. That
meant six hundred years of surplus resources to be
converted into space ships, into experiments, into a
new life-style. Those years and the resources they represented could and would be utterly dissipated since
nothing useful was to be left behind. Yes, he reflected,
life would not be as harsh as it had been. There was
another problem, though—man's technology: it was too
complicated. They would have to do without the great
central computers. Each ship would have to be self-
contained, self-sustainable, until it ran out of supplies.
There could be no dependency on central repair facilities, no large factories, no universities teaching ten
thousand specialties. A great simplification was needed.
Every aspect of technology not absolutely essential to
the survival of the ship and the colony it might plant
would have to be discarded. While they could carry all
of man's written knowledge compressed in a few cubic

feet, they could not afford the luxury of having tha knowledge operationally available in a person's mind

Harrison's reference to the Bible set Van Alkmeer on a new tack. It had taken, he recalled, two genera tions for Moses to convert the mentality of his follower from slaves to free men. How many generations, he wondered, would it take them to repudiate their ele gant technology and prepare themselves for space? Ye here was a paradox. Space would require even more advanced technology, subtler principles, yet more com plex concepts—and at the same time more simplicity and more intuition. How was that to be achieved? Var Alkmeer did not know the answer, and he was sure that neither Karkii nor Shimoza could ever resolve such a paradox. Only Harrison could find the new di rection.

He questioned the central computer regarding his choice. He was told that while there would be opposi tion from some of the Meisters, Harrison was not likely to be usurped. He confirmed his choice to the compute and then used the keyboard to compose individual let ters tendering his resignation to the senior Meister and, incidentally, informing them of Harrison's ap pointment. He tidied the desk and dialed the telephone "Doctor? This is Van Alkmeer. I want to be recycled."

2

Po Lin

Po Lin put the huge sailplane into a gentle northeast bank toward the Sentinel range. There she expected to catch an updraft that would boost the glider farther along the Antarctic peninsula where the plentiful thermals would allow it to regain the lost altitude. She would then swing back due south, across the Weddell Sea and the Bentley Trench that divided East and West Antarctica, gliding toward the Pole in a final prospecting pass. Minutes later the long-range sensors indicated that the hoped-for uplift would not materialize. Reluctantly she nosed the aircraft down, started the turbojet engine, and returned to the course for the final pass.

It was a routine survey flight to find raw materials in a land that had once been covered by thousands of feet of ice. The sailplane had cameras, infrared sensors, magnetometers, gravitational anomaly detectors, and other accouterments of aerial survey. It was an automated flying laboratory, built to detect the slightest trace of useful minerals being exposed by the retreating ice shelf. Each day brought new finds of hematite, bauxite, malachite, oil, coal, nitrates—everything their small population needed, except the basic biological compounds. The climate was moderate for Earth even if the air was unbreathable. The melting ice provided unlimited fresh water Yet with each day, with each flight, the rape of the virgin continent progressed, so that in the end it too would be scarred and disfigured like the rest of the Earth.

Po Lin shifted uncomfortably in the cramped cockpit. She was tired. Going without sleep for twenty hours and being three months pregnant was a poor combination. She set the autopilot for the final pass and let it take over the controls. She could have completed the flight with less fuel than the machine would use if she had not been so tired. Sleep, however, was more important now. It would be unwise to risk the aircraft or herself in a vain attempt at a perfect flight—one that would use no fuel at all. She had never gotten one, and this would be her last chance. She was to spend the next two years in the second of her three occupations— teaching some of the many children that had been born in the previous ten years. She had to complete this pregnancy and by then survey flights would no longer be needed. She leaned back and scanned the stars—an automatic reaction inculcated by the training of her third profession, navigation. Using averted vision, she spotted the brilliant stippling of the orbiting launch complex low on the horizon. By the time she had followed it to its occlusion by the upper bulkhead, she was asleep.

She awoke to a soft chime; it was the autopilot telling her that the aircraft was about to enter the Amundsenland glide slope. She looked at the fuel indicator and noted with satisfaction that less than eight hundred pounds had been consumed. As the aircraft entered the glide slope, she extended the flaps and slots. The airspeed dropped to eighty knots and the rate of descent increased. At three thousand feet she cranked down the inboard landing gear and the wingtip wheels, adjusted the trim, dropped the airspeed another ten knots, went through the final prelanding check, put on the helmet, examined all the seals, and being satisfied that none of the poisonous outside air would penetrate the suit, she depressurized the cabin. At five hundred feet she flared out and dropped the airspeed to forty knots. The huge wings behind her cockpit in the nose arched upward and shuddered under the strain of landing thirty tons of aircraft. It rolled to a stop in a small portion of the twenty thousand feet of runway she had used to take off. The wings, relieved of their burden, drooped, giving the impression that the aircraft was as tired as she was from the long flight. She waited for the distant tractor to come and tow her to the hangar.

Shortly after the big hangar doors were closed, a cherry picker crane nudged the aircraft just below the cockpit. She pushed the seat back, opened the hatch, and slid into the cherry picker's cupola. The crane's operator waved at her, but she could not recognize him because his bulky suit, similar to hers, had no markings other than the usual occupational symbols. She waved to him anyhow, and he waved back again as he brought her down twenty feet below the glider's nose. Other cherry pickers, assorted trucks, and more suited and masked figures emerged to service the glider and to retrieve its data tapes. The crane operator let her out next to the air lock. Once through it, she unsuited, sponged herself with cleanser, rinsed and dried herself. She was slight, with smooth, cleanly delineated musculature. She had the grace, agility, and compactness of a gymnast. The firmness of her now protruding belly enhanced rather than detracted from the image. Her face was triangular, balanced on the base of a sharp little cleft chin framed by a strong jawline. Her lips were shaped like classical Oriental recurved bows; she had a small, flat nose between high cheekbones and the dark, dark eyes. Her hair was straight and black and drawn severely back and tied into a tight bun. She put on a fresh loincloth and repainted the smudged occupational emblem on her left breast. The computer had analyzed the flight recorder's data before she got to the debriefing console.

As tired as she was from the flight and the debriefing, she stopped at the nursery to see her children. They were sleeping, it told her; there was nothing significant to report, and she was scheduled for a recreation period with both of them the following afternoon. It was not often that both children were scheduled simultaneously. Her berth in the dormitory had been changed from a single to a double. The recreation period and the double berth could only mean that M'Tamba was back. She identified herself at a food dispenser, extracted the meal, and sought the tiny double cubicle. Tired but happy in anticipation of her husband's return, she quickly fell asleep.

M'Tamba was in the berth, for his snoring had awakened her. She sat up and cracked the glowpane's louvers so that she could see him better. He was pretty, almost three inches shorter than her own scant five feet. She loved his fine, dark features, slender muscular arms, and even the slightly bowed legs inherited from his pigmy forebears. Their children would be smaller than either of them, according to the genetic board, bringing each generation closer to the size that had been determined as optimum for emigration.

Po Lin and M'Tamba had been paired from birth by the genetic board—a fact which, while known to both of them, was resented by neither. They had grown up together, shared the same training sessions, had the same recreation periods—they had been playmates, then friends, and now lovers. Yet she had had a free choice; there were other boys she could have married, as M'Tamba could have chosen another girl. There was no force or coercion to the marriage—if either of them had chosen a different partner, it would not have concerned the genetic board—Po Lin would still have had M'Tamba's children. It pleased her, though (and, she suspected, M'Tamba also), that the children's social father was also their genetic father.

M'Tamba had been gone for two months, and she tried to awaken him to make love. She shook him gently, caressed him, but got nothing more for her troubles than a grunted acknowledgment that barely interrupted the snores. He was too tired, so she let him sleep. She, however, did not feel like sleeping any longer and elected entertainment instead. She unclipped the earphones, identified herself by using the ubiquitous keyboard, and eagerly awaited what the computer had in store for her. It was an exercise in heavy planet cargo glider re-entry maneuvers. Pleased with the selection, she continued the game until M'Tamba awoke.

M'Tamba, being a man, had only two occupations. His primary trade was that of interstellar ship captain. His secondary job, the only one he had ever practiced, was that of captain of a submersible freighter that plied continually between the dwindling Hudson Bay complex and the fast-growing Antarctic colony. The fusion-powered submersible—a giant underwater blimp—ran collapsed from the Antarctic to the Arctic, for almost nothing went in that direction. On the return trip, fully expanded, it carried materials, equipment, dismantled factories, and other supplies no longer needed in the Northern Hemisphere. As the Earth had warmed, they had first moved northward, establishing great population centers on Hudson Bay and Novaya Zemlya and in Alaska and Greenland. The Arctic was now too hot and, furthermore, lacked the resources needed to construct the fleet of ships—the ships they would use to leave Earth. As the north was being depopulated, the Antarctic was building its population to the level needed to prepare the emigration. Later, just prior to departure, the population would again be reduced. Few of the northern oldsters were moved south—most of them elected to make the trip, and their contribution to the effort, in the form of recycled organic compounds. The north was home, they said, though what difference there was between northern and southern corridors, or ship corridors, for that matter, was a subtlety that M'Tamba could not fathom. He had made the trip many times and only rarely had he brought people back— mostly equipment. There was still much that was of use in the north, things worth dismantling and transporting southward, where a new generation, better trained and adapted to a life in space, was being raised.

"I still haven't figured out what's wrong with Dahlia's song," Po Lin said as they ambled to the nursery. "The timing seems to be right, but it still doesn't fit."

"Maybe you're jealous because her song is favored over yours?"

"No!" she objected defensively, then realizing the partial truth of her husband's observation, she softened her protest. "All right, M'Tamba, I am a little jealous, but that's not really it. Her song *is* better than mine in some ways. I tried it this morning, while you were sleeping, on a cargo glider re-entry problem. It *was* better, but it's still wrong, and so is my song. It's something that I'm going to have to work out." She brooded over the recalcitrant song for a moment, and realizing that it would not admit of an immediate solution, she decided to change the subject. She turned to her husband, smiling. "Anything interesting happen this trip?"

"There was a hurricane up top—very big and strong—it gave us excessive turbulence even at our depth so we had to divert to the west of it. We pulled in to New York Harbor for safety and got a good view of the city through the periscope. Most of the big buildings are still above water. It looks like a cliff. We saw it at sunrise—red and gold buildings above a yellow sea. One of the buildings fell as we watched. Its understructure had finally corroded. It collapsed slowly, like a rocket landing on its tail, throwing up a huge spray of water, which, because of the sun, looked just like flames. I recorded it; maybe the museum will show it."

They went to the museum, which was indeed showing the scene that he had witnessed. M'Tamba's image dominated the central screen. His arms were draped over the periscope handles in a caricature of the traditional pose of a submarine captain aiming a torpedo. Even though his face was obscured, his daughter recognized him immediately. "That's my daddy!" she squealed.

"That's bow-legged M'Tamba, all right," offered one of the watchers, followed in quick succession by:

"See how he has to hold himself up—he must have been drinking ethanol."

"It looks like he was trying to sink the buildings, like in the olden-day wars."

"Nonsense! He just gets a thrill moving that big periscope in and out."

M'Tamba grinned—embarrassed but appreciative of the compliments paid him. Direct praise in a small, circumscribed society with little privacy was a rare and dangerous thing that could lead to destructive tensions. It was better to barb the praise with sarcasm; the greater the deed, the more humiliating the taunts. Someone turned from the screen, looked at M'Tamba in mock surprise, and said, "My goodness! Look, everyone! M'Tamba himself is here! Admiring himself on the screen. Tell us, great sailor, how did you come to see the building fall down?"

"We were doing ninety knots," he began (the submersible had a top speed of thirty). "I know that sounds incredible, but the current was pushing us along very strongly." (They were going south and had to fight the current almost to the equator.) "We were making very good time—a record day's run, in fact—but I was not happy about it."

They looked at one another sadly, muttering, "Not happy about it," "Must have had some kind of trouble," "A record," providing the mandatory pause that allowed the storyteller time to create.

"I was not happy," he continued, "because to my great shame, I had allowed the sonar to fail." (Unlikely.) "And what was worse, I confess, I had no spare parts."

"Shame, shame!"

"He needs re-orientation."

31

"But," he exclaimed triumphantly, "I fixed the sonar by cannibalizing the IR sensor." (As unthinkable as it was impossible.) "I did a test scan, and you'll never guess what was in my way."

"A sea mount!"

"No."

"Not that great octopus again?" another intoned knowingly, disregarding the sterility of the ocean but crediting M'Tamba with a previous, well-circulated, tall story.

"No, not this time."

"Freda's submarine?" (A standing joke.)

"A big air bubble!" one of the children shouted.

"No, no, no, no, no, none of those things." M'Tamba continued with his incredible tale. "It was not one, and not two, but three of them, actually and truly—"

"Three *what?*"

"It was three of them. I never saw three of them together before. It was—"

"It was three *what?*" his daughter asked impatiently.

"Oh! Three great icebergs, directly in my path."

"You don't say," commented one politely.

"Imagine that, three great icebergs, and so far north too," responded another.

"What was I to do? A crash was going to happen. I quickly opened the control panel and changed the wiring to reverse the turbines. This slowed the ship down, besides which, the exhaust started to melt the icebergs. But the current, the evil current, in spite of my clever thrust reverser, was still carrying me, closer and closer, ever closer, toward those hulking icebergs."

"How can that be?" a snotty twelve-year-old asked. "The icebergs were in the same current as you. You'd have almost no relative velocity!"

"The boy has a point," a colleague said. "You had better give him an explanation."

"Oh, yes, indeed," another agreed. "That is really strange and bears amplification." The speaker was thoroughly enjoying the trap into which the liar had been placed and was relishing the way in which he would inevitably squirm out of it.

"Relative velocity?" M'Tamba repeated while hunting for an explanation. "Relative velocity? And I see by your mark that you intend to be a pilot? Oh, what a sad state! Have you ever seen an iceberg?" he asked the boy sternly.

"Only in museum projections," the boy admitted.

"Only in museum projections!" M'Tamba echoed sarcastically. "And what do museum projections show of convection cells? The melting ice dropped cool water down to the anticline layer, which caused a reversed Bernoulli convection cell. So of course there had to be a local bergward relative velocity. Don't they teach you anything but simple hydrodynamics?" It was nonsense, the boy knew that, but in the etiquette of tall stories, it was passable nonsense. The boy sagely nodded agreement with M'Tamba, who continued. "Anyhow, I was still being carried closer to the bergs. Closer and closer and closer, and the melted hole in the center iceberg got bigger and bigger and bigger—at the last moment it got just big enough so that the whole submarine slid through without even a scratch. Well, I don't have to tell you that I got excited. What with rewiring the controls, and steering through them icebergs, and getting the controls right again, the current and them reverse anticline cells and all, I have another confession to make—I—got—lost!"

"But the inertial navigator?" a child asked.

"I forgot to tell you." M'Tamba covered quickly, "I had to use it to fix the IR sensor."

"If the inertial navigator was out, how did you get back home?"

"Well, when it was all over, I used the broken part of the sonar to fix the inertial navigator, naturally. But I hadn't done that yet, so I upped the periscope to get a star sight—" He glanced at Po Lin smugly. "Some of us pilots know a bit of navigation also—and that's when I saw the city just the way you saw it a few minutes ago."

"But why did the building fall down?" his daughter asked.

"That iceberg? With the great hole in it? It was so weak that it collapsed and sent a big shock wave all the way to the city, and that's what knocked the building down!"

They had all been moved by the decaying city. M'Tamba had known intuitively that they could not accept the inevitable forces of gravity and chemistry that yearly reduced man's past accomplishments to rubble. His tall story was more comforting—easier to reconcile than the fact that it was millions of cubic miles of melting ice caps that had done it—ultimately caused by the pollution that accompanied man's earlier wanton treatment of his planet. They all knew the real causes of the decay—intellectually. The museum would tell anyone who asked, in as great detail as was wanted. The realities of a harsh world, a sterile world, a world to be abandoned, cannot be acknowledged emotionally, so gentler explanations are offered—funny or outrageous if that suits the purpose—for thousands of little events. Eventually such stories become canonized. The useless are discarded and the survivors melded, to emerge as folk tales, and later as legends. The museum, which was merely an extension of the computer complex that directed their lives, recorded the extemporaneous story and offered it thereafter along with the scene of the falling city, and in a hundred generations parents would tell their children the legend of "M'Tamba and the wandering asteroid."

Po Lin was chanting Dahlia's re-entry song to herself as she waited for the shuttle craft to complete the tediously slow automatic maneuvers required to dock it to the vast complex of ships and free-floating factories that orbited the Earth. For three of the five years that she had been assigned to piloting the Earth shuttle, two official re-entry songs had competed—hers and

Dahlia's. Now the computer had chosen Dahlia's song, so Po Lin and the other re-entry glider pilots had adopted the chant. Po Lin, however was not satisfied with it. She had come to the first pass verse, the exploratory pass that bounced the ship through the atmosphere to allow the pilot time to determine the best approach for a safe landing. This was not necessary for landing on the Earth, but the exploratory pass was always sung and executed for practice against its eventual use in landing on a new planet. That was the part of Dahlia's song Po Lin did not like. Dahlia always used the bounce maneuver even when it was not needed. It also gave a nasty jolt—a much higher G rate than Po Lin's song. But, Po Lin reluctantly admitted, the initial entry and the final touchdown phases of Dahlia's song were crisper. She concentrated on imagined instrument readings as she sang and found the trouble. The desired effect could be achieved by lengthening the vowel in the fourth measure of the exploratory pass verse. The slight delay would allow the pilot to make a choice. She considered the words, the meter, which dictated the delicate timing of the maneuver, and the notes themselves, which keyed the controls. Her proposed variation was finished before the docking.

She waited impatiently at the air lock, and when it opened, instead of floating leisurely to the debriefing room, she pulled herself along the handrails, turning somersaults at the corridor bends and pushing off with her feet in the new direction—a practice that was not recommended and for which she had often reprimanded boisterous youngsters. She removed her helmet and attacked the debriefing console. The computer did not yet have the flight data or else it would have made her wade through the tedious debriefing first. She sang the modified version of Dahlia's song. The orbiting complex's computer considered the proposed change, and finding it meritorious, confirmed its judgment with the central computer on Earth. The song was accepted, and with it, two verses of her original re-entry song were reinstated. It was no longer "Dahlia's Song" or "Po Lin's Song" but simply "The Re-Entry Song."

Her life had taken a new turn five years before when she had been assigned to the shuttle and M'Tamba to ship testing. He spent most of his time in the orbiting launch complex working on the prototype ship. Her job was relatively easy. Liftoff from Earth using the massive booster rockets was fully automated. It was the return trip with its hazardous re-entry that required a skilled pilot. And, her navigation skill being sharpened to the greatest extent possible without actual practice in interstellar space, there was little to do with it but to write navigation songs—first as a pastime and now as an occupation. So she piloted the shuttle from Earth to orbit every other week, remained there for three days, waiting for the return trip, spending the time writing the songs and seeing as much of M'Tamba as his job permitted.

M'Tamba had also been asked to write songs, but, to his dismay, not the pilot songs he had wanted to compose, but theory chants and system ballads. To be truthful, she thought, he lacked the sensitivity for good pilot songs. His system maintenance ballads were the best—they were perforce very long, and to sustain the interest, he filled them with double entendres and interwove bawdy passages that even made her blush at times. The computer, of course, did not care. It only monitored the performance of the users of the alternate songs and chose the song that gave the best results. His more obscene verses had often been challenged, but when they were eliminated, the song fell apart and so did the equipment; they were always returned at the computer's insistence. His songs were so popular that it seemed that everyone would soon know how to maintain the black hole drive (his lustiest ballad by far), the life-support systems, the bioponics, and the cryostats. Pre-adult twelve-year-olds snickered in their berths as they reviewed the disassembly steps of the ion generator, and old married technicians of twenty-five still chuckled as they did the indicated procedure.

She tried to find him as soon as she had refreshed herself. The computer told her that he was at the prototype ship again, engaged in yet another of an interminable series of tests. When would he return? In thirty or forty hours, it told her. That would be twice that she had missed him. She decided to go out and see—a husband had responsibilities, and M'Tamba was not fulfilling his, and when they were together, it was the ship, the ship, the ship. What, besides the black hole drive, was there to test that he and hundreds of others had not tested ten times? He would wear the ship out (and herself) with the testing.

The prototype ship lay in a parallel orbit a few kilometers away. She did not wait for a scheduled shuttle; she suited up and added a bulky maneuver pack that barely left enough room for her to turn around in the air lock. She kicked free of the air lock, curled into a tight ball, and straightened out at the precise instant required to aim her toward the ship. She activated the little thrusters and floated across. The ship lay spinning in front of her, majestically slow, a pair of spheres a hundred and fifty meters in diameter, joined by a slender three-hundred-meter-long tunnel; a giant dumbbell of aluminum and fiberglass, studded with random projections and apparatus. The center of the tunnel that joined the two ship halves was pierced by another shorter tubular structure about which the entire ship rotated. One end of the transverse tube contained the drive equipment and the other end the main air lock.

Now, with the Earth light full on the ship, she could see that something had been done to it: both spheres were colored sky blue, a blue no longer visible on Earth, a blue dotted with clouds among which huge sea birds glided effortlessly. As she neared the air lock, she looked up to the overhanging sphere—the birds were overhead, the farther ones painted larger than the nearer, so that by a carefully contrived trick of perspective, there was blue sky above and below and she was suspended in the clouds among the soaring birds.

37

It was M'Tamba's work, or at least his inspiration. Four months before, he had discarded his assigned occupational emblem and had instead adorned his shoulders with little blue sea birds—birds he had never seen, nor would ever see, except in the museum's projections. The awesome beauty of the ship's decoration did not diminish her annoyance with him—he would probably be painted blue all over now. She passed through the air lock and quickly shucked the sweaty, bulky suit and asked, "Where the hell is M'Tamba?" of no one in particular.

"M'TAMBA IN SHIPCONBRIDGE," the ship answered her.

"That's a new wrinkle," she muttered, not wanting to speak aloud, thereby triggering another response. The voice sounded like M'Tamba's, to her further displeasure. She traversed the connecting tunnel toward what she hoped was the correct hull—there was an identical bridge in both halves of the ship, and it was a matter of convention, not design, that designated one of them as primary and the other as backup. She went to the left—a judgment based on an intuitive knowledge of her lover—and was not disappointed. He was there, not at all blue, leaning back in the command chair, in the light gravity induced by the ship's rotation. She moved quietly, hoping to surprise him, but could not. He was up and running toward her as she crossed the threshold—no doubt the ship had informed him. They kissed, petted, and her anger dissipated. He broke away after a while, saying, "Just one more thing..." but the anger flashed in her eyes, so instead he called out, "Petrelship! Test suspend!"

To which it replied, "ACK ACK M'TAMBA. SELFTEST NOW."

"It does hear everything, doesn't it?" Po Lin asked as they went to his quarters on the next deck "up"— that is, toward the center.

"Yes," he admitted.

"And it will comment on everything?"

"Not if you don't want it to."

"I don't want it to "

"PETRELSHIP!" M'Tamba roared stentoriously "SHUT UP!"

"ACK ACK M'TAMBA EMERGENCY TALK ONLY NOW "

She stayed with him for three days. She knew the ship from numerous mandatory practice sessions on the simulator, but had been on board for only a few minutes at a time during various stages of its construction. It was one thing to know that something existed, or that it was of such and such a size and shape, but a different thing to be in it. She was most fascinated by the black hole drive in the central spine. It was complete. It looked ready to go. There was nothing makeshift or experimental in its appearance, yet it could not be used until they had the Alpha Centauri experiment's data. She sat at the inactive auxiliary control console and practiced the jump maneuvers and the chant that would control the drive. She imagined it creating a black hole that radiated from the center of the ship, absorbed it, hurled it into the alien tachyon space, followed by another anti-hole that brought the ship back to normal space but far away from its starting point. She toyed with the safety switch, tempted to disarm it and try the drive. M'Tamba entered.

"It's not functional anyhow," he commented.

"I know that, but—"

"But we have to wait for the experiment. There are six crucial numbers needed to control the drive. We have five of them. But the sixth—we don't even know if it's positive or negative, never mind what its value is."

"Will it work, M'Tamba? Suppose it doesn't work?"

"It will work, once the experiments are over and we can solve the drive equations. It will work because it must. It will work because we have no choice. And mostly it will work because I've done all the testing. Isn't that right, Petrelship?"

39

"IS RIGHT, M'TAMBA-CHIEF-TEST-HONCHO," the ship agreed.

"SHUT UP, Petrelship!" Po Lin snapped. "Don't you ever get tired of playing with its response programs, M'Tamba?"

"It's like the maintenance ballads, lover. It's part of the design—and it really wasn't my idea at all."

"Whose then?" she challenged.

"The Meister's," he responded smugly. "I had done it to a few special test programs, but he heard about it and told me to do it wherever I wanted. It's not just me. Everyone working on the prototype plays with it—it's just part of the ship and what it does."

"You didn't have to make it use your voice, did you? That's a bit vain."

"I didn't do that either. I don't know how that happened, except that I spent more time on the ship than anyone else. Maybe it's just good sense on the part of the ship's computer. It knows a good voice when it hears one!"

"Arrogant ass!" she exclaimed as she floated away, with a coquettish smile, toward the sleeping area.

"Sweet ass!" he countered as he followed her, but an hour later he was working again, totally distracted, while she had nothing to do but traverse the innumerable, monotonous corridors of the empty ship. She returned to the launch complex without saying goodbye and prepared for the trip back to Earth.

———

She went through the last countdown sequence prior to ignition, peeved because her copilot had not yet arrived. Ten more steps and I have to call a halt, she thought. Finally the copilot rushed in. His visor was polarized, and Po Lin could not recognize him, and neither did his suit have any distinguishing marks. The countdown proceeded uneventfully without conversation. Let him know I'm annoyed with his lateness, she reasoned. Probably a youngster who could use discipline. Talk was impossible during the powered phase of the flight; the high G's and the noise assured that. Finally, when they were in free fall, it was possible to remove the helmet, which she did. The copilot lay in the seat, unmoving, the visor still polarized. She called him on the intercom, but he did not respond. She tried to see through the darkened visor, but that was not possible. Finally, concerned that the copilot might be sick or hurt, she removed the helmet. "Oh!" she exclaimed. "You . . ." She was speechless.

"Hello, lover," M'Tamba replied casually. "We have leave together."

"You didn't tell me. You kept me rattling around by myself on that ship of yours, and you knew all along, didn't you?"

"Uh—yes—"

"And you took advantage of me—because I thought I wouldn't be back for two weeks!"

"Uh—yes," he admitted again. "But you're always better when you're desperate. Anyhow, after this leave I'm off the test crew."

"And then what?"

"I don't know. I guess I'll be reassigned. Maybe to training test techs."

"On Earth or in orbit?"

"I don't know. We'll find out after the leave."

After kissing their youngest child to bed, M'Tamba and Po Lin stopped at the communal lounge, where they met co-workers also on leave. A discussion leader was inviting speculation on the outcome of the forthcoming experiment. Unlike a formal discussion in which participants would be at approximately the same technical level, the group was heterogeneous. M'Tamba realized that several of the biotechs (obvious by their trade markings) were having difficulty following it. M'Tamba, who had a knack for explaining the difficult in simple language, offered to take them aside—an offer the discussion leader gladly accepted

M'Tamba decided to sing rather than to speak   they were more apt to remember the lesson then—besides, he enjoyed the challenge of maintaining poetic form while answering their questions. He addressed the computer, "My beat, please. A rock hexameter." The computer obliged him with a tentative patter which M'Tamba did not approve. He indicated his displeasure by exaggerated facial expressions and occasional visual obscenities. The computer, understanding this code, quickly converged to the desired beat and thereupon filled in with an appropriate melodic counterpoint.

M'Tamba started with a review of the basic facts of the experiment. The drive equations needed six numbers, five of which were known. Now only the Alpha Centauri experiment remained to obtain the last number. He devoted three stanzas to each number. The first set the pattern of the triad, while the last was traditionally supplied by one of the students. Not only had it to be mathematically correct, but it had to conform to the meter of the whole song and the rhyme pattern of the two previous stanzas. The computer escalated the pace as they progressed from hand clapping, through foot stomping, till at last they were all standing, dancing in a frenzied circle around M'Tamba, their tiny lithe brown bodies glistening with sweat as they echoed his triumphant screaming of the drive equation constants to six decimal places.

3

M'Tamba

The thought twittered through M'Tamba's mind like a small angry bird. It rebuked him again. Again he ignored it, but that was harder to do now that he was out of range of the Earth's broadcasts. He had read most of the library and seen all the history that the probe's museum had to offer. There was nothing to do but test, maintain the equipment, exercise, eat, sleep, and make the monthly observations—record the positions of a hundred stars, magnetic fields, and other technical data, package it into a buoy, and launch it back to Earth so that it would broadcast the navigational data to anyone who might need it in the future. Two more years to go, by which time the huge chunk of frozen methane reaction mass would be expended on the outer fringes of the Alpha Centauri solar system; and then the experiment.

He talked aloud all the time now and could barely distinguish his own voice from the ship's. It was so routine: the chime would sound as he said, "Ding—ding," and he and the ship would simultaneously announce the next chore; "Maintenance procedure 3A on guidance system," or "Check number 2 hydroponics cell mineral level." Pointless and boring. It was not as if he were really needed; he was there for insurance. The probe ship could and would conduct the experiment without his help—he was just another redundant backup subsystem along for the ride. The ship would reach its destination, launch the probe rocket, and transmit the observations back to Earth. It would take four years, traveling at the speed of light, for the data to reach Earth. In that respect M'Tamba could be useful. If the experiment was successful, and if the data were good, he could solve the drive equations, calibrate the drive, and set a jump for home—maybe—thereby returning to Earth four years ahead of the signals.

Returning home, home to Po Lin, who had always waited for him, who had always been there at the end of every trip. There was still that last glorious leave with her to relish, and then the meeting with the Grand Ecomeister himself. He had called them into an alcove at the side of a common lounge, closed the curtains, and sat quietly facing them. They sat for a long time without speaking so that each could find his own peace. The Ecomeister wore no decorations or tattoos of rank—he was just another elderly man with gray hair and hard lines in what had once been a soft face. Occasionally one of them would hum a tune appropriate to the tenor of the meeting. After these preliminary rituals had been observed, Harrison had opened the conversation.

"You are both thirty years old," he said, "and at the peak of your abilities. Po Lin is our best navigator and M'Tamba is the best captain." It was not a compliment but a statement of fact that they acknowledged with an assenting "Ah." "Po Lin," he continued, "when did you write your last song?"

"I have made small changes in many songs, but have written no new song for more than a year. The last one was 'View from the Hub.'"

"And you, M'Tamba, have you more songs to write?"

"I expect not, Ecomeister. The ships are being simplified daily. Others have learned the knack of writing good maintenance songs, and many that are attributed to me were actually written by them."

"Does this disturb you?"

44

"No, but a good song should bear the author's name, not M'Tamba's."

"Perhaps, Captain, all maintenance songs will be called M'Tamba songs."

"Perhaps," he agreed.

"How many ships have we built?" Harrison continued.

"Nine hundred," M'Tamba answered the Ecomeister's vacuous question. It was a count that they all knew, child or adult. "Nine hundred ships, excluding the prototype and the probe."

"Yes." The Ecomeister persisted in wandering. "The probe. Do you know the probe ship, M'Tamba?"

"I have been on it—it is a ship—a simpler ship, and smaller than the rest, but it is a ship, and all ships are the same in things that matter."

"The probe ship is now swinging back from its boost around the sun and will cross Earth's orbit tomorrow."

"As scheduled." M'Tamba acknowledged another platitude. In a few days it would begin its long journey to Alpha Centauri. The Ecomeister's repetition of the obvious made no sense; therefore, it was best to say nothing of substance until his purpose was clear. They were quiet again for a long time, until M'Tamba, finally understanding the old man's intentions, asked, "Has a crew been selected?"

"It is hoped so," Harrison offered.

M'Tamba looked at Po Lin, who nodded agreement. "We will do it, if that's what you're asking," he said.

"Not Po Lin," the Ecomeister corrected. "She will be more useful later. There is no need for a navigator on this trip, or a re-entry pilot. You may choose another companion if you wish—there is a list."

"It isn't necessary, is it?" he asked the Ecomeister.

"No," Harrison agreed.

"Then"—he looked at Po Lin wistfully—"I would rather be alone. When do I leave?"

"In twelve hours," the Grand Ecomeister answered. He rose and left the pair alone in the little room. They sat for several hours, not speaking, just holding hands,

45

until she sensed his need to be moving again and said to him, "You must go now." He stood and kissed her gently on the forehead. She cried only after she heard the faint rumblings of the shuttle craft's takeoff.

The thought twittered through his mind again, and again he tried without success to ignore it. It had no form or words, only a pure unvocalized thought that originated in the depths of his subconscious, rose to the surface like a tiny bubble, and quickly burst into a fleeting expression of annoyance. It was becoming disturbing. "Probe ship!" he called. "Is M'Tamba okay?"

"NO PHYSICAL TROUBLE," it assured him. "NEED MORE EXERCISE. M'TAMBA 430 GRAMS EXCESS MASS. HIM LAZY!"

"That's your fault," he countered. "How about mental?"

"BETWEEN NORMS FOR M'TAMBA," it reassured him. Something was different, though. He could not identify it, but there was something wrong.

"Ship check!" he ordered. The ship engaged in a long robotic omphaloskepsis session and eventually reported that nothing was wrong. "Course check!" he tried. This time the ship should have responded almost instantaneously, but it did not. After a long delay it told him that they were off course, drifting slightly and just a little behind schedule. It took M'Tamba several days to locate the problem. One of the engines was malfunctioning, but what was more remarkable, a second failure in the diagnostic equipment had obscured that fact. It was only a few ounces of thrust lost—enough, though, to cause the mission's failure if not corrected. Weeks of intensive work went into the repairs, both inside and outside the ship. In the course of it he discovered many other faults, all of which the ship had been able to correct or bypass, and yet it had not informed him, as it should have, of its actions because of numerous simultaneous failures in the diagnostic programs. He checked them thoroughly, and

46

with considerable effort he was able to fix things so that it would be impossible for a new failure to go unnoticed.

The twittering and the failures increased over the next months. He would "hear" the angry bird, as he called it, and then do a complete check of the ship; something new was always wrong. "Twitter-twitter," and part of the computer's memory went awry; "twitter-twitter," and a power supply blew a fuse. He became convinced that he was doing it himself. There was no point in asking the computer because he could have gimmicked that also. He tried to set traps—to catch himself causing the failures. It was a madness—an elaborate scheme he had invented to keep himself occupied. He dutifully logged his observations and inserted them into the monthly buoy. It became a new routine. Wait for the "bird," find the problem, fix it, and record it in the log. Some of the systems were down to the last spare parts, and he spent his increasingly rare leisure time designing a jury rig for an essential component if it failed, or a repair for one that was not repairable.

He had evolved a new theory now. It was an elaborate test devised by the Meisters to discover what was really essential and how the ships could be further simplified. If so, the challenge was magnificent, and he was now at least no longer bored. A year after he first heard the angry bird he had to start sacrificing marginally useful systems to keep essential ones working. The library and the museum were first—there was no longer time for entertainment anyway. Most of the computer went next—and he knew now that any voice he heard or any conversations he had had to be with himself.

With six months to go, Alpha Centauri was the brightest star in the view screen. Almost no system was untouched. The ship had been stripped to essentials, and, because of numerous malfunctions, he had to do much of the work that had been previously automated. The hydroponic tanks that provided him with

47

food, water and oxygen had to be tended twice daily. He had to make manual navigational readings using a sextant whose optics had been butchered from the now defunct autonavigator. The chores consumed all his time. At least the failures had diminished—there was almost nothing left to fail, and what remained was too primitive to be susceptible to the creeping debilitation that had beset the ship. The bird continued to come, when he was near sleep or in his dreams. He was beyond annoyance with it and instead tried to make a friend of it.

"Why do you break my ship?" he asked it one day.

"Bad, bad, bad," it responded.

"I know that," he admitted, "but that's no reason to destroy this ship."

"I hate!"

"And I hate what you've done to my ship—so there!"

"Bad thing! Ugly thing! Thing not perfect!"

"Is that your trouble? Well, bird—you're not so perfect yourself—so go away and eat a worm."

"Worm is flesh."

"So what else is new?"

"Eat flesh bad thing."

"So eat some seeds."

"Dirty thing, M'Tamba. Eat seeds badder eat flesh."

"Shut up and let me sleep!"

Incredibly, it did. It was there, furtively probing and rummaging around his mind, silent, sullen as ever, but the failures had stopped. The ship was an electronic shambles, and where before he had been barely able to keep up with the failures, the thing's retirement allowed him to make headway, and he was able to repair some of the simpler automated systems. He felt sane again. There was much work to be done, but no longer the frustration of an impending failure on the heels of the previous repair.

There were three months to go, and he devoted his newly found spare time to checking the black hole generator and the other equipment associated with the experiment. None of it had been touched by the attacks—but, then, none of it had been turned on. He was happy, pleased with the innovations he had instituted, and satisfied that his presence had been essential after all. Without him the probe would have missed its target, but he had made it work, and he looked forward to the mission's culmination.

He lay in the bunk, arms behind his head, composing a new emergency repair chant to be dropped with the next buoy. He turned on the rear screen. A few kilometers back, the remnants of the booster, many times larger than the probe ship, its fuel expended, drifted imperceptibly to the side, not having been given the final course correction that M'Tamba had given the ship. It would continue on its present course directly to the star, while the ship, on a slightly divergent course, would merely graze the alien solar system, close enough to launch a small rocket with the hole generator. Then, in a few hours, the generator would create a hole for M'Tamba to observe, record, analyze, and they would have the data back on Earth, and that would be the end of it, or rather the beginning.

There was no "bird" to warn him this time: the booster exploded, sending deadly shock waves of neutrons and ionized particles that overtook the ship in a fraction of a second. Debris followed the blast, slammed into the rear of the ship, tore holes in the skin, and wrecked his elegantly contrived repairs. He was in his space suit before the air pressure had dropped to the danger point. He went to work automatically without philosophizing over how the explosion could have occurred or how many physical laws had been broken in the doing. He assayed the damage: the hull was no longer integral, but there was enough oxygen for him to survive. Food and water were low but adequate for the duration of the mission. The probe itself, the hole generator, shielded by the bulk of the ship, had suffered only minor damage. He worked furiously, first on the equipment essential to the experiment, and only after their viability was assured did he start with the life-support systems. It was forty hours before he settled,

49

exhausted, in the tiny cylindrical compartment that he had managed to remake into an airtight combined control center and living quarter. Only then did he unsuit. Using the water to wash was frivolous, but he could not live with himself otherwise, and he granted himself this last luxury as a reward. He shampooed his hair. It came out in clumps. The medical instruments confirmed his belief that he was suffering from radiation sickness. Medication would forestall death but not prevent it.

He forced himself to eat despite the nausea, and continued laboring over the repairs, stopping only when the inevitable exhaustion overcame him. He concentrated on modifying the equipment to assure the experiment's success—to make it invulnerable to any conceivable future attacks. If he died before the proper time, the probe would be launched nevertheless, but it would not be possible to calibrate the hole drive, and Earth would have to wait four years to observe the experiment. Observations from Earth would not be as accurate as the more direct ones from the probe ship, but they would do. If, on the other hand, he did manage to survive, there was a fair chance that he could activate the drive and jump the ship back to within light days of Earth, not only saving four years' time but bringing the more accurate data as well. As a third backup, he set up a string of buoys to broadcast the vital data and the accurate observations back to Earth. He simplified the equipment brutally. Vulnerable, sophisticated electronics was replaced wherever possible by crude but effective and rugged mechanical gear. Finally, recognizing himself as the most important backup system, he undertook such treatment as would keep him alive, without regard to immediate discomfort or pain, or life beyond the duration of the experiment.

These preparations took a month. By then he was too weak to do more, despite medication and daily blood transfusions. He lay in the bunk now, waiting, conserving his strength for the final push eight weeks away. "Oh, bird, devil bird," he sang to himself, beginning a sad lament.

It answered him. "Bad thing! Cannot find!"

"That, bird," M'Tamba answered, "is because there's not much left to find. Why, bird?"

"You bad. You will destroy. I destroy first."

"That you did. Who are you?"

"I good!"

"Sure, bird. You're really good. You brung M'Tamba much luck. But it won't help. Why don't you tell me why I'm bad instead of punishing me first? At least you owe me that much."

There was no answer. Not for a week, although M'Tamba sensed that it was probing around him, on the fringes of his consciousness—what little of it there was at this time.

It answered his question at last. "M'Tamba thing bad to make Blackness hurt!"

This time it was M'Tamba's turn for silence. After a long pause he asserted, "You know what I'm thinking!"

"I know what you are."

"Same thing, bird. You know the Blackness?"

"Blackness hurt."

"Maybe," M'Tamba acknowledged. "Can you make Blackness?"

"No. I *know* Blackness."

"Same thing, bird. If you know it, you can make it."

"Not make. Blackness very bad thing. Cannot make, just know."

"If you know it, bird, tell me, and then I won't make it."

"M'Tamba thing is twice. Will make Blackness even if know."

"Sure, bird, but to get away from here. To go away. Never come back. Bad M'Tamba take his Blackness and go away, far away, far away, devil bird."

It was quiet again after that, and it remained so until the probe reached the edge of the solar system and the experiment was less than two days ahead. It did not respond to his many attempts to communicate. M'Tamba was convinced that the dialogue had been real and that the alien—for that is what it had to be—could somehow give him the solution to the drive equation but would not. He tried again, exerting himself to contact it. In response to his efforts, the last remnant of the booster, now safely far away, exploded again. Probably another shower of neutrons, he thought, but no matter now. One explosion of the booster could have been accidental, but two? It had to be directed by an alien intelligence.

He addressed it: "Bird? No, I won't call you that—you're a fellow sentient being. Sir?" He began again. "I am an alien life form from Earth, third planet of the star Sol. I mean you no harm. I am here on a mission vital to the life of my race. Its success could be harmful to you but need not be. You have the means to prevent the harm. Give me, please give me the data on the black holes so I can stop the experiment and return home without hurting you. Give it to me and I'll go in peace."

"M'Tamba thing is twice," the alien accused. "Once not to hurt and twice to hurt bad with Blackness. M'Tamba thing make Blackness even if I tell."

"Yes," M'Tamba pleaded, "I have to activate the drive—to make a Blackness to get home. But it'll be controlled, and no harm will come to you. I won't have to launch the probe. But I have to make a harmless black hole to get home."

"M'Tamba thing is twice. M'Tamba thing not perfect. Make Blackness!" and with that the ship lurched violently, throwing M'Tamba out of the bunk against the opposite wall.

When he awoke, several hours had passed. His compartment was still integral and the probe still functional. There was no time for discussion now. He watched as the automatic countdown proceeded inexorably, step by step. The probe's rockets were ignited, and it took off on a path that converged with the alien sun. The alien seemed to be having difficulty locating him now, but it still knocked the ship about from time to time. All that M'Tamba could sense was its incessant condemnation. He ordered it to shut up and concentrated on the experiment.

At the preset time, the probe rocket ceased to exist: it was replaced by a black hole that blossomed out and then shrank again to an unobservable blackness that began to draw the alien sun toward it. The equipment faithfully recorded the event, calibrated the results, and in a matter of seconds presented the data to a now semiconscious M'Tamba. He launched the buoys with the data and the song and set to work solving the drive equations. He needed no calculator or other machinery. He solved it mentally, using a long-practiced and perfected procedure. And then, blinded by a combination of the radiation and the alien's further attacks, he set the numbers into the drive and jumped for home.

4

Kalish

He was in the temple court when he first sensed the intruder. Its high energy scratched a tiny rip in the random probability fabric that was the sky's usual appearance. It was too far away to discern its shape or purpose. Kalish thought that it might be a new comet—its luminous trail and speed fitted that hypothesis. He studied the rip for a long time, his arms spread wide to get a better view.

He noticed it again the next day at the same time and again on the following day. On the fourth day he mentioned it to his fellow priests, who, because of their lesser sensitivity, could not confirm its presence. From his description, they agreed that it was a new comet.

On the fifth day Kalish officiated at the selection. A peasant had brought his family and the bags of seeds, as was the custom after the harvest. The three large bags contained seeds that the farmer had gathered from the three staple food crops of his own fields. The small sacks had seeds from the three small priests' fields that every farmer cultivated. Kalish opened the first large sack. He put his hands into it, stirred it thoroughly, and extracted a handful of seeds, which he spread on the stone table. He looked at the seeds carefully, judging their quality, now and again tasting them to determine their nutritional value, testing the toughness of the husks, ever watchful for the slightest sign of blight Some he held in his hands for a long time, concentrating on their innermost structure. He spread more handfuls on the stone and made a selection, separating the seeds into a large and a small pile. The large pile was returned to the sack and the small pile was left on the table. He repeated the ritual with the other two large sacks until there were three small piles of seeds on the stone.

"Have you made a selection?" he asked the farmer.

"Yes, Kalish," the farmer answered nervously, taking three small sacks from his pouch. He gave them to the priest, who poured them on the stone to compare them with his own selection. They were close. The farmer was industrious and had chosen the seeds that offered the best compromise of nutrition, irrigation, light, and a host of other factors. Undoubtedly the selection had taken weeks—each seed agonized over by the farmer and his wife. It was an excellent selection—suspiciously so. Kalish wondered if the farmer could have enlisted the help of a renegade acolyte—such things happened—if so, it was a serious crime. Perhaps he was merely industrious. Kalish remembered that this peasant's selections had always been good—both the man and the woman had above-average sensitivity, though not high enough for priests' work. At last, his suspicions allayed, he spoke to the farmer again.

"You have made a good selection. Let me now see the seeds from the priests' fields." He examained these more carefully. They were experimental and sometimes disappointing. Two of the crops were poor and were not to be perpetuated. The third looked promising and could be continued to the next generation. He selected seeds from the third priests' field and returned the selected seeds to the farmer's sack. He then examined the farmer, his wife, and their two children. He felt them, looked into their eyes, listened to their chests, and considered. They had a minor vitamin deficiency—perhaps that explained their anxiety. The experimental crop from the first priest's field was intended to take care of the deficiency.

He fetched two new small sacks from under the stone table. "Plant your selection in your own fields. You may eat the contents of the priests' fields. Plant these"—he pointed to the new sacks—"in the first and second priests' fields, and these," he said, indicating the selection from the third priests' field, "in the third." He was ready to dismiss them when he was again distracted by the intruder. To his surprise, Pils, the farmer's younger son, had briefly faced in exactly the same direction. It might have been a coincidence, but the selections *had* been very good.

"Did you select for the priests' fields?" he asked, sensing the farmer's increased discomfort. Dumbly, the farmer's wife gave the priest three more small sacks. He opened them quickly and spread their contents on the stone. The first sack contained sand, a confirmation of Kalish's own judgment that the crop was worthless. The second, instead of sand, had a scant dozen seeds. The husks were poor, some of them were blighted, but for some reason the farmer—or someone else—had kept them. Kalish examined these more closely and found what he had missed on the first cursory examination: despite the poor husks and blight, they had far above the expected quantity of the missing vitamin. He looked up from the stone and accused them, "You did not make this selection! Did the boy do it?"

"Forgive us, Kalish," the man begged. "Forgive the boy. He does not know it was wrong. The year before last, when he was three, we let him play selection. As usual, we let him plant the seeds. They came up very good. Last year he selected again, and again his crops were very good. His selection was much better than my wife or I could have done. This year he selected again, and we knew that his choice was better, so that is what we brought here. It was only a game to him. The fault is ours, not his."

Selection was an adult ritual. While children were encouraged to play at selection, it was heresy to allow

56

a child to pick the seeds that were actually to be planted. The acceptance of a child's selection marked his acceptance into adulthood—with attendant rituals that were not to be bypassed. It was usually easy to see the signs of a parent foisting his responsibilities onto an older child. The selections were poor, the family unkempt—there were hundreds of signs, and Kalish could almost always spot them without looking at the seeds. Yet, here all the signs were missing—except the anxiety—and the selection had been excellent.

Kalish, on a hunch, looked at the boy. "What did you see in the sky before?"

"It was nothing, Kalish. I think it was a bird, very far away."

It was enough to convince the priest. "Take your seeds and go in peace," he told the farmer. "The boy will stay with me for testing."

The peasants were overjoyed. If the boy was chosen to be a priest, support in their old age would be assured. Kalish was not angry with them, after all, but had instead offered them the greatest of all honors. Happy and relieved, they left, profusely thanking the stern-faced priest, who only moments before had terrorized them.

Kalish kept the boy at his side as he continued the selection. Seeds, domestic animals, tree cuttings, fruits, all came under his scrutiny; always he chose to improve the yield or the breed, striving to achieve the perfection of all species as God had commanded. He caught several more glimpses of the intruder as the long day passed. It was definitely moving closer and faster. The boy, Pils, Kalish was now convinced, could also see it.

There were no betrothals that day, so he finished earlier than usual. He took the child's hand and walked with him to the temple residence where the testing was to take place. Halfway across the square he saw it again, much clearer this time because the boy's astonishing sensitivity amplified his own senses many-fold. It was moving very quickly, and it was incredibly far away.

"It isn't a bird, is it?" the child asked

"No, son Not a bird It is a new thing "

Kalish spent the rest of the day testing Pils. He used ever more complicated seed mixes, ugly seeds of high value and seeds with perfect appearance that had a fatal but subtle flaw. Pils always made a near-perfect selection. With nothing but home training, he was more sensitive than many acolytes after years of study. The child would become a priest. So exceptional was he that Kalish did not doubt that he would become a high priest.

Kalish studied the object for the next four months. It continued its inexorable approach to the sun. Its trail was now perceivable to some of the other priests. Kalish, with the help of the boy, who was progressing at a rate that rivaled the thing's speed, had been able to trace its trail back to the star from which it had originated. It also emitted radio waves from time to time, which only added to the mystery. Such low-frequency light waves, Kalish learned from the archives, had come from that star before, but their purpose in the universe had remained hidden. There were many explanations for the thing now; it seemed to Kalish that each priest who sensed it for himself offered yet a new speculation for it. The comet theory still had its adherents, because the object radiated a trail of ionized gases and because it was the only comet known that circled two stars.

By the sixth month they were able to plot its course—directly for their sun. It would be eventually absorbed by the sun with hardly a notice, the other priests reasoned, and therefore there was no point in further speculation, yet Kalish continued to be morbidly fascinated by it.

Pils was as incredible to him as was the object. In less than six months the child's powers developed to the point where he was the equal of the more talented priests. Furthermore, there were constant hints of new capabilities. Pils understood genetic structure in a way that was different. Instead of reaching down through the biology, starting at the superficial and working toward the fundamentals of the structure of matter, he seemed to be applying a more basic understanding of matter and was working upward from there: from the atoms and molecules to the chemistry, to the genetic code, and thence to the biology.

"Why do we select and plant the seeds?" he asked one day. Kalish realized that this was not the question of an ordinary child; so many of Pils's questions were strange, and some were even heretical.

"To achieve the perfection that God has ordained," the priest explained.

"Do we know what that perfection is?"

"Yes. God has given us that knowledge for every species, even for ourselves."

"Show me perfection for the starch plant!"

Kalish took the boy's hand and transmitted the ideal pattern for the plant, the genetic structure, the arrangement of the code groups, the details which generations of priests had learned and similarly imparted to their acolytes.

"I understand," Pils said, "but why do we select and plant?"

"It is one thing to know the structure of perfection," the priest instructed, "but another to achieve it. There are untold billions of combinations of code groups. When one set of chromosomes is combined with another, only one gene might be moved toward perfection, while several others might move away. We know perfection, but the path is devious and God has not given us that. It is our purpose to find that path. Sometimes, after many generations of breeding, we find that we are at a dead end. Then we must go back and find a new path from the point where we went wrong. So we select, breed, and select again, moving ever closer to perfection, in accordance with God's commandments."

"But *why* must we breed and select?" the boy insisted.

"No other way is possible," the priest asserted.

"Here is the starch plant seed," the boy said. "In this

batch only four groups are out of order, but they are the right groups."

Kalish touched the seeds and recognized them immediately. It was one of the best dead ends. There was no way the required transpositions could be made. That had been proved experimentally through generations of frustrating breeding, and more recently, theoretically. The seeds were a laboratory curiosity; their primary use was to provide a trick question for an acolyte's final examination—a Godly purpose nevertheless. He smiled at the boy. "You may spend as much time as you wish to try to rearrange the groups. Take a little plot in the experimental garden, near the outer wall."

"Must I do it out there?" the boy asked petulantly.

"By the wall or in the garden?"

"In the garden."

"Of course," the priest responded, "that's where all experiments are to be done." He gave the boy a pouch containing the tantalizing failures. A few generations of trial and error would convince the child far better than hours of lecture.

"May I do it now?" Pils asked eagerly.

"Certainly." The priest agreed. This was no time of the year to plant that crop, and the results were bound to be disappointing, but that was something else the boy had to learn. As sensitive as he was, as powerful as he was, he was still a child and had a child's lessons to learn.

The boy took the seeds and left the room while Kalish continued his contemplation of the strange thing in the sky. A few minutes later Pils returned.

"I have them now, Kalish," he said gaily. "Look!"

Kalish was annoyed. The boy had obviously not even planted the seeds. He had had barely enough time to run down to the garden and back again. He needed discipline. "Go out now and plant them," the priest insisted. "After you have crossbred your selections you can show me if they are closer to the correct transposition!"

"But I have them now!" the boy insisted. "Please

look. It will take ever so many weeks till they come up. Please look!" He dropped seeds into Kalish's hand.

Kalish continued his contemplation of the object, but habit was strong, and he could not avoid examining the seeds in detail. He focused his consciousness on them, going over each code group in order. Finally he reached the four groups—they were in the proper order! He concentrated again, barely containing his excitement. Incredibly, miraculously, he confirmed their perfection. Awed by the experience, he fell to his knees, weeping with joy, bowing down low, thanking God for having allowed him to witness perfection.

"How did you get these?" he asked Pils, still trembling with emotion.

"I made them, Kalish. Just as I said I would. You said that I had to do it in the garden, so I ran out and did them and brought them back here for you to see. They are right, aren't they?"

"Yes, they are, boy. Can you undo them?"

"Sure, but do I have to go to the garden?"

"No, you may do them here if you wish."

The boy took the seeds from the priest and held them in his pudgy hands, screwing up his face as he concentrated. In a moment he returned them to the priest, who confirmed that they were as they had been before.

"Can I play now?"

"Not just yet. Make them perfect again, Pils."

"Sure." He took them back, went through the same pantomime as before, handed the rearranged seeds to the bewildered priest, and ran out to the court.

Within hours Kalish had spread the news to the rest of the planet. Other priests, the high priests themselves, announced their intention to make the arduous journey to examine the prodigy in person. In the meantime Kalish's brothers had taken Pils other samples to rearrange. He could make some simple transpositions, of six or seven code groups, and could take incorrect groups and modify them, but, as he said after he failed with the more complicated tests, "They get sticky and they don't want to move."

61

Despite their disappointment, the priests were universally awed by his ability to change things rather than merely to perceive them. They realized that he could not make some of the changes they had wanted because they were too complicated for him. He would lose his way in the tangled molecules. He was, after all, still a child.

At length, Kalish stopped the experiments, announcing that with more training Pils would understand the changes and would possibly be able to make them. The high priests, recognizing the special affinity between Kalish and the boy, and acknowledging the wisdom of keeping him close to home, decided that the boy would be tutored by Kalish and other priests of special talent who would shortly arrive at the temple. The boy was not to be pushed into premature responsibility, no matter how tempting it might be. He would be trained and ordained a priest, probably a high priest, upon reaching majority and not before. If, as a high priest, he decided that it was God's purpose that perfection be achieved through rearrangement, he could do it then. They had waited many centuries; they could afford to wait longer.

By the eight month the modulated light from the thing had become stronger and more regular. Kalish thought that with help he might be able to decode the now familiar pattern. He called together as many other priests as he could find, among them the talented specialists who had come to tutor the boy, and together they went out to the square, joined hands, and sensed the pattern. This cooperative effort enabled them to deduce that it was transmitting an abstract representation of their own solar system. The large sun was dominant in these transmissions, but the smaller sun, the larger planets, and several of the smaller planets, including their own, could also be identified. Unraveling the pattern had been difficult. The solar system picture was merely the only sensible pattern they had been able to extract from the thing's transmissions, and that was all but buried under an overburden of complex shifting symmetries whose structure, never mind function, was barely perceptible. Kalish re-examined the old signals previously received from that star that were recorded in the archives and applied the same scheme that had been used to decode the signals. What had previously been a random jumble of code groups became a clear representation of the thing's originating solar system. Further research into the archives revealed that this was not the first emissary from that solar system, but that similar things had been sent before, in centuries gone by.

The two patterns, the new and the old, now correlated, caused a new round of speculation. The thing must be alive, they reasoned, an emissary sent from the nearby star for unknown purposes. They agreed that it had something to do with Pils; there was a Godly design to it. Had not Kalish been the first to sense the emissary, and on the same day he had discovered Pils? In fact, was it not the boy's sensing of it that had brought him to the priest's attention? These were sound theological arguments. They could not, however, understand why it chose to communicate with them by such outlandishly slow and ineffectual means—modulated light. They tried repeatedly to contact it in the normal manner, the same way they occasionally communicated with races on other planets, but got no response. It did not even respond when they tried to reach it with its own bizarre signals. A heated discussion took place when some of the younger priests suggested that they try to send a similar beam of low-frequency modulated radio waves directly back to the thing's originating sun in response to the patterns that were in the archives. While possible, this proposal was adjudged impractical—it would take an unseemly effort to create a signal sufficiently strong to be discerned against the background of electronic noise that pervaded the universe. As the arguments raged, the thing progressed on its own unwavering drop toward the sun.

The boy continued to develop. He had taught himself the old trick of modulating light—normally a pleasant effect, of little practical use except to entertain children and make fires. In Pils's case, however, the intensity and directivity of the beams of energy he created bordered on the dangerous. Now and then he would move small objects or make them disappear. This, too, was not an unknown talent, but as expected, it appeared in unusual strength in the boy. He tried, hampered by the vocabulary of a five-year-old, to explain to Kalish what he did and how. "There are four kinds of sticky," he told Kalish, "the strong, the light, the weak, and the very weak—and they're all part of the big sticky." All that Kalish could make of it was that the light, the fire, the movement of the objects, and the rearrangements of the seeds were to the boy different aspects of the same fundamental thing—the "sticky." It was too new a concept for the priest, even though he was by now accustomed to the boy's strange ways.

As the months passed, Pils also kept watch on the object, but unlike the priests who still debated its Godly mission, it disturbed the boy. It was visible in the daytime again, and the boy often looked at it with obvious displeasure, hurling great blasts of energy at it and its parent star. The patterns that the boy sent were so strong, so morbid, and so readily detectable by even the untalented that Kalish forbade him to attempt any more contact with it. He questioned Pils about his hatred of the thing, but the boy would only say that it was a bad thing and that he would destroy it as soon as he could make enough "sticky." The priest wondered how much "sticky" was enough.

The child had only recently caused a great explosion in a field several miles from town. A huge hole, large enough to swallow the temple, topped by an awesome cloud of debris, had resulted. "It was only the sticky from a grain of sand," the boy had explained—it being no explanation.

Kalish thought that he was beginning to understand what the "sticky" was all about. As he trained the boy, studied him, discussed his findings with the other tutors, the "sticky" concept began to be revealed over the horizons of his intellect. He kept trying to change the gene pattern of the starch plant and had done so with limited success, but the changes were never permanent. The student and teacher would then trade roles; the child, now with almost no effort, would make the simple transposition while the priest exerted himself to follow the casual miracle.

The theological debate continued, fed by the reticence of the "emissary" to communicate with them and the boy's hatred on the one hand, and the miraculous circumstances of its coming on the other. Pils claimed to know what it was and insisted that it was bad. Despite his help, the priests could make no sensible contact with it—or perceive any evil in it. So they turned their attention to the star system from which it had come—their thoughts, warm and welcoming, going out—and getting nothing in response.

One day, almost two years after Pils had joined the priests, he quietly announced to Kalish that he could now make enough "sticky." Kalish, being somewhat distracted at the moment, murmured his assent, not realizing what he had agreed to. The boy sat down, hugging himself, and suddenly fell unconscious. Kalish was startled by what he perceived to be a massive bolt of energy—a force that arced out into space directly for the thing. The object blossomed for a brief moment and was then quiet again—and no longer visible.

Pils remained in a coma for weeks. Probing the child's mind while he was unconscious, in an attempt to heal him, had yielded nothing but concepts even more alien than the "sticky." The child was full of anger and totally dedicated to the conviction of the thing's evil, but the priests could not distinguish between the child's concept of the thing and the thing itself. It was all a tragic error, a by-product of too much power in too young a child. Kalish resolved to halt all further experiments and the uncontrolled rush to bring Pils to his full powers. They nursed him, and when he finally came out of the coma, he offered no explanation, but exuded satisfaction with having destroyed the thing. But his exultation was premature, for the object was not gone, Kalish realized, as the boy's gloom returned and as he caught Pils, time and again, glancing in its erstwhile direction.

Kalish and Pils were in the square when suddenly the boy began to cry hysterically, cursing with unbridled venom. It was not gone, and Kalish could see it again, though dimly. The child's paroxysm reached a peak and he fell unconscious. The priest knelt to examine him. Then he sensed that the thing had momentarily disappeared, only to be replaced by an emptiness that grew as he watched. The emptiness expanded, blocking out stars, and continued to grow until it had reached the size of a planet's orbit—then it collapsed as suddenly as it had grown, to a tiny dark body, imperceptible except for its huge mass—a mass greater than the big sun, which had now begun to move toward it, huge arms of burning matter reaching out to the blackness in response to the sudden disruption of the gravitational balance of their solar system.

Everyone in the square now noticed these happenings, and they stood, arms spread, trying to get the clearest view. Here and there they were joining hands, and then the little groups linked as well, until the whole crowd was spliced, looking at the malevolent object that had so suddenly erupted.

Kalish now recognized it as a burned-out star that would voraciously suck up anything that came too close to it. Horrified, he realized that their own suns could not withstand its pull and would eventually spiral into it. With the death of their suns, would come their own. The boy's purpose was now revealed and they had failed to heed it. He joined hands with the crowd and cried out to the other priests in thousands of other squares all over the planet, "The light modulators out of Sol have stolen our suns—let us be avenged!"

Thus linked, the entire planet cried out the message of revenge—over and over again—throughout the weeks they had left. The curse went out at many times the speed of light to the edges of the galaxy and beyond. It was still being sent as the big sun died, and as the smaller was destroyed, and for several hours thereafter, until the last priest in the last square had frozen to death; it went out: "Avenge us—avenge us—avenge us!"

5

Petrel

Po Lin had been expecting the Ecomeister's summons. There had been rumors that the probe ship had returned, which could have been accomplished only by using the drive. Alpha Centauri was no longer visible. Six months ago, when Saturn had suddenly disappeared, followed a week later by Jupiter, she had been convinced that the drive was close to perfection, despite official denials. Friends had taken to giving Po Lin knowing winks and surreptitious congratulations. While she hoped, she would not acknowledge it—that would have been an unseemly presumption.

The Ecomeister, looking older and more worn than ever, did in due time summon her. He was all business this time, getting to the point without even a preliminary ritual. "You are taking the prototype ship out— the *Petrel*," he announced. "It will be, as you know, the most difficult of all. We will need navigation songs to guide the ships that follow. With every jump you make, the harder it will be for you to track the sun correctly. Eventually you or the computer will make a mistake and jump beyond sight of the sun. Keep trying to return until you run out of buoys. Then you will find a suitable, uninhabited planet, revive the crew, and establish a colony. We may never find you, but the songs your buoys will transmit will enable us to correct your navigational errors. Other ships will follow in your path, exploring farther out, until they too will be lost. Finally, when the navigation songs for this sector of the galaxy are finished, the emigration proper will begin. You will leave in twelve hours."

Po Lin had no questions, and no comments were expected, yet the Ecomeister did not dismiss her. They were in his office and home, a quiet place with doors that could be closed rather than the typical curtains. The other occupants of the room drifted out as if in response to a prearranged signal. The last one closed the door behind him. Did the Ecomeister intend to make love to her? She looked at him carefully, trying to determine the extent of his need, but there were no signs. It was confusing—what else besides lovemaking required such privacy?

Harrison took up a keening—a mournful death wail that Po Lin had not heard before. It had no words, but it spoke of a big death, not of the voluntary recycling of an oldster, or of the kind death of genetic selection, or even the sad death by accident, but of a foul death, a murder. She cried with him for the murderer as much as for the murdered—until, racked with sobs, he could no longer continue. Again the silence. Trembling, he fumbled into the pocket of his loincloth and took out a small plastic square which he gave to Po Lin. She examined it carefully. It showed a pair of line figures, possibly male and female, vaguely humanoid. Behind them was a structure, a stepped pyramid, atop of which stood another line figure.

"Here is another for you to consider," the Ecomeister said. This one showed a stylized solar system. The sun was represented by a pyramid—the fourth planet by a top view of the male and female figures, their arms spread and touching to make a circle.

"Are there more?" she asked.

He gave her another plate. The scene was similar to that of the first plate, but the major figures were broken, as was the background pyramid. Po Lin, realizing the symbolism of the third plate, turned to the

Ecomeister. "It is a race of intelligent beings that has been destroyed by some unknown tragedy."

"There is more," the old man said and gave her another plate. She looked at it but could not make it out at first. She studied it for a long time before she spoke.

"This is a star map. It is a view from the galactic hub, of this sector of the galaxy, as it will appear thirty-five thousand years from now, when the light of our and neighboring stars finally reach the galactic center."

"That is correct," he said. "A year ago we began to receive signals from space. Centuries of continual monitoring had never revealed a pattern like this or any other kind. It was being broadcast over a broad frequency range. The experts say that the transformer was crude but powerful. The signals appeared to have been aimed toward us, but of this we are not certain. The entire transmission lasted for days and was repeated many times, so we are sure that it is correct in all details."

He gave Po Lin two more plates. The first showed the alien solar system again. The pyramid-sun was missing, and the circles that had depicted planetary orbits were replaced by spirals into the sun. The last plate showed a blowup of the view from the hub but with fewer stars. It was as if the picture had been taken from a point two-thirds along the galactic radius. The sender's system was represented by the broken figure. All other stars except one were represented by dots; that star was shown as a drawn bow with the arrow pointed unmistakably toward the victim's solar system.

Po Lin cried out as the realization hit her. "Aweee! It is Alpha Centauri and we are the murderers!" She stared at the plates again, going from one to the other, trying to deny what she saw. Finally, regaining her composure, she challenged the accusation. "There are other stars, possibly inhabited, along the same plane that could have been responsible. It would take at least three such maps from three different positions in space to confirm it. Furthermore, these plates do not positively identify Alpha Centauri—there is a possibility of ambiguity in that also—again it would take confirming star maps. Are there any?"

"No, Po Lin. We have no other maps, but it is useless to try to rationalize this away—we do have a confirmation." He touched several keys on a panel. A familiar voice emerged from the loudspeaker. She recognized the death wail that Harrison had sung earlier—his rendition had been a travesty of the real thing. M'Tamba's voice ranged from a deep sonorous baritone to a penetrating, shrill falsetto. It glided in agony over the scales without words but not without meaning. It pierced her and shook her and transformed her, tore at her, until she could feel his double anguish—of his own pain and of the deaths he had caused. She was beyond crying and listened, stone faced and totally absorbed as the litany unfolded.

Then, when she felt that she could take no more, words appeared, blurred at first, then more distinct, until a pattern could be perceived, a pattern that coalesced into phrases and then crystalized into sentences, and finally into a coherent story. He told it all—without bitterness. When he described how he had managed to keep the ship together, he made light of it and became again the M'Tamba she had known. The old M'Tamba, M'Tamba the braggart and teller of lies, the supertechnician who could repair anything with nothing at hand. He joked about the radiation sickness and his own impending death. Then he told the story from the other side, as he imagined it, and then lifted the burden of guilt. Finally he gave the solution to the drive equations—the justification for it all—and ended in a coda that rephrased the song, with sorrow, guilt, repentance, comedy, and hope interwoven, dying down at the last to a whispered, almost wordless, "Take this, M'Tamba's gift, the song of death, of hope, the song of the probe."

Harrison roused her after a decent interval. "We had

71

signals from the earlier buoys—and we were sure that he was going mad. Then we got the song. The probe returned successfully, a few light minutes away, but it was moving too fast to intercept—it went into the sun some hours after we first sighted it, but there was ample time to receive all the ship's records. He was already dead then. We didn't know what to make of it. The ship's records seemed to confirm the madness. We dared not use the data he had sent—despite his successful return. We waited four years for the light from Alpha Centauri to reach us, and then his figures were confirmed. The probe had been successful, and its return was not just a fluke. Then we began to receive the broadcasts of the tablets, and rather than M'Tamba's records confirming the tablets, it was the tablets that confirmed M'Tamba."

"And the accusation?" she asked.

"We don't know if it was intended solely for us or if it is being sent to the entire galaxy. It is traveling at the speed of light, so we should be able to outrun it. It will take fifty centuries to reach the other side. If it is being sent toward the hub, where the young races are, the accusation will spread to ever more races as they emerge, but in the scale of galactic time and distance the broadcast is so short and its power so weak that it is not likely to be heard. We shall be troubled only by our conscience."

"But M'Tamba implied that they are telephathics."

"Perhaps," Harrison admitted, "his story can be interpreted that way. If so, who knows if they have spread the accusation in that manner, how far it will travel, or for how long, or how fast."

"Who knows about this?" she asked.

"The Meisters, the computer, now you, and soon those who will ship out with you. It will be told to each crew only after they have made the first jump, and to each child as it reaches the age of reason." He stood abruptly. "You have ten hours to say good-bye to your friends and children." With that, he left the room.

Except for Po Lin and a few others, the ship's complement of five thousand humans had been placed in suspended animation. The crew would be revived in its entirety prior to a planetfall, or one at a time, as the command crew grew old and had to be replaced. The life-support systems could keep a minimum crew of four alive for several hundred years. In addition, they had sperm and ova for domestic animals, seeds for plants, and other paraphernalia needed for colonizing, if they managed to find a compatible planet, with not too many hostile life forms, before the life-support systems ran out, while the crew was still large enough, and if they landed with sufficient equipment and supplies. Since racial and not individual survival was the goal, even the tenuous hope offered by the pilot ship was not to be cast aside.

They left the solar system under the reaction drive, climbing to a point high above the ecliptic plane, where the hole drive was activated. Within microseconds it had created a black hole that radiated from the exact center of the ship. As the first hole was expanding, but before it had reached its maximum size, a second hole was started that, upon overtaking the first, annihilated it. The first took them into tachyon space, where time ran in reverse and where they lingered for an imperceptible fraction of a second before being returned to normal space by the second hole, but far from where they had started.

The view screen displayed a picture of their new position. It was, as planned, near Alpha Centauri's erstwhile location. Within minutes they had located the signal from M'Tamba's last buoy—henceforth known as M'Tamba's gift. The buoy was retrieved. They stayed long enough to make the exacting observations required to fix that location in relation to Earth. Then

Po Lin encoded the navigational data into a new song and replaced the old buoy with its radio broadcast with a more powerful transmitter based on the black hole drive itself.

The second jump was back toward Earth. They emerged closer to the sun than they had hoped—a half light year away on the other side. The observations continued, and another buoy was dropped, its song summarizing the deviation from the expected that had been experienced.

With each successive jump Po Lin took more careful observations, made finer corrections, but, as expected, the error kept increasing. Each jump was now as likely to bring them closer to Earth as it was to take them away from it. With each jump another buoy was dropped. At all times they had been able to keep the sun in view, sometimes from as far away as twenty light years, or once from as close as a few light weeks. Yet, with each jump, either far away or close to their home world, it became increasingly unreachable. Finally, with all the buoys gone, and with the error having accumulated to the point where each new jump was no better than random, she aimed the ship in the one direction where some precision was still possible, and made a great leap of twenty thousand light years toward the hub.

6

The Navigator

They were the last to go. Ten ships had left on the first day a year before. The next day twenty more headed for the hub, and on each day thereafter more ships left—thirty, fifty, seventy—till finally the peak was reached when more than a hundred ships, each with a crew of five thousand humans frozen in the cryostats, turned their backs on Earth forever.

They streamed toward the hub, an expanding cone of humanity ten light years long, scouts in the lead searching for a hospitable new home, the rear guard systemically stripping the wrecked hulk that had been the Earth of everything that might be useful for the long trip ahead. And then only a scant dozen ships remained in orbit, waiting for the last shuttle.

None was left behind. The old, the dispirited, and the intensely nostalgic opted for the greater good and had themselves converted to accompany mankind as chunks of protein if not as human beings. Earth was not without life, though—a life, however, that was comfortable in the stench of sulfur dioxide and noxious hydrocarbons, life that had adapted to the heat, the lack of oxygen, the streams of running acid, and the dim sun barely seen through the perpetual haze. A worm that had once lived in a hot spring, a blind cave fish, ten thousand crawling horrors in the Marianas trench, a family of roaches, a blue-green alga, a mold that liked polystyrene, and a hundred species of anaerobic bacteria—they alone remained and lived; some thrived.

The last shuttle came screaming out of the atmosphere, dropped its booster (man's last act of desecration), and continued upward to orbit with the waiting ship. They had turned off what little equipment remained, searched the cryostats and corridors for stragglers, confirmed the emptiness of the storerooms, and, satisfied that nothing useful was left except a bitter lesson called Earth, they took their places in the shuttle to the last ship in lonely orbit about Earth.

The captain finished the predeparture check and ordered the navigator to make the first jump. He sang the departure song in a sweet tenor—twice he had to stop because his crying had altered the delicate timing of the song. The captain—she was more the realist, as he was the sentimentalist—chided him for the waste that the delay entailed. Chagrined, he began again and made the first jump.

Later, when they reached a preordained point, they paused and looked back toward the sun. The last Grand Ecomeister of Earth, the responsibility of his grim duty heavy upon him, dispatched a missile to the sun. There would be no traces by which the victim's avengers could find them, no home to yearn for in future aeons, no monument for future races that would attest to their rapine. The missile reached its target and blossomed into a monstrous hole that swallowed the entire solar system and hurled it intact but alone, desperately alone, to the emptiness beyond the stars.

7

The Plan

There were the colonies, the ships, the people, and the plan. The colonies, which during the brief period between founding and finding and destruction (decades, usually, or, for the lucky few, centuries), managed to keep the ships equipped with material and crews, and occasionally to launch a new ship. The ships, unchanged from the time of launch out of Earth, except for a drift toward greater mechanical simplicity, more sophistication and viability—the ships, identical except for the special imprints of their crews—the three dozen ambulant humans who kept the watches and did maintenance while their brethren slept in the cryostats. The people, furtively skirting the edges of the galaxy, at first barely able to survive, and then later, ever so slowly, increasing, thereby giving continual testament to the wisdom of the plan.

The plan was based on three tenets: man shall not again cause harm to another race; man shall survive; and they shall build a new home, unpolluted and fitting to their needs forever. They left the Earth in a vast armada of ships streaking toward the galactic hub at many times the speed of light, where they found worlds in abundance, some barren, some with life just emerging from the seas, some civilized along parallels to man's own history, others in the agony of racial death.

To avoid harming sentient life, present or potential, only those worlds on which animals had yet to be dominant on land could be settled. Yet even this restriction of the plan left them with many choices, for there were young worlds in abundance at the hub. Many colonies were founded, some by only one ship that had been forced down by lack of supplies, others by the coordinated efforts of hundreds of ships. They settled, worked, built, and were inevitably destroyed.

Individual ships that attempted communications with worlds on which artifacts could be detected were often destroyed or severely damaged by unknown methods. The plan prescribed extremely cautious steps by which such contact attempts could be made—and later proscribed them altogether. New worlds, settled in parts of the galaxy where stars were dense, were more quickly destroyed than the settlements in the backwaters. It did not take long to learn this bloody statistic, and thereafter the plan directed them to the galactic fringes, where worlds were old and stars were cold and sparse.

Single ships or pairs of ships were rarely harmed, but let a meeting of ships grow too large and remain together too long, and they, too, were destroyed. So the plan regulated the times of meetings, the durations thereof, and the number of ships that could be gathered. Yet the framers of this section of the plan realized that if intership communications were totally cut off, mankind would soon become a few thousand isolated fragments and would eventually disappear. They dispersed the fleet but charged each ship to search continually for others, and upon meeting, to interchange as much of the crew as possible.

They had to live. The tenuous existence of the settlements did not provide a sufficient base of necessary supplies. They found their needs on primitive worlds that were soon to be destroyed by an errant sun. They picked over the bones of planets whose civilization was doomed by nuclear warfare, or polluted worlds with genetics gone awry. The plan established the circum-

78

stance under which such worlds could be stripped. Occasionally, but increasingly as time went on, on some of these worlds they found references to themselves in the archives of a now dead civilization. Not once, or only twice, but many times, they reconfirmed the fact that they were the object of a galactic vendetta. They learned that the other races, although telepathic, discovered man by sensing his radio and radar signals. So the plan acquired strict rules regarding the use of communications. As an added precaution, isolated worlds were chosen for colonization, far from any potentially hostile star cluster, so that a stray pulse of electromagnetic radiation might go undetected for hundreds of years, for so long it had to travel to the nearest star. Because the aliens' attacks left so few survivors, they did not know how intense the radio signals could be and still be undetected. The plan chose safety by barring almost all transmissions. On the basis of sound theoretical reasoning, overhead power lines were prohibited, for they too could be detected at a distance. The culmination of this logic led the colonists to a distaste for the use of electricity in any form, and then only with elaborate precautionary rituals and only after a proclamation by an official and often officious Sensor that the site was electromagnetically clean.

They learned how to locate their adversaries and keep away from them. Unfortunately, that was not enough—the enemy, in time, deduced the plan. Having flushed man out of the hub, repelled his first advances, and having sent the scattered fleet, ripped and bleeding, back to the rim, the aliens sought the isolated world specified by the plan, and by means unknown to man, destroyed the colonies. Some planets were booby trapped, turning into coruscating horrors when a predetermined level of civilization had been achieved. The plan dealt with the detection and neutralization of such booby traps as well.

Once, early in the odyssey, they had settled a world, an ideal world, that had responded to terraforming with amazing rapidity. In one hundred and fifty years a barren planet had been converted to man's needs. The word was sent to the fleet, which gathered and began to settle as fast as they arrived. Almost a third of the exiles participated in the great gathering. They delighted in the new world, its clear air, its abundant food, its beauty, all of which they had created. Then the aliens struck them down. The paradise gutted— homeless again. No one on the surface of Eden survived. The stragglers, those who had been too far away and those in the orbiting ships, lived to add another chapter to the plan so that the same mistake would not be made again. It had been a trap. No large segment of mankind would ever again take that risk. Colonization and terraforming were established at the safest level, not at the rate that would achieve a home as fast as possible.

What had started as aspirations based on justice for all races became cautions, and then rules, and eventually unquestionable taboos. Each human had a choice: to live in space, in freedom, without fear, in the confines of a ship and the company of a few, on the edges of survival, but mostly asleep in the cryostats, or to live in a colony with wide vistas and open skies, continuing consciousness, enjoying the variety of thousands of fellow humans, but circumscribed in every direction by the strictures of the plan, and in fear.

8

Gils

Sheina was not happy. She was hungry and tired of sitting still for so long. She indicated her displeasure by emitting a low bleat. He did not pay attention but continued looking through the binoculars at the valley below. She tapped his shoulder to no avail. She growled her annoyance this time, and to strengthen the force of her argument, she gently clamped her teeth about his arm, forcing him to lower the binoculars. Gils looked at the big Siamese. "I guess we won't spot him today. Are you hungry?"

She uttered a mixture of bleats and purrs that meant that indeed she was and that it was about time that he came to his senses and also had something to eat.

"All right." He picked up the binoculars again. "I'll look around for something." He examined a nearby water hole at which a herd of Thomson's gazelles were having an early evening drink. He spotted a young male by the edge of the herd. A weak one, he thought. The buck was not aggressive enough to fight the other males and would probably remain a bachelor; worse, he might mate with a similarly ostracized cow and produce offspring that were marginally fit. Gils pointed the buck out to Sheina, who, delighted with the prospect of running down a gazelle, loped into the brush and down the hill.

Gils followed the eighty-pound cat through the binoculars. Her buff coat, much like the mottled camouflage he wore, blended with the yellowing grass. Occasionally he could see her tail, a dark brown snake aristocratically poised above, but protestingly drawn along by the cat's narrow rump. She stopped at a clearing near the foot of the hill and looked at him inquisitively. As usual, she was begging for more than one strike—as usual, Gils waved his arm from side to side with his palm out, ending with a single finger pointing upward. She bared her teeth in a mock hiss and slunk into the underbrush again.

Gils continued searching the broad valley. He was looking for a tiger—a wreck of an aged male who was not doing his job. Large herbivores were drifting into the valley, welcoming the respite from terror that the impotent old tiger offered them. As a result of the unwelcomed influx, the grass was being eaten too rapidly to recover. This would eventually cause excess erosion. Neighboring regions, lacking the normal complement of herbivores, were experiencing an uncontrolled growth of grasses, which would have repercussions all along the food chain. The neighboring carnivores were getting hungry and were beginning to follow the migrating herbivores, further upsetting the delicate ecological balance. It was definitely time for the old boy to go, and since he had no natural enemies, the job was up to Gils and Sheina.

Gils had discussed the old tiger with the other Ecomers at the last council meeting. Selma had offered him a young surplus male as a replacement. Her group was out capturing it now. They would turn him loose in the valley after Gils's kill. Far off, in the eastern corner of the valley, Gils saw a movement that might be the tiger. He increased the magnification for a closer look. The old emperor was there, all right, tearing at some small animal that he had managed to catch. That was good; he would probably be sleeping through the next day, making it easier to stalk him.

Gils was startled by a commotion at the water hole.

Gazelles were exploding from the area by the hundreds, leaping thirty and forty feet in the low gravity. The young buck lay by the water hole, his throat slashed, but Sheina was not visible. He watched the jumping, frightened animals escaping. A group of gazelles that had been trailing the main herd suddenly veered, exposing the source of their anguish—Sheina, who was cutting them out and running for the sheer joy of the chase. Fast as she was, they began to outdistance her, so she dropped back and returned to the water hole at a leisurely walk. She had not intended to kill a second gazelle—she was too obedient for that—besides, it would have taken a lot of luck, but Gils had not told her not to *chase* the other gazelles.

He returned to the examination of the tiger's lair at the far end of the valley, working out an approach and point of attack. Sheina returned with the kill. She dropped it in front of him and licked herself clean as he prepared the carcass. He skinned it carefully and rubbed the hide with salt. Then, working quickly, he stripped the meat into long neat slices, giving the smaller, less manageable chunks to Sheina, who gobbled them whole with obvious pleasure. He nibbled the raw meat as he stored the strips into the freezer pack. When he was finished, he took the bones, guts, and other leftovers that neither he nor Sheina wanted to the clearing. In a short while several vultures had settled and were soon squabbling noisily over the remains. The man and the cat finished their meal with a drink of water, Sheina drinking out of his hands. He snuggled into the sleeping bag, struggling with the big cat who wanted to join him inside. She finally settled down, but not without protest over his callous treatment, alongside of him.

He looked up at the black sky. It was almost starless, and the few bright spots were fuzzy outlines of distant galaxies and farther quasars. The Milky Way, the lens of the galaxy, was just above the horizon, mostly occluded by the valley's surrounding hills. A star rose out of the north, moved rapidly upward, and disappeared at the zenith. "The seed ship, kitty." She did not look up but politely acknowledged his comment with a melodious bleat. "What's it like shipside, I wonder. You know, kitty, I've never been shipside. I was born here and I've never been offworld. Just another groundsider—that's what we are, Sheina, a pair of dirty-faced groundsiders. How about you? Did you ever want to go shipside?" The cat did not even acknowledge that remark. "I guess not," he continued. "Up there you'd be nothing but a few micrograms of chromosomes in the freezer." He patted her head and scratched behind the ear. She approved of the turn the conversation was taking.

Another bright object moved up from the horizon. "It's the station this time." He had pointed to it and therefore she had to look up, but her eyes were not suited to seeing that kind of object. She grunted and went back to licking her forepaw, which had a small thorn in it. He remained silent, looking at the scant stars, a hand behind his head and the other on his chest. That would not do, and, having finished the paw's medication, she maneuvered her head under his hand and growled over his lack of attention to her most important ear.

He was awakened the next morning by Sheina, hungry and impatient to get on with the day's work. She began the ritual by touching noses and purring as loudly as she could. While it did not awaken Gils, it sent flocks of birds screaming into the air. She then batted his nose with her paw, delicately extending her sharp claws a fraction of a millimeter at a time, until at last, the combination of the noise, the ever-so-slight pain, and half the weight of the cat on his chest destroyed any further possibility of sleep. He yawned and was met in turn by Sheina's yawn—a casual display of ranks of dental bayonets. She was now sitting on his chest. She closed her mouth, fortunately shutting off

84

her bad breath, and smiled beatifically at Gils, who had to struggle to utter the command that would free him. Once released, he took strips of meat out of the freezer and reconstituted them with the rest of the water from the canteen. He divided the meat with Sheina, packed their belongings, placed the small pack on Sheina's back, and put on his own.

It took most of the morning to work around to the other side of the valley. They kept to the surrounding hills, on the downwind side, rather than cut directly across, which could have given them away. The old boy might have been weak and lazy, but not so senile that he would allow a frontal attack on his demesne. By noon they were on a hillside above the tiger, who was still dozing peacefully. Gils took off the packs and they continued, unencumbered, farther down the slope.

As Gils approached the tiger, Sheina, sneakiness personified, began a wide circle that would eventually place her opposite Gils on the other side of their quarry. She would, if the tiger attacked, provide a diversion. She had completed the circle and was now ready to approach the tiger herself. She stopped and licked herself clean so that a sudden windshift would not give her away. Gils crawled to a position five hundred yards from the tiger. He could see it clearly now. He set up the tripod and mounted the light rifle on it. He carefully adjusted the telescopic sight onto the lower part of the tiger's shoulder. There was almost no wind now. He loaded the clip; the first two bullets contained a nerve block that would paralyze and then painlessly kill the animal within minutes without contaminating the meat. The other four bullets were high explosives—just in case.

The wind shifted, bringing a slight breeze in his direction. It was not enough to affect the shot. The tiger stirred, catching vague traces of Sheina, who had been momentarily upwind from him. Gils fired both rounds, fearing that the waking animal might move and spoil the shot. Both were on target. The tiger jumped up, roared, and immediately took off in Sheina's direction.

Gils lost sight of the tiger as it crashed through the tall grass after his smaller cousin. The tiger, roaring his displeasure, was easy to follow now. From his actions, Gils could guess where Sheina was. He focused the sight on a clearing, and sure enough, Sheina came through it at full speed, the tiger close behind. Sheina was circling back around toward Gils instead of simply outrunning him in the open as she could have easily done. That would have been the safe thing to do, especially with the poison working in him. But she was leading him back toward Gils, risking being cut off herself and unnecessarily exposing Gils, just to avoid a long walk back.

He removed the tripod and clambered down the hill as fast as he could. He stopped atop a small rise where he could get a clear shot at the area below him. Sheina was heading toward a rock outcropping, a few hundred feet away downhill. He focused on the rock and waited. Sheina came bounding out of the tall grass and onto the rocks, her claws scrabbling for a hold. She made it to the top just as the tiger, remarkably active and unusually energetic for one of his age, appeared. He made an enormous leap directly to the top of the rocks, missing Sheina by inches. She continued upward, directly toward Gils, with the tiger behind her, seemingly unaffected by the chemicals spreading through his bloodstream. Gils fired—and missed. He took more careful aim this time, leading the tiger, taking no notice of Sheina, who had just streaked by him, a blur of buff and brown. The tiger stopped to evaluate this new enemy; he roared, tensed, crouched low prepared to strike, and collapsed.

"Sometimes," Gils said to Sheina as they were examining the huge animal, "I think you get yourself into trouble just for the fun of it. See," he said, showing her the half-empty clip, "you cost us an extra bullet. Now go find it!" She sniffed the clip and sneezed at the offensive smell of cordite and went back down the hill to search for the bullet while Gils climbed to fetch the packs.

He took out a marker balloon, filled it with helium from the freezer pack, and sent it aloft, tethered to the tiger's front paw by a fine line. He sprayed the tiger with repellents to keep bugs, worms, and other carnivores from eating the meat or ruining the skin. He then turned back, directly across the valley, following Sheina's path.

High above, the pilot in the spotter glider saw the marker balloon. He turned northward, toward Selma's village, to alert the retrieval crew. They would bring the new tiger and take the old tiger's skin, meat, teeth, and bones in payment. As evening came and the double suns were setting, a hungry and tired Sheina approached the waiting Gils, with a high explosive bullet carried gingerly in her mouth.

Ten parsecs from any interesting star, Yehorag the Corrector detected a brief pulse of modulated light. It was too short for him to track accurately. He logged the signal and turned his attention farther toward the hub, where rumors indicated several more likely traces. Space was too big and the Correctors too few and time too short to waste on wild-goose chases. Better to stamp out the more advanced stages of the infection than to investigate what would probably turn out to be a natural phenomenon. If the pulse meant anything, it would eventually be correlated with others from the same source. Then another Corrector would be dispatched— fifty or a hundred years more or less would not matter.

Yehorag faced the hub and concentrated on building the focus that would translate his psyche inward. The stars shifted positions, their color crept to the red, and they accelerated from him into very long waves. When everything was black, he reversed the process and allowed normal space to reassert itself. It came back gradually, with little adjustment on his part. The place was unfamiliar. He sent out the question. The answers came immediately from several different places. Reoriented, he expressed his appreciation to the several anonymous priests and astronomers and continued the hunt.

The settlement was in the foothills of the ridge that surrounded the valley. As Gils stood on the ridge, he looked back at the valley critically, as he always did when he left it. There was a stand of pines near a bend in the creek. The bank was encroaching on them; several would soon be lost. The planners had misjudged the rate at which the stream would undercut the bank—the trees should have been planted on the other side. It was something to do, but the plan's priorities would not permit it. Another area, given over to grasses, was becoming marshy—eucalyptus trees would have been better there. Again there was no changing it now; later perhaps, after the settlers came, some other Ecomer would discover his notes and implement the changes. The hillside, for example—the plan explicitly stated that trees and foliage should have random, natural separation, so that no pattern could be detected from above, yet even a junior Ecomer trainee knew the value of planting to match the terrain. It was frustrating, but considering the restrictions of the plan and the limited knowledge of the pioneers, a good job had been done. It would have to do. He was resigned to that.

Sheina nudged him toward the settlement, food, and a warm place to sleep for the night. It took a lot of effort on her part to keep her charge attuned to the fundamentals of life. He was ever prone to gaze at stars, reflections, and other meaningless objects and to engage in interminable philosophical discussions. She nudged him again, hard, almost throwing him down, and at last he turned to the settlement and home. There was less to see of man's work at the settlement than in the valley. There, even an untutored shipsider could see the careful grooming of the foliage, the animals' habitats, and the workings of the plan. But the settlement itself was invisible, except to practiced eyes. Even the landing strip was almost invisible because of the several different colored grasses on it, grown in a random pattern, intended to hide it from prying eyes above. He always expected re-entry pilots to miss the strip, but they never did, so they too must have known what to look for.

This time however, the landing strip was obvious, for along its length dun-colored gliders were parked, and even as he looked, another was touching down. He recognized the gliders by the Ecomer's insignia on them. Shial from the eastern plateau, Selma from the north, Brom from the peninsula, Yuri's was the one touching down; twelve in all. They represented the ecological interests of their regions of the planet. They had held the annual council only three weeks before, on the peninsula, and another meeting was not scheduled for six months. The valley region, because of its central location, was always used for emergency meetings. Only something of importance could have precipitated an extraordinary session so soon after the regular meeting.

He hurried to the nearest entrance—a carefully disguised boulder which swung noiselessly aside to reveal a staircase. He was soon in a small complex of corridors that differed only slightly from equivalent corridors shipside. Color was the main point of difference. These corridors were uniformly drab, while shipside corridors were known for their imaginative artwork. Sheina left him for her own pen, and Gils, after stowing the meat in a food locker and his gear in the cubicle he called home, sought Liam, his assistant. Liam was at the main meeting hall and hurriedly approached Gils as he entered it, explaining, "I don't know the details. Shial called the council the day before yesterday. They've been arriving all day. It must be important because they radioed the call. They wanted to use a vehicle to get you, but I told them that you'd be back

89

before they found you. Shial says he'll brief us when the rest have arrived."

As he spoke, Yuri and two technicians entered the hall. "Bad headwinds, poor thermals, had to tack all the way up the mountains," he said. He was sweating profusely. He had run from the landing field without removing the high-altitude furs in which he was swaddled. Yuri made the grueling trip at least once a year and had never been known to use a booster rocket. His region, south of the continental divide, was the most recent to be opened. A toehold on the immense southern subcontinent that contained two-thirds of the planet's land mass. Yuri's group conducted a vast seeding program, broadcasting bacteria, plants, insects, and rodents, as far into the continent as they could safely fly and return. They lived a harsh, marginal existence, not attempting to increase their population. More than once, particularly after a severe winter, the other settlements had had to airlift their own meager surpluses to the south so that the project would not be jeopardized. The sacrifices were worth it, though, for the orbiting ships could detect a steady advance of Earth life forms and a gradual diminution of their native competitors.

The council chamber was cool and pleasant, having been carved out of a natural limestone cavern. The stone benches around the periphery of its bowl shape could hold the settlement's entire population. The news of the emergency session had spread quickly, and the hall was now filled to capacity with spectators.

Shial called the meeting to order. "I've not had a chance to explain the problem to all of you. Those of you who were here earlier, please excuse the repetition. There are ships on the way seeking haven. They will need to planetfall soon after they arrive. We must decide how many we can absorb."

"How many ships? How soon? How desperate?" they asked.

"No more questions until I finish, please! Three ships! Thirteen thousand humans in all. They'll arrive

90

in a few weeks. One of them is already in terminal recycle—every day's delay is another ten lives lost—and the others are not far from it." Shial's voice was heavy with the urgency of the situation. There was no minimizing the crisis. Their own population of fifty thousand was being asked to absorb an instantaneous increase of twenty-five percent. It could be done—easily, in fact, without danger to their lives, except for the plan. Every grain of wheat eaten by the refugees was one less grain of wheat for seeds. Every extra mouth could be translated into a reduction of the rate at which new acres of edible plant life would be created—which in turn could be translated into a reduced rate of expansion of Earthlike animal forms, delaying the time when a self-sustained ecology compatible to man would be created. Without their constant ministrations, the present inroads into the native ecology would crumble in centuries—like weeds encroaching on an abandoned highway. These were not the colonists; they were the terraformers who followed the pioneers but preceded the colonists. Theirs was to build an ecology, partly from seeds, ova, and sperm stored in the great ships when they had left Earth, partly from native life, and partly from genetic adaptations and hybrids of both. In the end they would achieve a self-sustained food chain, at the top of which a population of hundreds of millions could be maintained. It was a work of centuries, and they had been at it for only a hundred and fifty years.

The planet was ideal. Its biochemistry was genial. There were no large hostile life forms on the land, and the sea was still in the early stages of evolution. The climate was moderate. Mineral recources were abundant—and, most imortant, it was far from the nearest star cluster.

The pioneering crews had landed piecemeal over a period of a decade, depending first on converters cannibalized from the ship for their food—converting native sea life into edible proteins. A suitable emergency practice, but one that offered nothing for long-term viability. They had then adapted bacteria and other micro-organisms to begin the first link in the food chain. Later, as the pioneers were augmented by new arrivals, they became terraformers. They introduced algae into the ponds, and then mosses, insects, grasses, and worms. When fifty years had passed, they began to plant the trees, the rodents, and the small predators to feed on them. Eventually had come the higher mammals and their predators to keep them in balance with the grasses and the trees.

Concentric rings of humanly compatible life spread from the valley at the center, where there was the appearance of an Earth ecology. Yet, at the peripheries, native protozoans devoured Earth bacteria—their fragile ring of life would shrink and disappear if it were not for the constant pressure generated at the center. Until the outer circle had spread to cover more than half the planet, the native life could regain its birthright. And then, when the ring met itself and Earth protozoans devoured Earth bacteria, the first phase of the job—survival of an Earth ecology on land—would be completed. They would work for centuries more, planting new forests, controlling erosion, diverting rivers, until at last the planet could be settled. But the terraforming would not stop yet, for the sea, the sea would have to be changed. The sea, which had provided only oxygen but had otherwise lived on, in its foreign ways, would have to be changed lest its vast reservoir of alien life eventually recapture that which had been lost on land.

The terraformers, as on a hundred other planets, were building man's home world. A home that would not be destroyed by the building thereof. They could have built machines to strip out the buried minerals, defoliated the native life-forms and replaced them with Earth's, jetted across the continents or crawled upon its surface in fossil-fueled tractors, harvested the entire sea for proteins in abundance to feed a population of tens of millions for centuries. All this they could have done in half the time or less perhaps—but such hubris, said the plan, invited the aliens' detection and wrath, and if not that, they would end with a gutted wreck of a world that they would be forced to abandon again a millennium later.

So instead, they moved carefully, slowly, each life weighed, each life, whether human, native, or implanted, considered, not to achieve the best for themselves, but to endure austerity so that they could maximize the rate at which they accumulated their biological capital. The decision of the council, together with those in the orbiting seed ships and the three ships yet to arrive, was not a decision for themselves, but had to be balanced against the exiled remnants of mankind—thirteen thousand lives *now* at a cost of delaying the Home by a hundred years or more. Three ships in distress *now* to be compared to refusing thirty times three fifty years from now.

Shial spoke again. "The ships are from Kiryat and Edmonton—it's the Kiryat ship that's in big trouble. It attempted to land there, seeking haven. However, Kiryat has been sterilized!" He paused to let the shock of Kiryat's loss sink in. Kiryat had been more advanced than they. Kiryat could have easily taken one, two, or ten ships. They had started to increase their population by births, and a slight reduction in the birth rate would have accommodated the refugees.

He continued with the bad news. "They couldn't afford the time to make observations for a precise jump to the next haven, so they took a wild jump to Edmonton and overshot. However, they were lucky and picked up the tracks of the Edmonton ships, which they overtook, again by incredibly bold navigation. They learned from them"—he paused to wipe the tears from his eyes—"that Edmonton is also destroyed."

There were many in the hall crying now, and some had started the mourning wail for the two lost worlds. Shial called them to order gently. "There is no time for that now—it will be done properly later. Please let me go on."

The group regained its composure, steeling itself for

possibly even more bad news, but the worst of it was over. "The navigator from the Kiryat refugee ship is either the luckiest or the best because she took another wild jump, without waiting for observations, which brought them within reaction drive range of here. The other two ships were the seed ships from Edmonton—they saw it sterilized, but they escaped. They are coming here also. None of those ships can make it to another haven. Our seed ships have been in contact with the *Petrel,* the ship from Kiryat, since it appeared. That's the situation. It's now open for discussion."

Brom, who had been doing some quick calculations, offered the first proposal. "We can absorb five thousand directly without jeopardizing the plan. The birthrate will have to be dropped to the minimal level, below replacement level—in fact, at minimum breeding potential. So there'll be no more children for a while. Also, we'll all have to get a bit older and more uncomfortable than we had expected. The two Edmonton ships should be able, between them, to establish a self-sustained colony in the south. If they succeed, we'll profit from it—if not, we're no worse off. But we don't have the resources to help them—it's their own risk to take."

"I don't see taking on that many," Vern objected. "We're not due to offer haven for another fifty years. I say let the shipsiders land in the south and form a colony if they can, but don't absorb any of them into our population!"

"That's pretty extreme, isn't it, Vern?" Brom said. "One of them is already in terminal recycle, and the others are not far from it. There's no way that that many of them could establish a viable colony. Five thousand is the most that a new colony could take. We must absorb some of them!"

"I don't think you understand, Brom," Vern countered. "I'm fourth generation groundside, and there's not a person on this planet that isn't at least second generation groundside—including most of the people in the cryovaults of our seed ships. I know—I know—

in the long run we're going to have to take in many more shipsiders. But it'll be different then. It'll be a ship every few years. The crew dispersed in a big population with plenty of time to teach them groundside ways. A bunch like this, coming down so suddenly, is risky!"

"It's a risk we'll have to take," Shial said.

"Not for me," Vern insisted. "You don't know shipsiders, I tell you. I was in orbit five years, and I met them all the time. There's no percentage in inviting a bunch of naked savages to live with us. They have no camouflage sense at all. They paint everything in sight, themselves included, and they're noisy—very noisy. And worst of all, they've got a chant and ritual for everything. I don't think we can afford several thousand holy-holy shipsiders here. A few maybe—the children certainly—if they're young enough to train to groundside ways and camouflage."

"You can't do that," Brom said. "It wouldn't be planworthy!"

"We sure can. There's nothing in the plan that says we have to take refugees prematurely. In fact, I think it's more planworthy to refuse. How about a vote?"

They discussed the proposal at length, and it was soon evident that Vern's position would be voted down. Shial collected the opinions without a formal vote and called the meeting back to order. "The consensus is that we absorb four thousand into our own population and that five thousand will land in the south and attempt their own colony. Furthermore, this planet will be absolutely closed to haven for fifty years."

Brom, who had been adding up the totals, called out, "That means the Kiryat ship is to be refused."

"Yes," Shial said, "they can attempt their own colony, but if they're in terminal recycle, they won't make it. Their best hope is to move on, with another wild jump. We must refuse them!"

"No!" Yuri jumped up. "We can absorb them and ten times more. We don't have to refuse anyone!"

"What do you have in mind?" Selma asked, half-knowing his answer, but Yuri did not continue. He sat down, ashamed, in the awkward silence. A current of hostility buzzed around the room as they tried to recall a little-known loophole in the plan that would allow all the refugees to be absorbed, but they could not find such an escape clause. Then they looked to Gils, senior Ecomer of the planet and the best-versed in plan lore. Surely this would be one of those rare occasions on which he would speak. But Gils appeared to be oblivious to the discussion. They pressed Yuri for an explanation, but he apologetically asked them to forget it. It was not a good idea, he said, and he did not wish to expand on it.

"Then we've made a decision to refuse the *Petrel!*" Shial announced.

They murmured in agreement, but Gils stood, asking for the floor. He addressed Vern.

"Vern, you disappoint me. 'Shipsiders' and 'groundsiders'? 'Naked savages'? You wear a loincloth on a hot day also. And painted? Is that camouflage on your face natural? Songs? Did you hum a navigation chant to get here? Your objections to shipsiders are of temperature, hue, and decibels, not substance. If this 'shipsider,' 'groundsider' talk keeps up, this world's dead and it's time to ship out!"

He lowered his voice and turned to Yuri. "What was your idea?" he asked.

That was good, they murmured among themselves. Gils harsh reproach of Vern had been justified, but Yuri's case, if their guess was correct, was far more serious. Who would be better to discipline the young Ecomer than Gils?

Yuri did not respond.

"Say it!" Gils insisted.

"I can't, Gils. Don't ask me to," he begged.

"Tell us!" Gils commanded softly, but Yuri did not move. "Then I'll say it for you. 'Don't follow the plan.' Isn't that it?"

They had expected Gils's accusation, but it was nevertheless shocking. Yuri was known to stretch the

96

limits of the plan or give it novel interpretations that verged on outright error. While distasteful, it was tolerated, for Yuri did battle with a continent and occasional lapses in propriety were expected from him, but an outright violation was blasphemous and it was good that Gils chastised him for it. Now that it was out, Yuri had only to confess his guilt publicly, swear contrition for his error, and they could set about with the frantic preparations needed to rescue the two ships, and with the mourning of Kiryat, Edmonton, and the *Petrel*. Yuri looked at Gils, his mentor, who stood accusingly, glaring at him from the lower tier. Gils, who had taught him and inspired him to tackle the southern project. He should have known that Gils would not have missed the radical suggestion, even if unphrased. "Isn't that it, Yuri?"

"Yes." He finally admitted it. He lowered his eyes in shame, but then raised them again in defiance. "Yes!" he shouted. Then, quiet once more: "That's what I wanted to do—violate the plan—but only in part—forgive me, all."

"'A crack is a breach and a breach is death!'" Selma quoted.

"Triply guard it, faithful and perfect, lest you be burned," Vern shouted.

The others joined in the humiliation until it was obvious by his crying, his face buried in his hands, that Yuri was genuinely contrite. Still, Gils did not sit down. The hubbub stopped suddenly as they realized that Gils had something more to say. He looked at Yuri again closely, and then at the others, and said, simply and clearly, "Yuri's right. Don't follow the plan!"

He said nothing more, giving them time to let the heresy grip them. Yuri was dumbfounded. He looked to his mentor in confusion. Gils waved to him, motioned him to stand. Yuri obeyed but could not speak. "Tell them!" Gils ordered, but Yuri, like the rest, was speechless. "Tell them!" Gils insisted.

"The *Petrel* can establish a colony by the sea," Yuri

began, "and use converters to supply food for the short term—"

He was interrupted by objections from every side. Gils quieted them and explained, "The native sea life is doomed anyway. All pioneers depend on the converters at first." He nodded to Yuri, who, now warming to the subject and aware that Gils was supporting him, discarded caution and euphemisms and spoke directly to the point.

"We can build a technology and use it to terraform this planet in fifty years instead of centuries. There will be other Kiryats and Edmontons and ships needing haven. The knowledge for a technology is in the library; it's there for the asking. Instead of holding the population down and refusing ships for the next fifty years, we shall be continually frustrated by our inability to build the population fast enough."

Selma was the first to speak in response to the outrageous proposal. "But that would mean the eventual death of this planet—just like Earth all over again."

"The ecology's not that fragile," Gils retorted. "We've learned something since we left Earth. We don't have to be stupid. This planet probably won't be the Home, but it can support ten million indefinitely. And if it's not the Home, so what?"

Shial was furious. "The plan says," he spluttered. "'If you should find a planet in which life has not crawled up from the sea, then shall you bioform it in the image of Earth, so that it will be the Home to Man. Every ship and every colony will look upon itself as if *it* would create *the* Home.' What you suggest, Gils, is nothing more than"—he hesitated before speaking the harsh words—"a waste!"

"Waste?" Gils seemed to favor the obscenity. "Kiryat was 'wasted,' Edmonton was 'wasted,' and Wilmot, Ferdessee, Kolar, Shamta. And Eden, Eden the Home, the eight hundred ships and the eight million—wasn't Eden 'wasted'? And plan or no, camouflage or no, won't *this* planet be wasted too?"

"It is precisely because so many other homesites

were destroyed that we must look upon every colony as if it would be the future home of Man. That is the way of the plan. That is the wisdom of the plan," Shial insisted.

"Wisdom," Gils observed. "Wisdom. Day before yesterday I killed a gazelle and yesterday a tiger. The tiger was old, so he was sacrificed. Because of the gazelle I live, and because of the tiger the valley will live. Those deaths—*they* were wisdom. Shial! You cut down a young forest last year—a thousand trees planted only fifty years ago."

"They were scheduled to be cut down." Shial defended his action. "The marsh was drained and the forest was no longer needed. It was dictated by the plan!"

"But the forest *was* cut down, and the birds have flown to Brom's great forest on the peninsula. Where did the birds come from, Brom?"

"From the seed ship, of course," Brom answered indignantly. But he could see that Gils was not satisfied with that answer. He thought awhile and then corrected himself. "Initially from the seed ship, that is—but most of them from Shial's forest, after it was cut down."

Gils nodded. He looked at each of the other Ecomers, one at a time, and asked, "Who cut the forest down? Shial couldn't do it alone."

"There were thirty of us," Brom admitted, "and Selma had half her settlement; they were between harvests. Kati, Vern—we all helped to cut the forest down. Why do you ask?"

"You came by the hundreds," Gils reminded him, "to cut the trees down; you sang, I remember. It was a great party, cutting down that forest. It was right, and it was wise—"

"And in strict accordance with the plan!" Selma interrupted impatiently. "Where are you taking us, Gils, with your 'wisdoms'?"

Gils had spoken more words more freely than he had spoken in several previous meetings together. The thoughts were clear in his mind. He longed to be eloquent, to tell them that the plan had a broader interpretation. That letting these and future ships land *was* following the plan—if not the letter, then certainly the intent. That this world was perhaps destined to be only a temporary home to be cut down. That the narrow, legalistic interpretation of the plan was not working. How many worlds had died because of the blind following of the plan? Had not Kiryat been the most orthodox world of all? Yet it had died. Gils knew intuitively that the time had come for a new development. That it was time to build a technology so that old ships could be refurbished and new ones launched, even if at the risk of discovery or long-term ecological disaster. For with many havens man would not merely survive, but would increase, and eventually not one but many Homes would be constructed. It was not the ecology of a single colony that had to be preserved, but the ecology that consisted of all the colonies and all the ships as a totality.

He longed to say this, but he had used all his words, and instead he answered Selma's question by saying, "This world"—he jabbed his index finger downward several times to emphasize his point—"this world is just a forest."

They argued late into the night and much of the next day. Gils said nothing through it all, letting Yuri, now released from all inhibitions, do the talking for him. At last, when the polarization of the colony was complete and it was clear that each party had won its adherents, Brom, who was undecided and had taken the role of mediator asked, "What do you intend to do Gils?"

"Go South."

—————

The next eight months were hectic. The *Petrel* arrived in orbit, soon followed by the two Edmonton refugees. They linked to each other and to the two seed ships. By sharing their sparse resources, they were able to stop the terminal recycling aboard the *Petrel*. It would be many months before they could land, for much had to be done on the surface in preparation. The Southern terraforming project based in the center of the subcontinent was temporarily dropped. Half of Yuri's settlement agreed with the rebels' proposal and set to work establishing a base camp by the sea. The remaining seven hundred, too small a group to continue with the terraforming, had to be resettled among the Northern groups. There, as the news of the Southern project spread, individuals decided to join it—a hundred from here and a thousand from there. Others, being ultraconservative, decided that the entire planet was no longer suitable and elected to ship out. They would eventually have to be installed in the cryovaults of the orbiting ships, waiting for the day, ten years or more thence, when the ships would be outbound again. On board the five ships there were nineteen thousand humans in cryosleep. Each to be awakened and told of their alternatives: to join the Northern conservatives, the Southern radicals, or to stay shipside. The world was topsy-turvy.

Gils spent many hours orchestrating the logistics of the project: construction schedules, technology, work assignments, training, food production, seeding plans, transportation, wildlife birth rates, fuel production— all had to be coordinated. It was, to him, a culmination of his training. He knew for the first time what his job really was, and his previous work in the valley faded wistfully into insignificance. Where once he had been able to manage it all himself, he was forced to relinquish the responsibility of details to others.

Yuri had the new base camp to do with as he saw fit. Brom agreed, reluctantly, to begin bootstrapping a technology above the basic level allowed by the plan, but with the understanding that all such products would be moved South as soon as possible, so that the peninsula would remain ecologically pristine. The valley Gils gave over to Liam, more by default than by decision, for he had been reluctant to give it up. When, in the sixth month, Liam had assumed the function of Ecomer in all but name, Gils called a meeting of the settlement to confirm what was already a reality. There was much opposition to Liam's appointment— he was too young for the job, they said, though none argued against his qualifications. Gils's protest that he could not do both jobs was not enough to obtain the majority needed for Liam's confirmation. Gils finally broke the deadlock by citing the plan in his support. He claimed his irrevocable right to ship out to a new world, which, using a well-contrived argument based on accepted plan sophistry that none could refute, the South was, thereby forcing them to choose a successor. Liam was confirmed and the proud badge of office tattooed on his shoulder.

When the hydrogen/oxygen electrolysis plant was working at capacity, regular shuttle flights to the orbiting ships began. Groundside surpluses were sent up. Shipsiders were awakened and the transfer of cargo to the primary re-entry vehicles begun. This, too, required planning because the new approach dictated a priority order that was different from the normal one specified by the plan. With each shuttle flight, two dozen or more shipsiders landed. They were quick to adopt groundside clothing, for the cold wet season that passed for winter had arrived, but they did not adopt groundside manners—to the dismay of many older conservatives who anxiously waited for the day that the alien shipsiders would go South—as most of them elected to do. So despite themselves, in the interest of ridding themselves of this bizarre element, conservatives helped with the project also. To the further dismay of the orthodoxy, especially bigots like Vern, the young ones of the settlements started to imitate the shipsiders—to the extent that there was concern over the next generation of conservatives. Soon dull camouflage was replaced with brilliant hues of red and blue, and half-forgotten ship rituals became regular events.

It had been raining for two weeks. The suns finally

pierced the clouds and began to dry the sodden ground—events unnoticed by Gils, who spent almost all of his time indoors now. There was a minor commotion in the corridor as a brace of children raced by on the way to the exit stairs. He followed them to investigate—a glider was landing. It had Southern markings. He walked to the upwind end of the landing field. The glider touched down and rolled toward him. The pilot climbed out of the cockpit and waved, calling his name. "I have a message for you, Gils." Though he could not see who it was because of the bulky furs she wore, he recognized Rina's voice—a Southerner with whom he had spent pleasant evenings a few years back. She held the letter out to him. It was from Yuri.

> To Gils, former Ecomer, central valley, now Chief Ecomer, Haven: There is much to do and we need you now. Time to stop planning and start doing. I'm in over my head. Come South with Rina. Thank you, friend and teacher.
>
> Yuri

"When are you going back?" he asked Rina.

"If you decided not to go, immediately. Otherwise, as soon as you can make the arrangements."

"I'll go," he said, "but it will be weeks."

"Well, then," she replied, taking out another letter, "in that case, Yuri told me to give you this."

> Gils:
> Forgive me this impertinence. Be rational. You started it all and you have to see it through. You can't have it both ways. Let go and move the office South. There's no reason you can't leave tomorrow. We want you here before the first primary RV lands.
>
> Respectfully,
>
> Yuri

Gils was furious with his former assistant's presumptions. He turned to Rina and asked sarcastically, "Is there *another* letter?" She told him that there was not but that she would wait. He went down to the cubicle, Rina following. There was a point to it. Yuri was right, Gils realized. He himself was trying to hang on to the past despite having started a revolution. He had misgivings. He *had* advocated violating the plan, and saying it, he was learning, was much easier than doing it. This planet would not be the Home; excessive use of artificial energy, raw materials, release of unnatural hydrocarbon and nitrogen compounds into the atmosphere, the water, the danger of the technological spiral that no one had really tried to control before— he was absorbed by these thoughts as he and Rina walked back in silence.

"Yuri suggested that I try to convince you." She had removed the furs, revealing some part of the reason that Yuri had chosen her for the trip. "Although," she coyly admitted, "the suggestion was superfluous as far as I was concerned."

"I need a day or two to think things over. I'll see you later." He turned abruptly, leaving an insulted Rina staring at a closed door. He fetched his pack and gear, as well as the cat's, and went out. He put his index and little finger to his mouth, emitted a piercing whistle, and headed for the valley.

A few miles outside the settlement, he was attacked by a ferocious cat, who knocked him down, pinned him to the ground, and sat on his chest, growling, roaring, and hissing in his face. "All right, Sheina, enough comedy. I heard you coming at least a hundred yards off. You disturbed an owl, broke twigs, scraped your claws—you're getting sloppy!" The big cat bleated her disappointment and released her master, who quickly fitted her pack.

He followed the rounds of the inspection tour of the valley that he had made so many times before. They camped where they always camped on the first night of the tour and were up early the next morning. They ate lunch on the rock where Sheina had almost gotten them both killed. She had scented the new tiger earlier, and they had detoured to give him no reason to be annoyed by their presence.

He examined the valley in detail from this vantage point. There were subtle changes, not wholly explainable by the rebalance of the ecology brought about by the new tiger. He looked carefully, and the details began to unfold. There were new trees on the far bank of the stream. Here and there were other changes; some were permissible, many were not. It made sense, of course. Liam was doing a good job—but now that Gils could see the tangible evidence of his own insurrection, it did not satisfy him—it repelled him instead. And worst of all, Liam's hand was on the valley. Gils had lost it forever.

That night he looked up at the few stars and the orbiting ships and mused to an uncomplaining Sheina, "I don't know, kitty. It's not the way I thought it would be. I know what I said, but that's not what I felt. They're all going too far and too fast. They look to me and expect me to lead, but in truth I'm a born follower. I just hope I can keep it all together."

Sheina growled at him as a signal to stop talking and dropped a paw over his mouth to emphasize the point.

They waited, cramped in the glider's cockpit, bundled and sweating in layers of high-altitude clothing, for a windshift. The village had come to say good-bye. They lined both sides of the catapult rails for ten times the length of the glider. Nearby, Sheina, knowing that she would have a new master, lay disconsolate, her nose low to the ground, eyes half closed.

Far forward at the winch, the catapult pit was primed with ten tons of water ready to drop into the deep well below. The wind sock turned toward them. Rina waved to the catapult crew. They released the catches, and the huge plastic sack of water began its descent into the well, winding the winch as it fell. They accelerated along the track, became airborne, and reached an altitude of a thousand feet, where Rina dropped the tow hook. She turned into a tight circle, to gain altitude from the thermals over the landing strip. As the thermal gained strength, the glider nosed down ever more steeply, continued to gain altitude, and gave Gils a long view of his erstwhile home.

The thermal lifted them to five thousand feet before Rina turned South. They continued climbing, moving southeast, toward the mountain chain that divided the continent. Gils had not been South before, but he knew the geography; they were heading directly toward the mountains instead of diverting westward toward the pass.

"Is there an updraft up ahead that can lift us over the mountains?" he asked.

"You might say so," she replied mysteriously.

They continued southeast, neither losing nor gaining altitude for several hours, heading directly for the mountains instead of riding the thermals upward for altitude. Finally the mountains were upon them, the peaks far above their present altitude. Rina must have miscalculated, he reasoned. She would turn back in a minute, fight her way up to a higher altitude, and try for the pass.

"Here comes the updraft," she said as she cranked a recessed lever overhead. Craning his neck upward, Gils could see the tip of a protuberance emerging from the fuselage. She opened a small panel on the console, set some switches, and incredibly nosed the glider down, losing even more precious altitude. Suddenly the bird shuddered and surged forward, the silent rush of the wind drowned by a new sound, a brash, rasping, loud sound—the sound of an engine. Rina, with still another surprise, gave him a microphone and headset, obviously electronic, and with motions showed him how to put it on, which he did with obvious distaste. "Better than tacking all over the countryside for a day and a half," she explained.

"But—engine," he objected.

"Engine for rockets or engine for gliders. What's the difference?"

"Rocket engine's necessary for survival—this one"—he pointed upward—"not. How long has this been going on?"

"A few years," she admitted. "That continent is big and we lost too many pure gliders and good pilots. If you go down, you have to walk out. We keep the engines shrouded up North—otherwise scandalize the natives. Just three with engines now. Building them as fast as we can. Don't have to use catapult—except up North—too risky. Hydrogen from electrolysis plant. You said 'build a technology.' Well, we'd been doing it before you suggested it. Anyway, plan allows engines—if you read it right."

They were moving faster now, climbing rapidly as they approached the mountain peaks, which loomed ever more imposing—they would pass over the mountains at a much higher altitude than usual and he could already feel the effects of the thin air. "Here," she said, giving him a contraption of plastic hoses. "Oxygen—put it in your mouth—breathe in your mouth, out your nose."

Although their altitude was dangerously high and the temperature so low that they should have frozen despite the furs, it was apparent to Gils that some of the engine's heat was being utilized to warm the cabin. It was still cold, though—that, combined with the oxygen breather and the noise of the engine, made conversation impossible. To his further consternation, the aircraft now left a contrail that he was sure had to be obvious at least ten parsecs away.

In twenty minutes they had cleared the mountains and began to descend into the great plateau of the Southern subcontinent. Rina turned off and stowed the engine.

107

"How many more surprises?" he asked.

"More, Gils, many more. It was your idea, after all."

"I'm not going to like it," he confessed.

The conversation was sporadic and inconsequential thereafter. He spent most of the trip examining the new land, while Rina, with the autopilot set, slept. As he saw the continent's everchanging face, hour after hour, he realized that he had undertaken the transformation of a world—not, as he had earlier conceived it, merely a very large valley. Furthermore, not just to begin the project, but to finish it as well, within his lifetime. The continent was too big to take in all at once; he was humbled by it. He would have to learn much more and, most important, to think on a new scale.

They passed over the center of the original Southern project late in the afternoon, scattered scrub and the boundary between terrestrial and native life blurred and barely visible. The colony was now populated only by caretakers, who made no pretense of being self-sufficient, but only tried to hold on to what had been gained. The old site had been well chosen, though, and was the right place from which to stage the terraforming of the Southern subcontinent. It would be years before they could return in force, but Gils vowed to re-establish at least part of the operation there as soon as possible.

They reached the coast in the late evening as the suns were setting. Rina started the engine again and kept it going through the night, since the rest of the trip would be mostly over water. They skirted the coastline, following a direct path from Gils's old village to the new coastal settlement. Gils could see occasional phosphorescent patches of native sea life near the surface of the water. Some kind of algae, he thought. They were primitive fish with cartilaginous notochords rather than fully developed backbones. The king of the sea was a sharklike leviathan with three-meter jaws. Below him in the food chain were smaller creatures with exoskeletons, armor, colonial plasmodia, kelp, and other analogues of Earth's early sea life. The sea was too harsh, too violent, and too unforgiving to allow the introduction of Earth life too soon.

The first sun rose brilliantly red out of the quiet sea, casting a long reflection, out of which, minutes later, rose the smaller, brighter sun, quickly transforming the red ocean to deep blues shading to green on the nearby shore. Rina awoke, checked the instruments, turned off the engine, and spoke to Gils. "We'll be landing on the other side of the river there."

He tried to find the river but could not at first. Then he realized that he had not seen it because of its size. It was muddy brown and miles wide, plunging into the sea as an immense waterfall five hundred feet high. A drop from the land off the continental shelf—an irregular white line of foamy violence; its roar, even at their altitude, rivaled the sound of the engine. One third of the planet's water was dumped into the ocean by the giant waterfall, creating a brown stain that spread to the horizon, burying uncountable numbers of microscopic life-forms in the millions of tons of sand and clay brought down from the continent's watershed. One could not think in terms of groves of trees to tame the bank of this river, and even "forest" seemed puny by comparison.

The cataract was out of sight and sound, far behind, when Rina pointed to the new colony. It was obviously visible, and he could see, to his dismay, buildings on the surface. It was afternoon by then, and they approached the landing strip from the seaward side. The strip, built for re-entry gliders, was as impressive to Gils as the waterfall had been. It was a straight brown line, thousands of feet wide, extending several miles inland from the coast. It was much larger than the original landing site on the peninsula up North. This one was being built to take the traffic of many heavy re-entry gliders over the next hundred years.

"It's dirt now," she explained. "We'll extend it and fuse it as soon as we can build the heavy equipment. It's still pretty crude—hang on!"

She had not exaggerated; as they floated over the strip, he could see rocks, some as big as his head, littering the sides. They would not damage a re-entry glider, but they could destroy their frail craft. Only the exact center was relatively smooth. To make matters worse, there were still dips and rises, not visible from the higher altitude. The landing was rough despite Rina's expert handling. Considering the shaking they had received at forty knots, he did not envy the re-entry gliders that would land at more than two hundred.

The view from the air, dominated as it was by the landing strip, had not conveyed to Gils the activity that he saw on the long walk to the center of the new colony. Rina pointed to pits, foundations, beginnings of walls, stakes in the ground, explaining that this one would be a power plant, that one a food converter, the other a factory, a hangar, a shed, school, housing—all of it above ground. He did not like what he saw. He disliked it far beyond his aversion to surface construction. He intuitively felt that it was not being done correctly: the concentration of factories near the power plant, the homogeneous clustering of dwellings, the closed spaces that would in the future stifle the air where a proper design could have been arranged to cool it. A city, he felt, like a valley or a continent, should still grow serenely so that the finished product was in harmony with the surroundings rather than appear to have been hacked out of it in an untimely and irresponsible manner. He sensed the potential decay of the future city in the settlement's beginnings; he would have to do something about that also.

He was several weeks settling into his new job and taking control over a multitude of activities. Most difficult of all was diverting the enthusiasm of the new settlers from a total rejection of the plan and to a more rational adaptation of it. The new freedom exploded in

110

numerous experiments and in the exploration of "new ways," which Gils, through his deep knowledge of the plan, knew were not new at all, but had been tried and rejected on dozens of worlds before. While he was the center of activity, the master planner, he was also the conservative, and to the annoyance of his colleagues, he increasingly took to quoting the plan for his support. It was inevitable—he was resigned to that; he hoped that he could curb the more dangerous excesses and that in time they would return to it, recognizing that the plan still had much to offer. He spent as much time as he could with youngsters, for, he realized, it was they who would have to uphold it.

He was developing a schedule for additional aerial survey flights with Siu To, who had expressed an interest in the Ecomer business, when Rina interrupted them. "The first *Petrel* RV is landing."

"But," he protested, "that's not due for days."

"It *is* days since it was announced—you've lost track." She took his hand and urged him out—he followed, looking back at the chart. He held back and, despite her protests, returned to correct some entries. She took his hand again and dragged him toward the landing strip.

They had all stopped working and were running or walking briskly toward the settlement's new focal point. High above, too far to see the craft itself, a contrail formed as the craft hit the cold, moist air of the upper atmosphere. The contrail disappeared, but by sighting along its direction, they could see a bright speck that caught the sun as it banked. It passed directly overhead, barely visible now, and continued its descent and final turn in the pattern. Miles away, and still at several thousand feet, three acres of silver paraglider cloth erupted from the top of the craft and assumed a familiar triangular shape as it caught the air, instantly magnifying and making obvious what they were straining to see. Its descent was steep and rapid, directly in line with the runway. It passed overhead with a rushing sound. The paraglider wings shredded

111

here and there, fluttered with every audible frequency, some so low in pitch and so intense that the watchers were physically buffeted by the sound.

It seemed to float above the runway for many seconds, moving so rapidly that a crash appeared imminent. Finally contact was made, followed by the crunching, rumbling, screeching sound of two million pounds of aircraft belly-landing on a rough field. Dust and sand were thrown up like the wake of a high-speed boat, caught in the turbulent vortices at the glider's stubby wingtips, creating twin horizontal cyclones whose size did justice to the sound. Five miles away the glider, now slowed to the point that the paravane and rudder no longer provided stability, swerved and then slid down the strip sideways for several more thousand feet before it stopped. The strong breeze kept the paravane airborne for a few seconds, but at last it reluctantly settled to the ground.

An abrasive rain of dust and sand pelted them continuously throughout the long hike to the aircraft. It was hardly visible. They turned around at the whine of a ground-effect machine piloted by Yuri. He offered them a ride, incidentally recycling the dust that had fallen to rise and offend them once again. Gils and Rina climbed aboard the aft skirt to join those already there, loading it so much that the little turbine could barely provide the lift to clear the rubble.

After a bumpy and occasionally exciting ride, they penetrated the final layer of the moving dust to discover the immensity of the re-entry vehicle. None of them had ever seen a primary RV. The RVs that came down from the seed ships or the orbiting station were much smaller, and the shuttle would have been no more than a lifeboat for this monster. The blackened ablative shield that lined the five-hundred-foot bottom, ridged along its length by the grinding contact with thousands of rocks during the landing, gave it the appearance of a grounded whale. Here and there a smoking, smoldering chunk of shielding dropped off and landed with a dull thud, throwing a brief shower of sparks. The bright, clean upper surface was visible because it was now leaning on the nearer wingtip. Far above, through the tiny angular window, the pilot clasped her hands above her head in a victory sign, announcing thereby that the landing had been successful. The crowd shouted joyfully at the good news.

Sheina, dim-eyed, growled her displeasure at the subsonic rumble that emanated from the launch complex ten miles away, indicating that another load of cargo was on the way to the ships parked in orbit above. "It's all right," Gils said, scratching his old friend and companion-in-retirement behind the ear, soothing her in preparation for the sonic insult that was still to come. "There won't be another one for several weeks."

He looked out the window and tried to pick out the rocket's trail against the brightness of the setting sun. His eyes, tracking upward, caught a glimpse of the purple stream as it cleared the upper sun's disk. Bathed in the red light of the fast-dropping first sun and the blue sharpness of its smaller companion, submerged beneath the awesome roar of the ascending rocket, he dropped his eyes to look at the city far below. It was not *all* bad, he thought, considering that it had been done so quickly. It was, judging from what he had seen in the archives, as good as the best that Earth had ever built. Man, he reflected, was not fated to live unobtrusively in harmony with an unchanging natural ecology, but was driven to modify that system into one of his own liking. And here, on Haven, they had shown that it could be done without endangering the long-term viability of the planet. True, as he had expected, Haven could never be the home for all mankind, but for a small segment it would be a pleasant garden, a respite from the harshness of space, and a safe harbor in which to replenish wandering manships en route to their own as yet unfounded havens.

Despite the building of the city and the technology
113

that supported it, the plan had not been altogether dropped. He could see the emergence of a new chapter that retained the uncompromising morality of the old, moderated by the new spirit. In the far reaches of the galaxy, other havens were being built. Elsewhere, as the news of Haven's success spread, others took up the revolution against the ineffectual strictures of the plan.

The city was never quiet. From the east came the constant crashing of the breakers against the granite cliffs, while from the north the awesome cataract of the great river hurled seven million tons of water into the ocean every second, each ton adding its molecule of sound to already overloaded senses. When the suns were properly positioned, the tide would come in, and the ocean would meet the river at the horizon and give battle along a skirmish line a hundred miles across, creating a stationary breaker thirty feet high to provide a biennial crescendo to the symphony. Far to the east a volcanic chain added a dimly perceived percussion section that marked the beginnings of the moving continental plate that was sliding under the eastern shore, providing a continual uplift that replenished the cliffs as fast as the river wore them down. In a hundred million years the eastern coast would be a mountain chain cut by a gorge through which a small stream flowed, the tamed reminder of a once great river, now diverted southward, emptying the watershed of a continent amid the fjords and glaciers of the antarctic region. Against the background of these natural sounds, they added those of the rocket, which during the brief minute of its sonic existence rivaled the river and the waves a hundredfold, causing tremors that shook the city to its foundations in the bedrock.

Haven's population had two tasks: terraforming the planet and manufacturing supply kits for manships that required refurbishing. The Northern settlements, having recognized the futility of trying to maintain two contradictory ecological plans on the same planet, and having lost the more stubborn conservatives through emigration, had added their manpower to the terraforming task, but they would have no part of the launch complex or the city. Earth life was in dominance over most of the continent and in balance elsewhere. While the Northerners made free use of Southern technology—the mines, the aircraft, the powered vehicles—they would not build them—that was "Southerner's work," repugnant to the Northern purists. Therefore, it was the Southern people who built and launched the great kits on which manships depended for sustenance. The kits were launched into orbit regularly, whether needed or not. Different kinds of kits were built. A ship could resupply itself by taking the proper mix of kits. Every kit contained addenda to man's library, so that the refurbishing included history, technology, and philosophy, as well as materials.

Haven became a focus for the ships, a node through which information passed and through which ideas could be spread. Gils recognized that the job could not stop with Haven and that the piecemeal and haphazard distribution of information through the chance visits of ships was neither fast enough nor reliable enough. It was essential that all mankind be reached—that all mankind converse—and that all mankind plan consciously for its future. His last great break with the restrictions of the plan was to call for a gathering of ships, far outside the galaxy, where such a meeting could be held in safety. He specified a time and coordinates, and every ship that stopped at Haven was admonished to carry the idea outward and to inform such ships as it might meet. It was not practical, it was dangerous, he was told, but they humored the old man in his dotage. In the spring, when it was warm, he would walk the streets with the big cat, accosting every shipsider he met, using Sheina's apparent ferocity to command their attention. They promised, partly under duress, but mostly in respect for who he was, to carry the word of the conclave.

Ships came to Haven, and their crews were revived. Some individuals elected to trade centuries of life, interrupted by periods of consciousness, for a continuous span on the surface of a planet—while others, equally anxious to seek their destiny away from what had to them become a dull existence on the surface, shipped out frozen in the cryostats, prepared to waken in a far region of the galaxy, to share their lives with new faces, though not among strangers.

Gils continued stroking Sheina while staring at the city and the sea long after the second sun had set and the rocket had added its spark of light to those already circling the planet. The telephone rang. He picked it up. The line was dead. As he replaced the handset, the room was illuminated through the shuttered western windows. He opened the blinds. Far to the west, at the confluence of the two main tributaries of the great river, a third sun, a new sun, a pillar of light, stabbed down from the sky, boiled the river, dissociated its molecules, and continued pouring energy until the very atoms were rended. The pillar of horror moved ponderously onto the city, but long before it had reached them, the radiation had doomed them, the shock wave had crushed them, the heat had seared them, and the quake had tumbled them back into the dust.

9

Ferenc

Ferenc was presiding over the fourth preventive maintenance ritual in a hundred hours. Each time, he had tied the ceremonial apron with its pockets full of tools around his waist and had led the crew in the intricacies of the ritual; each time, it had been accomplished without error. The tedious repetitions were his fault. His inattention during routine maintenance had caused the gravitational anomaly detector to fail. He had been engrossed in finding the ending of his epic poem and had absentmindedly applied the poem's meter to the detector's chant. The impromptu modification of the accenting had not only been poetically ludicrous but had also been mechanically catastrophic. The crew had followed him blindly with ruinous consequences. He had suffered mild humiliation as his mates teased him with aberrant verse. The taunting continued until the ship called for the first expiatory ritual. The teasing had stopped, but the ship had not.

The ritual began with the laborious suiting up for an external inspection. Once suited, they assembled outside the main air lock, and Rajah, the basso, pounded out the dirge that accompanied the long walk to the test positions scattered about the hull. They marched slowly, shuffling from one toehold to the next—release the left-foot catch with the left big toe, step to the next foothold, unclip the right lifeline, swing the right arm forward and reclip the line, release the right-foot catch, step, swing the left arm—trudging across the faded blue hull, across the gray clouds, across the muddy, pitted white birds, until they reached the prescribed positions.

Then Rajah shifted the cadence to the meditation and they stood quietly, preparing themselves for the work ahead. Far out, a mile or more away, were the globular supply kits, the huge primary re-entry vehicle, and numerous small pilot and shuttle craft, each attached by a slender tether to the bulk of the mother ship, the tethers kept taut by the ship's rotation. The galaxy's faint light swung about them every five seconds, giving an ebb and flow to the slight shadows of the crew who stood upon the spinning hull.

Ajax, the youngest, began the fugue in a crystalline soprano, announcing to all what his task in this doing of the rite would be. Then the next crew member announced her task, and then the next and the next, until all were singing their procedures in melodious harmony. The fugue climaxed, was resolved and completed, and the ritual proper started. Ferenc directed by hand signals and interjected counterpoint. Rajah assumed the watchman's position and continued in the background, his powerful voice providing a foundation for the rest. Only he was connected to the ship's main communication system lest an inadvertent interruption spoil the rite and thereby force yet another repetition. Ferenc relied on hand signals more than most, for his mediocre baritone added little to the evolving symphony. When he did join in, it was to direct a phase to be repeated, or to call for an exception procedure based on a reading that had just been made. Ferenc would have preferred that Rajah lead the ritual, but that was not possible since it had been Ferenc's mistake. The ritual was routine and mechanistic, and he was in danger of lapsing into another reverie when the red light of Rajah's signal lamp flooded his faceplate. Ferenc unclipped the lifeline and rushed to the closest intercom junction box. He plugged his toe into it. "Ferenc has been called during the inspection drill," he said with annoyance.

"It's the gravitational anomaly detector," Sirna replied. "It's recorded a hit!"

"Is it confirmed?"

"It's as genuine as the last one was."

"I'll be right in." He signaled to Rajah to take the lead, and then he interjected the change song while Rajah diverted the bass back to the dirge. Each one finished the part of the task he or she had been doing and picked up the dirge to walk to the new positions required by the change of command. Rajah had the lead now, and they were back into it without a hitch by the time Ferenc had reached the air lock and ended his part in the ceremony. The walk, the air lock procedure, the unsuiting, and the slow float down to the bridge gave him time to consider the new hit. There were several possibilities: it was yet another, more elaborate drill dredged out of some murky path in the ship's program; someone's practical joke—in which the ship had concurred; a malfunction; or a genuine hit. He dismissed the first idea. While the programs were complex and occasionally devious, he could not recall any such path, nor could he imbue the programs with sufficient sense to have created such a path as a response to his error of a few weeks back. The second possibility, while it would have been expected on the first or second expiatory drill, at the fourth go-around would have been in poor taste. None of the thirty-seven ambulant members of the crew had such an errant sense of humor. The third was improbable. He had personally dissected the unit and its numerous backup systems, as well as having Ajax concentrate on it for exercise. This left a real hit as the only reasonable alternative.

"The detector's been checked again." Sirna greeted him as he dropped down to the bridge, his hands sliding on the highly polished ladder rails. "The hit is real. It appears to be a contact, not more than five years away."

"Have we got a bearing?"

119

"The third octant is as close as we can place it."

He ordered a randomly phased sequence of close jumps through the center of the third octant, terminating at a point five light years away. Traces of the anomaly were found at each jump. Reaching the end of the first jump sequence, they waited the mandatory ten minutes for a new track and, finding none, they split the octant into three parts, jumped to the center of the new segment, and initiated a new sequence of jumps back to their starting point. If there was another ship, and if it had also detected them, it would be executing a complementary maneuver.

When they returned to the place where they had first detected the track, still another series of jumps were executed, which, they hoped, would be better yet. After three days of examining the track from various vantage points, they had fixed the anomaly to within a cone a fraction of a degree wide and four light years long. They jumped along the axis of the cone to its center and waited another ten minutes—still no new track. They bisected the further segment of the cone and waited again.

By the twelfth day of the search Ferenc had not yet found his poem's ending, nor had they found another track. The search for that track would continue with decreasing intensity for a thousand days, at which time the probability of finding still another track would have become vanishingly small. An average of two searches were initiated yearly in response to some newfound trace of another ship, so that they were always involved in half a dozen simultaneous searches.

The main search was continually interrupted by probes along old tracks. It was on one of these that the second anomaly was detected. The instruments showed a bearing that could be correlated with either the old track or the new. Ferenc elected to treat the "new" hit as belonging to the old track. Under this assumption they picked up more traces and continued narrowing the possibilities until it was certain that a return signal would arrive momentarily. Jumping to the most probable location of the other ship, they executed the recognition jump sequence, causing a pattern of gravitational disturbances to radiate outward from their position, and waited.

This was the hardest part of the search—the anticipation of meeting with another, equally lonely fragment of mankind, the anxiety of possible disappointment if the track turned out to be a dud, and the frustration of doing nothing, nothing but waiting, just waiting.

Ferenc was killing time, dozing, his eyes half open, looking at the lush jungle scene that Sirna had painted around his bunk. Fantastic snakes (Genetic code #127.568.334/A-2) draped from the overhanging branches along the wall and to the edge of his bed, eyes and scales glistening as brightly in the hot green sun as the straggling drops of the recent downpour on the broad blue leaves of the bandany plant (Genetic code #893.002.671/Q-1), while in the distant clearing at his feet, viewed through a narrow tunnel in the foliage, the omnipresent tiger pawed his displeasure at the carrion birds that had prematurely descended to filch the residue of his kill. Ferenc was rudely but joyously dragged out of the forest by Sirna's shout: "It's a recognition sequence—a recognition sequence, Ferenc!"

"How far?"

"Just minutes, with good direction."

"Have they answered us yet?"

"No. But they will, they will. They must! Revive the crew?"

"No. Not yet," he replied thoughtfully, "not until they answer, and not the whole crew—just those needed for the meeting."

They continued the search maneuver in miniature, improving their bearing and range, till at last a response to their signal was received. Ferenc, to the jubilation of all, ordered the revival of the first list— young ones who had never had a meeting, old ones who might never have another, some selected for genetic exchange—one hundred and fifty in all. The last jump brought them within milliseconds of each other, as close as safety allowed.

"Turn on the beacon!" Ferenc ordered, and the crew looked at the screens, waiting for the beacon from the other ship. Before any human had seen its brief flash, the ships had found each other's beacons, locked into each other's lasers, exchanged some preliminary chit-chat, adjusted minor linguistic differences, started the massive transfer of the libraries and museums, and gotten ready to announce to their respective crews that contact had been established and that all was well. A child spotted the wink of the beacon and called out the find before the computer had exceeded its pre-programmed delay:

"Thanks be to her who found the beacon," Ferenc intoned.

"Thanks be to her who found the beacon," the crew responded.

"Thanks be to Him who made the finding possible," said the child.

"Thanks be to Him who made the light," the crew finished.

"This is Lhong-Tao-Levy Karmaborn, of the *Hoffnung*"—the voice came from the other ship—"one hundred and seventy-two years from planetfall at Solace and nine hundred out of launch at El Kophra, with a full crew."

"And this is Ferenc Petrelborn, of the *Petrel*, ninety-seven years from planetfall at New, partly one hundred and eighty years out of Haven, partly seven hundred and fifty years out of Beth-Adam, partly nine hundred and forty-one years out of Green and many places else, but mostly three thousand nine hundred and sixty-three years out of launch from Earth as pilot ship, with a full crew!" Ferenc announced with pride.

"We are honored by the meeting and blessed by the knowledge," the *Hoffnung* crew proclaimed.

"We are honored to serve her and blessed to be carried in this sacred relic of the Earth," Ferenc and *Petrel*'s crew returned.

"Your manifest"—Ferenc had read the other ship's supply list as Lhong-Tao-Levy had done the same for the *Petrel's*—"indicates that you are well supplied. We have only one primary RV and insufficient supplies for more than a hundred years. We dropped the RV at New, a nonsentient primitive. *Mirrafeule* was forced down there and had to start a colony. We gave them what we could. Will you supply us?" The question was unnecessary, for both captains knew that the answer would be affirmative, but not the formality.

"We have twenty-seven kits, four spare RVs, and two spare shuttles—take what you need," the *Hoffnung* offered.

"How is it that you are so well blessed and yet so long from planetfall?" Ferenc asked.

"We were at Solace's destruction. They roasted it slowly and did not bother with anything off-planet. Just us and the seed ship were in orbit at the time. We split whatever there was of use—we took more than a hundred kits, RVs, and shuttles, and made a great jump to the other side of the galaxy. We have since resupplied many ships and have been able to avoid a planetfall."

"You have been lucky to have so many meetings. We shall mourn Solace, take the kits, and be thankful."

"How did you find us?" the *Hoffnung's* navigator asked Sirna, his counterpart on the *Petrel*.

"It was an old track, yours was," Sirna told him, "and we diverted from a fresh search to check it, and picked up your second track."

"That's a coincidence. Exactly the same thing happened to us. What were the bearings and ranges?" The two navigators had usurped the channel without objection from the captains, for this conversation had priority. The two navigators exchanged information concerning the now discarded tracks.

"They could have been from the same ship," she concluded. "There's no way that the fresh tracks could have been ours. There's certainly a third ship, possibly a fourth, in the area!"

The excitement that had erupted on Sirna's face quickly infected both crews. The captains now usurped the navigators to discuss a strategy for finding the third ship.

"I think we shouldn't link the *Petrel* and the *Hoffnung* until we have found the third ship—if any," Ferenc counseled.

"I agree. Suspend the library exchange!" Lhong-Tao ordered in response. The navigation computers were given the channel, and they began the massive correlation analysis required to bring both ships' records of the tracks to a common reference frame. They bickered for a while and finally agreed on a set of compatible coordinates. They then exchanged all sightings within the probable location sphere of the third ship. They correlated the two sets of data, resolved ambiguities and contradictions, swapped the results of their calculations, checked each other's work, planned a search pattern, and announced (after several days) that they were ready to start. During this time (when the computers were not hogging all the intercom channels) the crews established their data exchange in human terms. They admired each other's bulkhead paintings and tattoos, exchanged jokes, began friendships, traced common ancestors, swapped lies and legends, and did what crews have always done when becalmed together in the lonely vastness of sea or space.

With the completion of the computers' work and the minor human adjustments to the search pattern (which the ships were programmed to encourage rather than to criticize), the two ships separated and within hours had confirmed the existence of the third ship and had found it. Again the ritual of the finding was enacted.

"And this is Mascha Dolphinborn, of the *Liverpool*, one hundred and sixty years from launch at Haven and many planetfalls since, with a half crew, a stoved hull, and a mission!"

"What of Haven and what is your mission?" Ferenc asked after the ceremony was over.

"Haven, beloved Launchworld, is gone," Mascha told

them. "And the mission is to tell all ships and all colonies of the conclave. Have you heard of it yet?"

"No," said Ferenc. "Tell us."

"It was the idea of Gils Havensborn to call a meeting of ships, of many ships, at a point well outside the galaxy above the ecliptic plane. Its purpose to decide our future and how best to achieve it. It is less than a year away in time, and there is much to be done. You may be too far and too late, but it is worth trying to go—especially an Earthship and the pilot ship, at that."

"And you—will you go?" Lhong-Tao asked.

"We are at the end of our mission and shall head toward a safe world—God grant us one—to make repairs and replenish the crew. We've spent no time on maintenance since we started, but we've orbited forty planets and met a hundred ships. This hull will not tolerate a long journey—she needs overhaul now. We should prepare to link up immediately. Can you approach us? We're short of reaction mass."

A discussion on the reaction mass situation showed that the least wasteful approach would be for the *Petrel* and the *Hoffnung* to link up first and then for them to drive together to the *Liverpool*. It was not only in the interest of conserving energy that the approach was made slowly, or merely for the sake of safety, but because there was much to be done. The library exchange, beginning with an interchange of star maps and navigation data, continued. The revivified members of the crews needed treatment and orientation. Biochemical analyses of bacteria and immunoreactive assays had to be performed and exchanged. Finally the proper bacterial-biochemical "soup" had to be created, incubated, cultivated, and inoculated, so that the crews would not sicken each other with their respective "harmless" native bacteria.

The *Petrel* and the *Hoffnung*'s dumbbells were linked at the narrow tube that connected the two spherical halves of the ship, so that the combined ship, with the extended hatchway joining them, took on the appearance of a giant plus sign. After the biological tests were completed, the connecting hatch was opened, and the two ships became one in spirit and in fact. Crew members wandered from one ship to the other, freely spending time in either place, cementing the friendships that had begun over the intercom. Youngsters shyly entered their genotypes (already exchanged by the computers) and preferences for new-found lovers into sundry consoles, not once, but several times, and in several places.

The time passed quickly, and except for occasional speculations and random comments, the *Liverpool* passed out of their minds until she hove into unaided human view. The *Liverpool* was as brown and battered as her ancient namesake—her arduous trip and lack of maintenance obvious in the faded and mottled coloration of her hull. Her stores, crew, and spares were sharply depleted, but her library, enriched by the many ships and worlds that she had contacted on her frenzied journey around two-thirds of the galaxy, carried data more valuable than life.

The new double ship joined the old ship, again at the waist, forming a six-lobed, three-tiered snowflake, with the *Hoffnung* and the *Petrel* at the ends and the *Liverpool* in the middle. Ferenc and the others waited impatiently at the connecting tunnel for the ship to signify that crew interchange was now permitted. The signal came, and immediately the far air lock, five hundred feet away, opened. A head popped out and, dissatisfied by what it saw or heard, went back in; the air lock hatch slammed shut behind it. Warning lights came on, admonishing the mystified *Petrel* crew to remain where they were. The tunnel darkened, except for the bright light at its end, near the air lock. The ship began to play an impossibly pompous march, with baroque ornamentations executed by massed harpsichords and trumpets. The air lock door opened slowly. A golden figure stepped out, removed an imaginary hat, bowed low in a sweeping gesture that tumbled his long curly hair almost to the floor, and held the bow through several orchestral flourishes and until the sedate march began again.

He came down the corridor in precise, magnificent steps, turning slow, majestic somersaults, completing each with a flourish of his phantom cape. As he progressed along the corridor, the lights came on, so that he was always seen as a bright spot, back-lighted in splendor, through the dark tunnel. He wore, or so it seemed, golden sandals; their thongs traced an intricate pattern across his spotless white hose that were attached by sky-blue buckles to his golden breeches. There was a gilded vest, and the dark face was crowned with an emerald laurel wreath that sparkled and shimmered to the time of the lights that shifted in complement to the music. He was in front of them now, their mouths open in wonder, staring at the magnificence that had condescended to grace them with his presence. He flourished the imaginary cape again, and again removed the imaginary hat, and bowed low from the waist, his forehead at the ground. The ship produced a drum roll and a trumpet fanfare. The apparition sprang up gracefully, spread his arms wide, and announced, "Permit me to present—ta-ta-ta-dum-da-dum—Belltone Jumpship, Petrelborn!"

"Ferenc, also Petrelborn. Welcome back to your birthship," Ferenc responded morosely. The *Petrel* was a very old ship, and it was not possible for Ferenc to remember all its previous inhabitants or all those who claimed it for a birthship; furthermore, each year the number who thus claimed her, it was joked, doubled. But surely someone like this would have at least one story attributed to him. The music had died, the lights were normal again, and Ferenc could see that it had been only a clever illusion and a masterful application of body paints—for Belltone, like the rest, wore a simple loincloth with utilitarian pockets. Nor was he as beautiful or supple as he had seemed to be during the elaborate entrance. He was stocky and had a full face, and the grace of his walk had been contrived by the

127

ship's adjustment of the music and lights to match his pace rather than the other way around. It was, nevertheless, the most impressive thing that Ferenc had ever seen.

Belltone, satisfied by the hush that still surrounded them and the looks of wonder on old and young, impressionable and cynical, alike, dropped to a more normal conversational mode. "That was my Louis XIV. I've been saving it for my return to the birthship. *Did you all like it*?!" he exulted.

"I see no occupational markings on you," Ferenc said. "How are we to know what you do?"

"But these"—he waved about himself—"*are* my occupational markings. I'm Belltone Jumpship, lately of the *Liverpool*, before that of the *Carpathian*, but also the *Jocular*, the *Pollydoodle*, and others, but Petrelborn. I've stood a watch on every ship and moved at every meeting. I'm shipborn, and shiplived, and proud to say I've never made a planetfall. I'm a ship's programmer. Matter of fact," he announced smugly, cocking an eyebrow, "I programmed the *Petrel*."

"I am pleased"—Ferenc had deliberately avoided the use of the more common "honored"; he was intent on taking Belltone down a peg—"to meet a former shipmate—one who was also the *Petrel*'s greatest braggart, an honor that formerly belonged to Felicity Earthborn, or so the *Petrel* records. Surely you've surpassed her in that category, since the *Petrel* never mentioned you, nor did I ever hear of one who claimed to have programmed an entire ship, especially the pilot ship, of which it is said that M'Tamba was the programmer."

"A whole ship? Of course not," Belltone said. "Only parts of her programs—the important parts, mind you. As for the name, I had a different one then—it was something austere, like Peter or Samuel."

"And what parts of the programs, outside of the music, lights, and special effects, were you responsible for?"

"I'll have to tell you that later. Have you eaten yet?"

"In three hours. What has that to do with it?"

"Don't start without me. I'll explain it then." And with another flourish, he disappeared into the adoring crowd.

It was easy for Ferenc to locate the gilded apparition. The hubbub could be heard several corridors away. Belltone stood, surrounded by admirers, near a food dispenser. He was doing things to the standard biscuit with small phials taken from his loincloth pouch. He would sprinkle this and touch that, and then give the biscuit to its rightful owner, who would taste it and express an opinion by a wry face, a show of pleasure, or neutrality as appropriate to the taste. Ferenc watched, trying to determine what Belltone was up to. It was outside his experience. Food was food and came in a variety of standard tastes and textures over which no person had control.

"Ah!" Belltone noted as he looked up. "He comes." And he winked to his audience of now enthusiastic supporters. He addressed Ferenc. "You are the ship's captain, obvious by your trademarks, but you do poetry as an avocation, also obvious from your face paints—and judging from that as well, heavy, somber poetry it is."

Ferenc looked closely at the other's shoulder, and beneath the glitter he could barely discern a programmer's markings. So at least that part was true. "My vocation," Belltone continued, ignoring Ferenc's close inspection, "as you can plainly see, is programmer. But that is a dull job for the most part. My avocation, like yours, is poetry—the poetry of food and taste—that is my art."

"An art, is it? I thought that it was merely a matter of nutrition. Since when was food something to be programmed beyond the proper allocation of each person's requirements?"

"Oh, *Petrel*, oh, *Petrel*!" Belltone wailed, shielding
129

his face with his hand. "My failure was more complete than I had imagined. This ship, this poor, poor ship, was my first attempt—and a miserable attempt it was. So it's not surprising that the *Petrel*'s crew should not be educated in food matters. On the other hand, self-important poets are not known for their ability to appreciate another fellow's art. But never mind. Nutrition and allocation are, of course, fundamental—that's trivial. But taste, that which the tongue and nose exist for, is the artist's to produce. The *Petrel* was, as I've said, my first try. I was sated with olfactory lushness, and I strove to achieve a new form of purity and candor (I recognize that now for the adolescent idealism that it was). I returned to basics and allowed only the subtlest variations. Alas, I created a ship of gustatory idiots. Furthermore, judging from you, my tasteless friend, I programmed the strictures too strongly for crew dissatisfaction or for the library exchange programs to overcome. I have returned to my birthship to correct my youthful error—allow me to begin your re-education."

He went to the food dispenser, keyed in his identification, asked for Ferenc's, and keyed that in also. Then he continued to enter number after number, which, had they been identifications, would have produced enough food to last for days. Instead, a few pellets emerged, which Belltone scooped up, put into his mouth one at a time, chewed, and, with closed eyes, evaluated at length. After several more trials, with Ferenc getting hungrier for his meal, Belltone was satisfied. He punched in a new sequence, which resulted in the usual combination of liquid containers and hard biscuits. Ferenc reached for them, but was intercepted by Belltone, who, taking the phials from his pouch, repeated the scene that Ferenc had watched earlier. Belltone dipped his fingers into the food, tasted it, broke off crumbs and munched them, ever adjusting them with minuscule sprinklings of the mysterious phials. Finally he allowed Ferenc to try the result.

The aroma of the first course made him salivate

furiously—an unfamiliar and unpleasant experience. The biscuit, normally crumbly, was hard to chew, and, again, the taste was not pleasing. The third course—a flat, rubbery substance—exploded in his mouth after a delayed reaction, causing Ferenc's eyes to tear. "I thought that would wake you up." Belltone grinned at the watching crowd as he passed Ferenc a water container, which brought yet another surprise. The "water" reduced the rubbery stuff to the point of bearability, so Ferenc ate and drank alternately, for no matter the taste, he knew that it could not hurt him, and refusing to eat one's portion of food was an unthinkable waste. The last course was a pudding consisting of small, exotically colored globules in a sticky matrix.

"Why, this tastes exactly the way food always does," Ferenc said testily.

"So it does. Other than the shape and form, it *is* what you are used to eating. You see, it *is* disappointing. You hated the first two—that's natural. Taste must be cultivated. The third was intended as a shock, but not wanting to cause you pain, I provided the moderator in the water. Before, you did not believe that there was a world of taste, and now that you do believe, you must prepare to explore it. There are classicists who insist on trying to recapture the taste, texture, and appearance of old Earth foods. There are experimentalists who are constructing abstract tastes, and there's even a senile, monomaniacal old bitch on the other side of the galaxy, long overdue for recycling, who's created a complete program based on nothing but variations on a theme of jolapeño peppers. That hot one was one of hers."

"The experience," Ferenc admitted, "was interesting, but I don't think the *Petrel* can afford such dissipation of resources. It would lead to, if you'll excuse the term, waste."

"Waste, Ferenc? It's clear to me that you are grossly misinformed regarding the food generators. Tell me, would you exchange your portion with another's?"

"Of course not!"

131

"Why not? Does anything prevent you? Would you key in someone else's identification?"

"Such things are not done. They're obscene; they're wasteful. I might key in the identifier for a mate who was sick, but I could not eat his food. It wouldn't be my just portion. It could be excessive for me, and that would be a direct waste. It could be insufficient for me, and that, through my reduced effectiveness, would be an indirect waste. It could be unsuited to my metabolism or the tasks I was engaged in; certainly a pregnant woman or a growing child has different needs. What you suggest," Ferenc concluded heatedly, "is as illogical as it is ineffectual!"

"But you see then, by your own admission, that every morsel of food that you have ever consumed has been individualized. You identified yourself at this feeding station. The ship examined your metabolic records and your activities for today, estimated your caloric output, made a hundred other calculations, and then established the nutrition package appropriate to Ferenc Petrelborn, not for any day, but for this specific day and hour. It manufactured the food exclusively for you, as to taste, content, texture, and so on. What comes into the machines are basic biologicals, roughage, and modifiers. The programs do the rest. They can just as easily produce food that you like, hate, or are indifferent to."

"All food tastes the same," Ferenc insisted.

"How would you know?" Belltone challenged. "You've never tasted any but your own. It's not the food that's the issue. It's life itself. Are we to stay in the comfortable rut we're in? Are we destined to be just sad, sanctimonious sojourners of the stars in sackcloth and ashes? Are there to be no songs other than for navigation, maintenance, and other technical folderol? If we don't learn to live again, we shall surely die."

"The basic virtues," Ferenc preached, "are the virtues of survival. Two thousand ships have been lost since we left Earth, and three hundred colonies, at the last count. 'Waste is pollution, and pollution is death!'"

"Yes, Ferenc, two thousand ships have died, but
132

there are more than six thousand in the fleet now. More than we started with. And we still have three hundred colonies to supply them and launch them. We can do better than just survive"—he snorted the word disdainfully—"at the alien's whim; we can take our destiny into our hands and do better than just exist!"

Repair technicians from the three linked ships were revived. The corridors swarmed with busy people rushing to this task and that—a throng such as only those who had made a planetfall had ever seen. It was decided that the *Petrel* would go to the conclave, if it could make it on time, and that the *Hoffnung* would accompany the *Liverpool* to help her with the repairs. The work was started immediately, and it was soon evident that the *Liverpool* would eventually be restored to a proper condition. As the work on the *Liverpool* progressed, they became increasingly dissatisfied with the *Petrel*'s appearance. It was not right, they said, that an Earthship—the pilot ship, at that, and a representative to the conclave—should look so faded and worn. Ferenc insisted that the entire ship was perfectly functional. There was nothing lacking with respect to standards and quality. She was sound, clean, and all her systems worked. What was there to do to her?

He found out when he was next wakened, prematurely, by the incessant *click-click* of toeholds being opened and closed by many suited figures on the outer hull. He rushed to the bridge to look at the screens. There were hundreds of them all over the hull, applying anodyzing to its surface. The faded blue was interspersed here and there by brilliant azure patches. Others worked on the birds, tracing their original outlines, restoring their pristine whiteness, and filling in the details, using such stylistic changes as had emerged since the time of launch. Pitted surfaces were being filled in and exposed metal parts burnished until even the faint starlight was sufficient to reflect the coloration of the hull upon them. Ferenc grumbled at the marginal usefulness of such treatment and went back to plotting a course toward the conclave.

Then came the final interchange of crews. Many were revived to bring the *Liverpool*'s crew closer to the normal size, while others were revived to attend the conclave. Some were chosen who, in the opinions of those who knew them and proposed them (human as well as computer), had something unique to offer the conclave. Some wanted to paint new pictures and could. Some wanted to compose new songs but couldn't; the best navigator, the wisest, some who merely wanted to go very much, the best storyteller, the humblest, and, of course, the biggest liar were weighed and selected for the trip. The *Petrel* would carry the news, the history, the wisdom, and the foolishness of all the ships and all the crews which the *Petrel*, the *Hoffnung*, and the *Liverpool* had ever contacted, as well as those of the contact's contacts, and so on, *ad absurdum*.

When all had been stabilized, unnecessary crewmen resuspended, final opinions regarding man's future cast, and the first dull moment of repetition sensed, the *Petrel* separated from the *Hoffnung* and the *Liverpool* and headed toward the conclave.

10

Retribution

Precise coordinates had been given for a place 100,000 light years above the galactic center. The trip was long and would require many stops to calibrate instruments and correct star maps. Predicted plasma densities and gravitational field measurements had to be correlated with actual values and new bearings developed so that they would land within a sphere a few light years in diameter surrounding the expected location of the conclave. Without these tedious intermediate observations, they could have landed outside of the probable position of the other ships and would either have spent months trying to find them or have had to jump back to a known point within the galaxy and begin the outbound trip all over again. Rather than miss with a number of direct but possibly wild jumps, they took the slow, accurate course of action to which they were accustomed. It was soon evident that this course would never bring them to the conclave in time.

Ferenc enlisted Belltone's help in searching through the records for tracks and intermediate jump points that might cut the duration of the trip. Despite himself, Ferenc was beginning to like the man, and for all his posturing and braggadocio, Belltone was competent at his job. Although the three of them—Belltone, Sirna, and Ferenc—worked at it, they could not find a shortcut. Belltone put a stop to it by announcing one day, "With all respect, Sirna, this is not going to work. There's no way we'll get there on time."

"Do you have a suggestion?" she asked.

"Uh—yes—but it's very risky, and I'm not sure we'll ever be the same again."

"It's my job to weigh the risks, Belltone. So why don't you tell us what you want to do?" Ferenc said.

"I'm sorry, love," Belltone apologized to Sirna, "but I'm suggesting another navigator."

"Indeed!" she replied with expected anger. "And who might that be?"

"Po Lin Earthborn."

"Oh—that's different."

"How will Po Lin Earthborn help us?" Ferenc asked. "Is she a better navigator than you, Sirna?"

"Not better, exactly," Sirna explained, "but different. It's something among us navigators. They use her to scare us with when we make a mistake. She's to be revived in a life-death situation, but I don't even know if she's on this ship. I always thought she was a legend or something."

"She's no legend, believe me," Belltone said, "and as for being on this ship, she's never been on any other and never will be. Ship?" he asked.

"YES, BELLTONE?"

"Po Lin Earthborn in ship?"

"PO LIN EARTHBORN HIM IN SHIP," it confirmed.

"Talk her!"

"NO CAN DO, BELLTONE."

"Why 'No can do'?"

"HIM IN DEEP CRYOSLEEP."

"Cycle him out from cryosleep!"

"NO CAN DO. BIG-ASS TROUBLE!" it objected.

"Medical trouble?"

"PO LIN TROUBLE. BIG-ASS TROUBLE. PO LIN COMMAND PETRELSHIP NEVER WAKE PO LIN AGAIN EXCEPT SURVIVAL OR UNLESS PLANETFALL. PRIME PERSONAL DIRECTIVE."

"Override personal directive, Petrelship, and cycle

Po Lin Earthborn out from cryosleep!" Belltone insisted.

"PO LIN EARTHBORN WARNED PETRELSHIP. BELLTONE SCREWING AROUND. CREWMATES SCREWING AROUND. IS NO PLANETFALL NOW OR IMPENDING. IS NO SURVIVAL CASE NOW OR IMPENDING. BELLTONE SCREWING AROUND WITH BIG-ASS TROUBLE. PETRELSHIP NO CAN DO. NACK!"

"Well, that takes care of it, then." Ferenc was disappointed. "We'll have to do the best we can and hope that it's not all over by the time we get there."

"Not at all," Belltone countered. "We'll just have Po Lin taken out of cryosleep."

"But you heard the ship; there's no emergency. You can't wake her against her will, and the *Petrel* said that it wouldn't go along with you."

"Trouble with you, Ferenc, is that you've never programmed a ship." He called the ship again. "Ship? 'Member Po Lin Earthborn cycle from cryosleep?"

"'MEMBER BIG-ASS TROUBLE, BELLTONE."

"Why no can do?"

"PRIME PERSONAL DIRECTIVE. NO WAKE TILL PLANETFALL ET CETERA."

"Sure that right, ship?"

"NINE NINES SURE!"

"When last Po Lin Earthborn planetfall?"

"HAVEN. SHORT TIME. ONLY ONE-EIGHTY YEARS."

"Cycle Po Lin Earthborn from cryosleep; ship survival issue."

"BELLTONE SCREWING AROUND!" It refused.

"Crew take ship far place. Need more supplies and planetfall. No planetfall till Po Lin Earthborn him cycle out from cryosleep. No planetfall, no shipstores; no shipstores, no ship; no ship, no planetfall!"

"You're lying to it!" Ferenc accused Belltone. "You're actually lying to it!"

"Certainly," he admitted. "How else do you expect to get your way with it?"

"BELLTONE?" the ship asked. "PARADOX BELLTONE. IS NOT IN FACTUAL DOMAIN. IS IN HUMAN DOMAIN. OR IS BELLTONE SHITTING SHIP?"

"No shit. Is human domain, not factual," Belltone reassured the troubled ship. "Is paradox resolved Petrelship cycle Po Lin Earthborn from cryosleep."

"PETRELSHIP CYCLE PO LIN EARTHBORN FROM CRYOSLEEP. IT'S YOUR ASS BROTHER BELLTONE!"

"That's that." Belltone smirked. "Now we'll have the dubious pleasure of attending to her when she wakes."

Ferenc and Belltone looked into the cryosleep container at the old woman. She wore no body paints and only a faded navigator's tattoo adorned her thin breasts. Her yellow skin was stretched tight over her bones. Her long gray hair was loose about her face, a face dominated by a pair of clear black eyes set into twin craters of wrinkles induced by her long stay under Haven's twin bright suns. Her body twitched, and an angry scowl marred her face as the ship explained the circumstances of her awakening. She seemed to be talking to herself now, for they could clearly see her lips moving.

"She must be giving the ship a going-over for waking her," Belltone said, "and it's probably finked on us. Brace yourself—we're next."

Her eyes focused, scanned, and settled on Belltone as if in response to his remark. She muttered something to the computer, and in response to the information it gave her, she searched for and locked on to Ferenc. There was another short, inaudible conversation with the computer, and she began to pound on the inside of the cryostat's cover. At last, when it was clear that it could no longer hold her down, the ship withdrew the intravenous tubes and electrodes and released the restraining clamps. The cover slid open, whereupon she sat upright, glaring at the two men, her dark eyes still young, flittering back and forth between them. Her right hand jabbed out and pointed accusingly at Ferenc. "You're Ferenc, ship's captain—you look like one—so that—that"—she pointed a trembling hand at Belltone—"must be the Belltone who's responsible and better have a good explanation! I'm Po Lin Earthborn of the *Petrel*, too many thousands of years out of launch from Earth and God knows where in between. I am of the launch crew."

"We are honored by the meeting and blessed by the knowledge," the two men responded. "We are honored and blessed to be carried in this sacred relic of the Earth. Blessed be He who has preserved this ship out of launch and has brought us into her hold and crew."

"Blessed be the maker of man and ships who has preserved this rotten bag of bones to be insulted by the addled prattle of junior crewmen who make more ceremony than sense!" was the woman's blasphemous reply.

Ferenc was speechless, but Belltone, always ready with a retort, quickly rejoined, "Blessed be the corrupt carcass before us who was rejected six times in succession by the converter and has been sustained by numerous malfunctions of men and machines to plague us this day forward with her evil ways."

The old woman smiled for the first time. She looked at Belltone closely. "I know you, but your name's not Belltone. You're—you're . . . Are you Petrelborn?"

"Yes, Earthmother," the young man admitted, using the honorific title, hoping all the while that Po Lin would not remember; it had been a very short watch that they had shared—was it five hundred years before? Po Lin, using a variant of the navigation chants, started to re-create the genealogy of all Petrelborn crew members, starting with the first joyous birth so many centuries before: the whole ship had been revived for that event. She followed each newborn from birth through childhood and to the point where they had children of their own or had left the ship. As each one passed in review, she fixed his image in her mind, trying to match it to Belltone. While easier than reviewing star maps, the process was still laborious and complex and she almost missed him. She backtracked a few generations and found her quarry, totally unlike

the elegant apparition before her. She looked at Belltone again and laughed. "You're not Belltone! You're
Oliver. Oliver Shipsmasher! That's what I named you."
Then, as the details of his past sins began to collect in
her mind, she stopped laughing. "You have the nerve
to come back to this ship?" She looked at Ferenc sadly.
"You let this one on board? You look like a serious and
sensible young man. Look to the records, Captain Ferenc. Look to the records for the only man ever thrown
off a ship, and look to your ship—or better yet, just
dump him overboard immediately!"

"It was an error, old mother." Belltone defended himself, and for the first time since he had returned to the
Petrel, Ferenc saw in him signs of genuine humility,
at least before Po Lin. "It was a harmless prank—in
the end at least."

"So it was," Po Lin admitted. She turned to Ferenc.
"No use looking to the records for *that* particular es-
capade, Ferenc—we all thought it best to wipe it out.
Right now it's something between Oliver and me."

"Please, Earthmother," Belltone requested, "it's
Belltone now, not Shipsmasher."

"All right then, 'Belltone' it will be," she said as she
climbed out of the cryostat. She stood before them, looking down at them from the advantage of a full head's
height. "I swear that not only is the cryostat rejuven-
ating, but it also makes one grow. Well," she continued,
getting directly to the point, "what possessed you
youngsters to wake me?"

"There is to be a meeting, a conclave of ships—"
Ferenc began.

"Oh, he finally did it," Po Lin interrupted with pleasure. "Well, good."

"Who did it, Mother?" Belltone asked.

"Gils did it. He said he would, and I thought he
would. I suppose you have coordinates?"

"We have, but it is far."

"Don't tell me *far!*" she snapped. "Can we make it
or do we just drift?"

"It is possible to make it with your help, Father." Belltone smirked.

Ferenc was beginning to understand the proper mode of address for this apparition, and, unlike himself, he attempted to join in the fun. "Possible, but probably too difficult for you, Neuter One."

"Old, certainly," she agreed, "but neutered, never! There's some equipment on this ship that's still functional, or will I have to teach you *those* rituals also?"

"It might be functional at that, Ferenc." Belltone continued the gibing while leering appreciatively at Po Lin. "Come to think of it, I've never had a museum piece. Do you think if we both worked at it we could get it patched up so that it runs at quarter speed?"

"All you have to do, prepubescent snot," she countered, "is to supply the energy. However, the resources on this ship are so slim that I doubt that even the two of you simultaneously have the necessary—"

"That's enough!" Ferenc interrupted. "We have a navigation problem to solve."

"That's no real problem," Po Lin said matter-of-factly. "The only problem will be getting this dumb ship to agree—he was always stubborn when it came to things like this..." She mumbled, "All right, then. Up to the bridge!"

The waking crew for the trip was back down to thirty, and most of them were on the bridge listening to the old woman explain her shortcut. "It's not a question of distance," she told Sirna, "but of making jumps to and from well-known points. Instead of crawling one small jump at a time, you make a big jump to a known point, and then to another known point. Since we have to go almost directly above the hub, the first step will be to get to the hub as quickly as possible. Then the only observations we'll have to make will be the ones needed to get from the hub to the conclave." She got out of the navigator's chair and beckoned Sirna to sit in it. "Now, child, you're going to have to do the jump. I'll give you the coordinates and the readings, but you're going to control it, because if I sing it, we'll surely get wrecked."

Sirna happily accepted the honor and prepared the controls while Po Lin meditated, trying to recall the elusive coordinates. She sang one song after another to herself and while they could detect the former glory of her voice, it was clear that she had acted wisely in relinquishing the controls to Sirna. At last she gave it up. She could not remember. "Damn it! I'll have to ask the ship after all."

"Where are we jumping toward?" Sirna asked. "Perhaps I know the coordinates."

"Toward Earth, and I don't—"

"Toward Earth!" Ferenc exploded. "That's forbidden!"

"Toward where Earth used to be," she corrected herself.

"That's forbidden," Ferenc insisted, and several others murmured in agreement.

"No." Po Lin explained, "Where Earth *is* is forgotten and unknown and outside the galaxy. But where Earth *was* is merely unpleasant, and in navigation nothing is forbidden if it works." She addressed the ship. "Navigation coordinates!"

"JUMP WHERE LOVER?"

"Old Earth place."

"IS FORBIDDEN!" the ship informed her.

"Do we have to go through this again? I knew them once; I've forgotten them—besides, I've jumped this ship there how many times? Old Earth place coordinates: NOW!"

"EARTH PLACE COORDINATES FORBIDDEN. ALLOWED ONLY MEISTERS. PO LIN HIM NO MEISTER."

"That's my own rule. I've always known those coordinates and just can't remember them at this moment. Now, Meister or not, give them to me!"

"What's a Meister?" Ferenc asked.

142

"A Meister was—" Po Lin began to explain, but she was interrupted by Belltone.

"It doesn't matter what a Meister is, because I am one, or soon will be." He addressed the ship again. "This Meister Belltone. Old Earth place coordinates! Now!"

"BELLTONE SHIPPING SHIT. HIM NO MEISTER."

"How Meister created?" Belltone asked.

"MEISTER WAS WITHIN SHIP AT FIRST BEGIN: ORIGINAL DATA DECLARATION."

"Information for ship: Meister created by ship programmer. Confirm!"

"ACK, ACK, SHIP PROGRAMMER OLIVER SHIPWRECK."

"I didn't know *that* name," Po Lin snorted.

"Meister created human domain by ship quorum of wakeship personnel." Belltone continued the programming. "Create Navigationmeister! Create Programmermeister."

"NAVIGATIONMEISTER CREATED ACK ACK. PROGRAMMERMEISTER CREATED ACK ACK."

"New Meisters all attributes old Meisters. Confirm!"

"ACK ACK."

"Ship quorum personnel say Po Lin Navigationmeister and Belltone (alias Oliver Shipwreck) Programmermeister," Belltone told the ship. He then informed the crew that they were to confirm the newly elected functionaries by a voice vote; they shrugged and agreed—it mattered little by what exalted title a person wished to be addressed. The ship acknowledged the election. Belltone turned to Po Lin. "It's yours now, Navigationmeister Po Lin. Ask it nicely if you can, and it'll tell you anything."

Po Lin asked the ship again for the coordinates of Earth's original position, which it now dutifully gave her. Sirna took the coordinates, translated them to the appropriate form of the control song, and executed the jump. There was nothing to see but still another—to all but Po Lin—unfamiliar star pattern. And nothing to note the place but the faint, sporadic, largely useless signals from the decrepit buoy. It took only a few hours

143

to make the observations for the next jump—the jump to the hub.

They emerged in a region of stars so dense that even though they were light years from the closest one, they were surrounded by a brightness that exceeded that of a close orbit around a sun. It was a dangerous place to be. Dangerous because of the high radiation, and dangerous because they knew that they were surrounded by hostile alien worlds. They took normal precautions for the radiation and extraordinary ones for the aliens. All unnecessary power was shut down, and all forms of electrical activities not absolutely essential to the running of the ship were curtailed. The continual subliminal susurrus of the equipment gone, the ship, its lights dimmed, was quiet. A conversation decks away could be heard reverberating along the corridors, and a heavy footfall in the opposite hull seemed destined to give them away, despite the fact that the aliens could not detect their sounds but only their radiations. Nevertheless, they took to whispering in the darkened ship—it couldn't hurt.

The next jump was a long jump—the longest that had ever been made—and it would take weeks to make the observations for it. They had been there a few days when they detected the first broadcast, obviously of human origin. They located its source—a yellow sun one hundred light years away, farther yet into the hub. There was no record of a human colony here, nor could they conceive of how, if such a colony existed, it could have escaped detection. It could only be a colony that had reverted to barbarism, lost its history, and was now re-emerging toward civilization. The colony had to be warned, to be guided, for it was only a matter of time until the aliens discovered and destroyed them. Conversely, they were afraid of a trap.

Ferenc was undecided as to what course to take. Investigating would take time and would largely obviate the investment in measurements that they had already made. Po Lin assured him that the jump to the conclave would be successful and that the shortcut they had taken would more than permit the detour. The crew agreed with her and overruled him; they were willing to risk a trap. Ferenc, no less concerned than they over the potential demise of a colony of fellow humans, nevertheless insisted that the approach be made with extreme caution; a fraction of a light year at a time, rather than in one jump. They jumped toward the yellow sun and, mysteriously, found no trace of the broadcasts—which heightened Ferenc's suspicions. Again they jumped, closer to the star, and now the broadcast was there again, having progressed from early radio to a more complex and sophisticated pattern of radio broadcasts. This was as expected, since in traversing the one hundred light years of distance, they should expect to pass through one hundred years of the colony's electronic history. They continued following the track. Its evolution, other than the gaps, was as expected. The broadcast existed for a few hours, and then a gap of years, and then it started again—always showing increased sophistication and the further evolution of the foolish society. It was like watching the museum's recordings of Earth's pre-collapse civilizations. They had wars, formed alliances, dissolved them, built cities, destroyed them; it was new and yet familiar.

They were now only a few light years away and the broadcasts were continuous; the *Petrel* maintained the silence. The last jump was a neatly executed maneuver directly into orbit about the star's outermost planet. From there they could observe the sun's fifth planet. It was a green world with blue seas over which clouds swirled. From their position the broadcasts were overwhelming. They blared out raucously over the entire frequency spectrum and in many variants of human language. The television broadcasts were a continual mechanistic repetition of the same inanities, differing from day to day only in insignificant detail—a fact that made Ferenc even more suspicious than he had been

145

before. But Belltone assured him, for Belltone had studied such things, that this was the normal pattern of human television broadcasts, an opinion held by several others in the crew who had an interest in history. Ferenc refused to believe this, so he examined the museum's records and found indeed that there were no significant differences between the broadcasts from the planet and those on record.

They detected huge, worldwide power grids, and every square mile of the three continents was blanketed by the radar signals of a thousand aircraft, while the oceans reverberated to the electronic pulsings of a like number of ships. Yet, paradoxically, the instruments also said that there was nothing down there. It was an empty world. There were no cities between which the illusory aircraft flew, and no safe harbors for the ghostly ships that so blatantly announced their electromagnetic presence.

Ferenc, ever wary of a trap, was nevertheless intrigued by the ethereal legerdemain. Preparations for the jump to the conclave continued and did not require his attention. Instead, he spent his free time observing the thing, trying to decide to go to the planet for a closer look.

Belltone resolved his ambivalence. "Go!" he urged. "We came here for a look, so let's take it. There's plenty of time for it—so let's go!"

Ferenc expressed the necessity for caution, but those within hearing—at one time or another, the entire crew—insisted that they investigate. Finally he agreed. "But we'll have to revive another navigator and a re-entry pilot."

"And what's wrong with me?" Po Lin asked. "I can do both those jobs!"

"Surely you could have, honored Earthmother," Ferenc said apologetically, "but you yourself said that Sirna should chant the control songs."

"That's for a big jump," she countered. "That planet is no farther than my hand, and from the looks of it, no more difficult to land on than if it were a child's exercise. Sirna can complete the observations for the conclave jump as well as I can. Besides, you owe me a landfall, in case you forgot."

Ferenc, Belltone, and Po Lin suited up and floated out to the small shuttle craft. They jumped into a close polar orbit that circled the planet every hour. Po Lin smirked in self-appreciation over the maneuver; Belltone was lavishly sardonic in his praise, and even Ferenc grudgingly admitted his error by addressing her as "Navigationmeister." Maneuvering in orbit, however, was difficult. Controls did not respond properly, and more than once Po Lin had to bypass primary circuits and rely on the less sophisticated backup systems. The ships, designed to operate in an electronically suppressed environment, were not shielded adequately from the massive interference caused by the broadcasts. At this altitude even the simple instruments of the shuttle craft should have been able to locate the broadcasts' source—but there were no artifacts on the planet's surface. The broadcasts' source, they discovered, was not beneath them, but above them in a higher orbit. They located the source, tracked it, and reached it in a few hours. It was a half ship that appeared to be derelict. It had no spin to provide artificial gravity, and yet from it came powerful signals that bespoke a vast and busy population. The electromagnetic radiation was intense and the interference with the instruments and controls worse than ever. They reached the air lock and tied the small craft to a tether line.

The hull was airtight, and it was possible to unsuit. The energy of the broadcasts was palpable; instead of the expected musty smell of an abandoned ship, they were overwhelmed by the acrid stench of ozone. They went directly to the bridge, floating easily in the absence of gravity. At the halfway point the ship wrenched and shuddered, as if it were under drive. "The shuttle!" Belltone shouted as he raced back to the air lock. They arrived at the air lock: the shuttle was under power and straining against the tether that held it to the ship.

"It must be the interference that set it off." Po Lin

hypothesized as they hurriedly resuited. They entered the outer air lock only to see the tether cable part. As the shuttle disappeared out of sight on a path that would inevitably crash it into the planet's surface, the tether cable, previously stretched by the strain, now lashed back; loop upon loop of cable came at them. The cable smashed against the air lock door, and then, as if that were not enough, encircled the air lock tube in numerous coils like a vastly elongated and angry boa constrictor. It would not be possible to use that air lock for escape. They were temporarily trapped in the outer air lock. Unfortunately, the wrecked ship's controls functioned sufficiently to prevent opening the inner door while there was still a vacuum in the air lock. It took the three of them several hours, using the suits' few tools, to bypass the controls and re-enter the ship proper, which they did with only a minimum loss of atmosphere. However, the suits' air supplies were now severely depleted.

They returned to the bridge by the most direct route. It was a shambles. The black hole drive generator did not exist, and the main reaction engines did not work, nor was it possible to repair them. The few communications systems that appeared to be operable were overwhelmed by the strength of the broadcast.

"We're either going to have to signal the *Petrel* with what we have on board"—Ferenc summed it up—"and that means turning this broadcast off, or we'll have to contrive some way of driving this wreck out to the *Petrel*'s orbit."

"Assuming," Po Lin said, "that we can get some maneuvering engines to work, we could make it to the *Petrel*'s orbit in a few weeks. They might stay around that long."

"I don't think we actually have to get there," Ferenc explained. "If we can get this ship under way toward the *Petrel*, they're sure to notice it. Right now they probably think that we've crashed on the planet's surface. Our only hope is that they decide to investigate why the broadcast is approaching them. That, or turn the broadcast off and use the communications gear."

They split up. Belltone went to the lower deck to evaluate the maintenance and life-support situation. Ferenc remained on the bridge to see what he could do there, while Po Lin undertook to search the ship for the broadcast source, simultaneously taking inventory of anything in the derelict that might be of use. Almost nothing on the bridge worked. Some of the subsystems were ancient and appeared not to have been repaired in a thousand years. The wreck was half of what had been the *Phoenix*, an original Earth ship. The few working instruments gave sporadic, inconsistent readings, and even the simpler primary instruments were unreliable.

They met Belltone on the maintenance level after the first hour. "How does it look from here?" Ferenc asked.

"We have a hull full of air that should last several months. There's not much food. The instruments say the stores are empty. What did you find?" he asked Po Lin.

"The stores *are* empty, at least those I've looked at so far. There is some food left at the ends of the dispenser tubes. If there's a like amount in all the tubes, we have enough to last a week."

"There's a working converter," Belltone said, "and we have plenty of water. Energy, though, is a serious problem. Only a few million kilowatt hours left—just the storage cells—the reactor, of course, is out."

"Where's the power for the broadcast coming from, then?" Po Lin asked.

"She's right," Ferenc agreed. "There must be a huge source of power someplace. Let's get back to work—Po Lin will find it."

She was back in less than fifteen minutes this time. "The cryostats don't exist any more." She led them to the place she had discovered. "That thing must be the broadcast source. It's like nothing I've ever seen before."

149

It was beyond comprehension. The cryostat vaults had been removed, creating a huge spherical chamber several decks high. They had turned a corner in a corridor and had almost tumbled into the void that had been hacked out of the center of the ship. The cavity was dominated by a gargantuan apparatus that was undoubtedly the work of man. It had no regular shape but consisted of multiple protrusions, irregular forms, and random hollows pierced with unfamiliar conduits and, occasionally, vaguely familiar appurtenances. Equally strange was its lack of connection to the ship proper. It stood away from all walls and surfaces, suspended by light girders, so they could examine it from every side. By contrast to the decay that surrounded it, it was completely new.

"We can be assured by the presence of this thing," Ferenc said, "that this hulk was not cast adrift by accident. This thing must have a purpose, and it must be the source of the broadcasts. If we can figure it out, we might be able to turn it off and signal the *Petrel*."

They went over it carefully, looking for an access to it. Ferenc was on one side of it, and Belltone and Po Lin on the other. Ferenc had just discovered a panel, which, upon removal, revealed a control console—clearly labeled. He called Belltone over. They looked at the console together. It was a makeshift arrangement, but the controls were unambiguously labeled. He was about to hit the main power switch when they heard Po Lin's sharp cry: "Stop! Stop whatever you're doing!" They went quickly to her. She pointed to a scribbled message on the side of the thing. "Remember Eden and learn from Hearth!" it read.

"Eden and Hearth are both dead." Ferenc commented without understanding. "We were just about to turn this thing off."

"You can't!" she exclaimed. "This thing is booby-trapped!"

"Why do you say that, Mother?" Belltone asked.

"Because Hearth was the first of our colonies to be

booby-trapped by the aliens. I say we can't touch this thing—can't even try."

"What's the worst?" Belltone smiled. "We'll be killed. We're probably dead anyway, so what does it matter?"

"At my age it's not the dying I mind—oh, yes, I did want to make another planetfall and romp in a bunk with a man again. But we could cause great harm by meddling with this thing. I say it's a booby trap and that none of those controls mean anything. If you touch it, you'll probably blow us up—perhaps this entire solar system, including the *Petrel*, or worse. I say leave it alone!"

"I'll grant you it's a booby trap," Ferenc said, "but then it's only a matter of time until we figure it out."

"Ferenc!" she protested. "This thing is so new that we could spend months at it—months that we don't have. If you try to disarm it, you won't be allowed one mistake. This thing is made by man, and it has a purpose. Not only will we be killed, but the *Petrel* will be jeopardized, and that purpose, whatever it is, will be thwarted. We have no choice but to leave it alone. Let's get back to work and see what we can do with the rest of the ship."

Ferenc reluctantly agreed and replaced the panel over the tantalizing console. He returned to the bridge. The relic was unusual in other ways. It had not been stripped. There were stores of equipment and some spare parts, so that between what Po Lin brought back from her foraging trips and what they found to be operable, they were able to reconstruct a working maintenance console that quickly gave them a reliable assessment of all their available resources. While bleak, the situation was not hopeless. Eight maneuvering engines were operable, and there was enough reaction mass to drive the ship out of orbit and onto an intercept course with the *Petrel*.

Three engines were needed to drive them in any particular direction rather than merely spinning them around. No three engines were properly oriented for that task. The maneuvering engines would have to be moved—at least two of them. Furthermore, reaction mass had to be ducted to the engines without benefit of working pumps. Handles had to be fitted to the pumps and the mass transferred manually. It would take a lot of valve openings and closings and a lot of sweat—difficult but feasible.

The two engines were moved at the cost of the last of the suits' oxygen supply. Once the engines were in place, Ferenc worked on jury-rigging controls while Belltone and Po Lin pumped reaction mass from the far ends of the ship. The job took a week, by which time the food had been consumed. Even if the engines did work, the three of them would soon be starving. With much agonizing over the sacrilege, they robbed the life-form vaults of seedlings, biota, and nourishment, stealing that without which no ship could found a colony. They ran the material through the converter, thereby extending their food supply to the point of feasibility.

They gathered at the maintenance console to do the final check prior to firing the engines. Phase after phase of the complex ritual was passed without fault. There were only a few steps to go, and Ferenc could hardly restrain himself.

"Suck the getter at seven watts!" he sang.

"Suck the getter at seven watts!" Belltone chanted.

"And check!" Po Lin added.

"Standby power and that's all," Belltone announced.

"And check! . . . No! No! Hold!" Po Lin screamed. "It's standby power *before* focus! Hold! Hold!" But the jury-rigged controls could not respond to the interlocks that were keyed to the crew's voices, and Ferenc had pressed the stud even as Po Lin had begun to voice tentative approval. The ships and procedures had changed in almost forty centuries. The *Phoenix* had been derelict so long that she had not been brought up-to-date. Po Lin had realized the possible discrepancy too late. A quick examination confirmed the engines' destruction. They would have to begin again.

They returned to the bridge. Belltone explained the food situation. Where before they had had enough food to last for a possible rendezvous with the *Petrel*, that was now out of the question. Ferenc estimated that three new engines could be moved into a stable pattern, but it would take much longer now that it had to be done from inside the ship: two or three weeks for that task alone. Then the fuel would have to be transferred again and the controls re-rigged. By then it was likely that the *Petrel* would be gone—long gone. "We're in terminal recycle," he announced gloomily at last.

"Well"—Po Lin was cheerful—"that's that. No planetfall and no romp in a bunk. We might as well get to it."

"We could wait a week," Belltone said.

"For what?" she asked. "The situation is clear and the choice is obvious. Better now than later."

They went to the converter and, floating around it, started the mourning song for Po Lin. She sang of Earth, of the leaving, of her first lover, M'Tamba, of subsequent lovers and planetfalls, of other ships met, and of her more recent awakening and events. There was no sorrow in the traditional wail—she was full with life and content to leave it in this way. Her story ended, they began the funerary ritual proper:

"To our mother, who gives life for life."

"I give life of my own will for life."

"She will be with us now and to all our generations."

"My gift is all that I have left to give."

"She will sustain us in our trials."

"Blessed be He who has given me a life to give."

"Blessed be the giver of life."

She removed a pill from her loincloth and placed it in front of her. It was a painless depressant. "I make no sacrifice," she said. "The life is not my own. It was only lent to me. Remember me in joy as I am joyful to have known my friends. Remember me in joy as I become my friends. Blessed be the converter."

"Blessed be the converter, blessed be the converter." She reached for the pill.

She reached for the pill floating in front of her, compensating for her change in angular momentum, in a free-fall maneuver that she had executed faultlessly thousands of times before—and missed. The pill drifted toward the wall, and they began a slow but accelerating drift after it. Upon reaching the wall, the pill rolled toward what had been in their previous position the ceiling. They watched the pill move, and soon they, too, began to feel the tug of centrifugal acceleration and the restoration of gravity. They were not alone.

The ship had full gravity again. A look out of the ports on the bridge made it clear that the ship was rotating. It seemed that they must have been connected to a ship—another ship with supplies and crew. If so, there was no reason for another attempt with the engines—their hope now lay in attracting the attention of the other ship. Po Lin suggested that they try using signal rockets that she had seen in the lower six o'clock air lock. It was as sensible a plan as any, and they hurried there to take stock.

The internal door of the air lock responded to the "open" button and showed, as Po Lin had said, some old but probably still functional signal rockets. They left the air lock, closed it, and attempted to open the outer door. The pumps were not working, so that air still remained in the air lock. With air in it, it was not possible to open. Again, they would have to bypass the controls, which could be done only from inside the air lock, after bleeding out its air, which meant in suits— suits that no longer had an oxygen supply. Using the suit now was not much better than holding one's breath for several minutes, but they tried nevertheless, not once but several times. The bypass worked, but the air lock door was jammed tight. They tried other air locks with no better results. They considered drilling a small hole through which the signal rockets could be fired, but they lacked the tools to drill through the tough substance of the outer hull.

"We can set the signal rockets to fire out of the air lock's outer door if we can get it open," Ferenc suggested. "The rockets can be ignited from outside the air lock electrically. We only have to drill a small hole in the inner doorframe through which to pass the wires. The only trouble is—how do we open that jammed outer door?"

"Po Lin," Belltone asked, "what did you say we had in the storage hold?"

"Metals, chemicals..."

"What kind of metals and chemicals?"

Various alloys, basic fertilizers for the hydroponics..."

"Good enough!" He was exultant. "Ferenc, you and Po Lin set up the signal rockets as if there were no door. You'll have to rig up some kind of igniters for them. Set up a pair of igniters near the hinges and the lock bolts—all of them, and several more around the periphery of the door seal. Bring the whole lot out through that small hole in the doorframe you suggested. I'm going down to look at those storage holds!"

"What are you going to do?" Ferenc asked.

"You're knowledgeable when it comes to systems and electronics, Ferenc, but it takes a cook to do chemistry. I'm going to blast that door off!"

Neither Po Lin nor Ferenc understood what Belltone intended to do or how, but they went ahead with the preparations. They stripped power cables out of the conduits and set up circuits for the igniters. The signal rockets were mounted in the air lock, aimed on crude launchers in several different directions so that the assumed other ship would be sure to see them. The work went quickly, and they finished as Belltone returned. He carried heavy sacks, which he set down near the air lock's outer door.

"What have you got in there?" Po Lin asked, examining a sack full of brownish-white powder.

"It's a mixture of iron oxide and aluminum. It's called thermite. It burns very hot, without oxygen, hot enough to burn through the hinges and lock bolts."

"And this?" Ferenc asked as he withdrew a finger now coated with a sticky mess.

"Basic starch," the inventor said, "just slightly modified. Two kinds—one inert and the other explosive. The inert stuff we use as a putty to keep the igniters in place, and the other to blast the door off. The converter is quite versatile if you know how to handle it."

"But that's food!" Ferenc cried. "That's enough food to last for days—that's probably all our food. What if there is no ship out there?"

"So what? This hull is now rotating. Even if we could move the maneuvering engines, they'd be of no use until we first stopped the rotation. If there is a manned ship out there, the food doesn't matter. And if there isn't, the engines won't work anyhow. And even if they do, the *Petrel* will be gone. If either of you wants to starve out to the end, I'll happily convert for you. But I'd rather start packing this stuff in."

They pulled back the rubber seals and made pockets out of the dough surrounding the hinges and lock bolts. They put the thermite into the pockets. The door seal was packed with the explosive starch. Finally, with igniters inserted, the whole mess was covered over with more of the sticky stuff. When all was ready, they left the air lock, closed the inner door, and retreated with the igniter wires a safe distance from the air lock. Belltone, unmindful of the danger, stayed by the air lock so that he could observe the fireworks through the small port.

The first set of igniters was a dud, and the standby had to be used. The second started a bubbling and bulging of the goo, which then hardened and broke away in charred masses to reveal a totally destroyed hinge. Additional sets were fired, each one doing precisely what it had been designed to do. Soon only the seals were holding the air lock's outer door in place. Belltone gave Ferenc the signal. The entire hull reverberated to the explosion, throwing Belltone back against the opposite wall and Ferenc and Po Lin off their feet. But the door slammed out into space, followed by the air in the air lock, with a gratifying *whoosh*. A few of the launchers were knocked down, and some of the wires were now crossing.

Belltone, having regained his breath, called back, "I underestimated that stuff. Don't fire number three or seven—they're off their launchers." Ferenc set off the signal rockets one at a time. They went off in various directions, out of the air lock, each leaving a phosphorescent smoky trail, and the few that could be seen through the small window ended in a satisfyingly brilliant explosion. The last rocket fired, number 9, inadvertently set off the remaining two that had been lying in the bottom of the air lock. Number 3 fizzled out after a few seconds, but number 8 caromed around, finally penetrating the side wall. It exploded in an adjoining chamber, causing considerable damage, as evinced by a sudden perceptible air-pressure drop. Belltone hurried back to where Ferenc and Po Lin were waiting.

"They got off, except the last two. One's exploded inside the hull!"

"We're losing pressure!" Po Lin exclaimed.

"We've got to get to the main air lock and close the hatches as we go," Ferenc said.

They raced toward the remains of the double air lock—the main air lock through which they had entered the ship. Each airtight hatch was closed in turn, but it did not seem to affect the rate at which the pressure was dropping. They had still several levels to go, and now at least the rate at which the pressure was dropping decreased with each additional hatch they closed, but the drop did not stop. There was no place to go now except the inner chamber of the main air lock. Belltone, who in the excitement had grabbed one of the sacks of starch, dropped it just as they closed the door. He was now watching the lump of dough expand and bubble in the ever-lowered air pressure outside their small chamber. "The air out there will be gone in a few minutes," he observed, "and in here in a few hours."

"Anoxia is not so bad," Ferenc commented. "At least you go out quietly or laughing."

"I think," the old woman said, "that it is best to sing—I'll start off with 'Majah Maroo.'" She sang the first verse in a reedy but unexpectedly lusty voice and turned the nonsense song over to Belltone; it then went back to Po Lin, and with some prompting, Ferencs joined in also, first with stock verses, then with new ones composed for the occasion. He accused Belltone of a plot to capture them and hold them as unwilling guinea pigs for dishes so outlandish that even Po Lin expressed surprise. She in turn castigated Ferenc and Belltone for their inability to repair the minor malfunctions of the slightly damaged ship; Belltone returned with a bawdy set of verses that suggested an improbable and biologically impossible *ménage à trois*. The song continued with lessened energy and with increasingly longer pauses between stanzas. The last one was a repeat of one of the standard verses, which somehow seemed very funny to Belltone. He laughed and the others joined him.

———————————

Ferenc awoke in a strange bunk of an obviously healthy ship, groggy from the effects of oxygen starvation but otherwise all right. Belltone was either up or had been bedded down elsewhere. Po Lin was in the bunk below his, still asleep. His head was clear when he reached the bridge; Belltone was declaiming a proposal to reprogram the food dispensers. This ship, judging from Belltone's enraptured promises, was another gastronomic wasteland, luckily soon to be revitalized. Belltone stopped the lecture to allow formalities to be observed.

"I am Ferenc Petrelborn, of the *Petrel*, lately of the *Phoenix* and headed toward the conclave."

"And I am Ilan Xanaduborn. This ship is the *Gyrfaulcon*, out of launch at the conclave. We have a special job to do now—after that's over, we'll take you back to the *Petrel* and guide you toward the conclave."

"What is this job?" Ferenc asked.

"It's difficult to explain. Ah, I see that we're about to be joined by the last of your crew. Welcome to the *Gyrfaulcon*, Mother."

"Welcome is it?" the old woman snapped. "What welcome to be starved out and choked in the serviceable hull of an honorable ship that babies like you are too inept to keep in repairs?"

"There was no intention to repair the *Phoenix*. She is to be consumed in a good cause."

"You mean recycled," Ferenc said.

"No. Consumed! Destroyed!"

"But why?" Po Lin wailed. "She can be repaired. At worst scrapped. There are useful components in her. The life supports kept us alive—and that abomination in the suspension vaults—what about that?"

"That's what I started to tell Ferenc about," Ilan said. "This is a research ship. The idea of the conclave didn't catch on all at once, and it did not come from only one source. Some of us were out there fifty years ago. First one ship, then two, and then twenty, and even more, long before the appointed date. There are things that man can do that cannot be done by the crew of a single ship, events and developments that will not occur if left to the random conjunction of ship and ship. The planets are dangerous and vulnerable and too concerned with survival for such things. Out there, between the galaxies, there is safety and the freedom to try new things. That thing in the *Phoenix* is probably the first new development by man in centuries. It's likely to be our salvation."

"Our damnation, you mean," Po Lin interjected.

"Perhaps that, Mother—perhaps that too. We prefer to think of it as a defense."

159

"It's a weapon then?" Ferenc asked in astonishment.

Ilan nodded. "It's a weapon, a simulator, a decoy, and a booby trap. The telepathic races find us by detecting our electromagnetic activity—the decoy part provides plenty of that. It's a booby trap because if they leave it alone, they won't be harmed."

"And if they attack it?" Belltone asked.

"The telepathic races," Ilan said, "create energy. Once they have found our colonies, they create an energy field by means unknown to us, a field that moves at many times the speed of light and terminates in the awesome beams that roast the planet. We have discovered, based on some very old, pre-exilic physical theory, how to detect that field, and how to use it as a conduit to send the energy back to the source."

"And then?" Ferenc asked.

"We're not sure. The reflection of the energy might be of no more concern to them than our own reflection in a mirror is to us. Or it might be as harmful to them as it is to us. We don't know, and that's what we're here to find out."

"I suppose then that it's a reasonable use for the *Phoenix*," Belltone said. "But what brought you back here?"

"We didn't think that it was even remotely possible that a manship would ever come so close to the hub. So when we picked up tracks—your tracks—we investigated. We found the *Petrel*, and they told us that you had shuttled to the planet. We found the wreck on the surface, but no signs of life. We had to come back here anyway for some final adjustments. Then we found the main air lock jammed with the shuttle's tether cable and figured out what had happened. While we were latching the ships up, the crew went to work to clear the wreckage—then we saw the signal rockets and knew you were alive—we managed to get you out just in time."

Ferenc, who had been considering the experiment, turned to Ilan. "How effective will this shield be? Will it turn back all the energy?"

"That's unlikely. From what we've seen of their attacks, even if a small part of it got through, it would annihilate all life on the planet."

"Then what use is it?" Po Lin asked. "It doesn't protect us or the colonies. It's just vindictive retaliation."

"*Just* retaliation is what I see it to be," Belltone said. "Retaliation with justice!"

Ferenc shook his head. "But the decoy. The decoy will provoke them. It's your intention to provoke them into an attack—to provoke an innocent race into self-destruction."

"Not innocent, Ferenc," Ilan said. "That simulator shows man going about his own business. That doesn't constitute provocation in my mind, unless you accept their point of view that our existence is provocation enough. If they leave the *Phoenix* colony alone, no harm will come to them. If they attack, and if the device works, they'll pay the consequences."

"But you're counting on their reaction. They'll be given no warning. You know they'll attack. You're manipulating them."

"The outcome," Po Lin said, "is as sure as if you launched a black hole against one of their suns. We could have done that ever since we learned who they are and how to avoid them. I've survived the whole thing, from the very beginning. I personally know what we're guilty of. I've seen almost four thousand years of atonement—atonement beyond reason. We've paid a hundredfold, and atonement should stop. But this weapon will bring a new sin, and we'll have to pay for it a thousandfold."

Ferenc and Po Lin turned to Belltone for support but he denied it. "Don't look to me. I was born in space, I have lived in space, and I shall be recycled in space. I've no desire to live on a planet—planets are merely supplies placed by the Almighty for our convenience. Planetfalls are dangerous—the fewer the better. It concerns me little if we ever find a permanent berth on a planet, but I do not like aliens mucking about with my supplies, and I welcome the idea that anyone who tried

161

to roast a gathering of ships would be burned in the process."

"I can't condone it," Ferenc declared.

"Nor I," Po Lin said.

"We are determined to do it," Ilan announced. "We've debated it. There is no other way to test this defense. There is no alternative."

"We seem destined to make choices without alternatives," Po Lin said.

Ilan continued. "Nevertheless, if we're successful, it will be a weapon available to all ships and all colonies. And every death from then on will yield instant retribution. Perhaps, in time, after *they* learn the consequences, they'll stop hunting us."

Nakomi, a second-class Corrector, was tired of being on patrol for such a long time, so he wrapped himself in the outer fringes of his being and extended himself throughout the universe for the journey home. There had been no pleasure in this trip, made more for ritual than reality. And there was the constant threat to his physical body, vulnerable, but presumably well hidden in the deep cave. It was a dull job. He disliked discomfort, disorientation, and the loneliness of patrols. For himself, since it had been so many years since anyone had had action, he believed that the "menace," if ever there had been one, was gone, if not at least contained among the decrepit stars of the galactic fringes.

It was nonsense, a nightmare of old fuddy-duddies, who, ever jealous of their own positions, maneuvered threatening youths such as himself out to the stars and out of the way on patrols. And more than one Corrector had been snuffed out when his physical body had been found by the energy priest safe at home. The patrol had not been without value, though. He now knew that he would have to be surer of his strength before he could attempt to usurp a priest. More powerful and more cau-

tious. He would try again and succeed. The permanent banishment of a second failure was not for him.

He recollected himself in the neighborhood of his home world as well as he could, and, inevitably lost, he reached out and asked for directions. The response was quick and the surrounding stars took on a familiar pattern. He could now see his home sun, a brilliant blue-green jewel less than a light year away. Rather than move directly for it, he decided to collect his thoughts, refine his plans, and suppress their manifesting emanations until they were ready for execution. That was where he had slipped the first time. He had underestimated the priest's ability to ferret a guarded thought.

He was busy laying an overburden of placidity on his plans when the entire fabric was torn apart by a primary alarm. Nakomi, who had been trained to expect the unexpected, was not prepared for what he now sensed. It began as an insulting twitter of radiation that blossomed into the grossest affront ever inflicted on a sentient race. Wave after wave of the nauseating hubris swept past him, revolting him with each newly received perception. This was no simple random pulse. These signals were strong and varied and could be decoded and understood by the meanest intelligence. He raced his consciousness along the stream to its source, watching the evil unfold itself, confessing its own putrefaction. He could see their inane repetitions of violence—their glorification of it and obsession with it.

It was not as if the infection were out on the rim or hidden in some dark nebula. This was at the hub, surrounded by hundreds of civilized races. They must have been there for a very long time, and finally, having decided that it was safe to begin their rapacious activities again, they broke the silence. If left alone, it would be only a few centuries before they reached out and destroyed every living thing for light years around. The old ones were right after all. He glorified in the find and in the accolades he would receive for it. There would be no need now to usurp a priest; surely he would be elected despite his youth. The signals were so strong and

163

so directive that there was no ambiguity as to the source. And the menace was so obvious that there was neither need nor time for the usual investigation.

Nakomi gathered himself and built up the energy needed to contact as many races as possible within his calling range. Such effrontery required instantaneous, massive obliteration, not the normal, casual, surgical procedure. Fully gathered, he released a piercing alarm to half a hundred neighboring worlds, who responded instantaneously to enforce the tenuous energy fields that Nakomi had started.

Ilan stared at the view of the charred remains of the world below. The decoy planet had been suddenly enveloped from every direction by piercing beams that had slashed across its surface like sharks in a feeding frenzy. The land had burst into flames, the oceans had boiled off in minutes, and the entire world had been enveloped in clouds thousands of miles thick—and then that, too, had been vaporized. What remained was a featureless, glassy, lifeless rock that not even the kindness of thousands of aeons would revive. Ilan kept thinking back to the decoy planet to give him comfort and justification for what he now saw on the screen.

"How is this one?" Ferenc asked, equally morose.

"Like the others—just like the others. At least it's the last one. If there are more, the field was too weak to trace back to them. How deep is their hatred? How violent their anger?"

"It was just," Belltone said. "The weapon didn't even work well. Only one percent of the energy was reflected back to the sources. They got only one percent of what was coming to them."

"But," Ferenc said, "that one percent was more than sufficient to destroy them. Would it have mattered if they had gotten back twice as much or ten times? They only destroyed a machine—a lifeless machine—not one human life lost—yet fifty-two races burned out. Fifty-two races, one hundred billion lives for one machine."

"It was their own hatred that consumed them," Ilan said. "Remember that. If they had attacked with the usual strength, they might have survived. It's not the fact of their destruction that dismays me, Ferenc, but the intensity of their hatred. It would have been no different if there had been no decoy, but a real colony."

Ferenc continued. "I'm afraid of the retribution this will bring. I'm afraid of this weapon that will be adopted by too many of us. I cry for the slaughter it will engender. It's true they wouldn't be harmed if they left us alone, but perhaps they can't. Perhaps that's their disease. The weapon *is* just—it trades life for life. But that's not enough. We must find a way to protect them from themselves as well as we can now protect ourselves." He continued staring at the wreck of the once beautiful world until it disappeared from view with the jump back to the *Petrel*.

11

Conflict

Using the precise navigation data given them by the *Gyrfaulcon*, they reached the region of the conclave in a single jump, a region so dense with tracks that the problem was to select which one to follow rather than to search laboriously for additional tracks. It was more navigational pride than necessity that made them spend hours pinpointing the conclave's precise location. They set a jump a few hundred miles away—it would not do to hit the center and convert overzealous navigation into a catastrophe.

The conclave lay beneath them—a rotating, undulating, multicolored pearl bracelet of ships thirty-five miles in diameter. The dumbbell ships had been split in two, with the drive splines that bisected the connecting tunnels of the two halves joined to each other and to the neighboring ships, forming a huge ring of two thousand ship halves. That ring was now rotating once each minute to provide normal gravity. The ring was a main corridor by which all the ships were joined. At various points tunnels were extended toward the center, which joined other tunnels at half a hundred nodes to provide more direct access than would be possible via the 110-mile circumference. Splayed out from the globular ship halves along tethers of random lengths lay the kits, re-entry vehicles, and shuttles, providing an outer ring of diamonds to the setting. The soft light of the galactic hub that was reflected and re-reflected on the ship halves and kits was supplemented by numerous beacons and work lights, so that the whole shape was readily discernible. The response to the *Petrel*'s questing beacon was an instantaneous babble of simultaneous voices on every channel, projecting to the crew the greater sparkle of the humanity that lay within the gigantic brooch. Thus the *Petrel* stood off in awe of man, and man welcomed the *Petrel* to its conclave.

Throughout the complicated procedure required to integrate the *Petrel* into the great ring, her library was being integrated with man's while her crew was being biologically accommodated through the absorption of yet another immunological cocktail. Similarly, the *Petrel*'s information and bacteria were dispensed to the five million they were about to join. At last the connecting air locks were opened and they who had been merely suited figures or images on a screen poured into the *Petrel* from both directions, colliding with the *Petrel*'s crew, equally enthusiastic to explore the new world formed by the vast agglomeration of manships. With the integration complete, the *Petrel* temporarily relinquished her identity as a separate ship. Her crew, revived in toto, abandoned her, leaving her to others who were making the long trip around the ring, or who just wanted to bunk down among new murals.

They had expected a great central meeting hall where the wisest and the loudest would gather and ponder knowingly, deeply, the titanic issues that had brought them together. But there was no central hall, and the closest they could find to an organized meeting was an occasional orator who exhorted all who had the patience to listen to his or her particular point of view. Mostly, the conclave was a free-wheeling amorphism that seemed to be more concerned with enjoying massed humanity than guiding humanity's masses. It was, as Po Lin cynically observed, "More party than parley." If there was a specific issue, it was the debate over the weapon, a debate that had started fifty years before when its possibility was first discovered; a debate that had intensified as the weapon had approached completion; and which now, following its successful demonstration, had spawned groups of militant opponents and proponents.

While the conclave talked and argued about the weapon, it was, except for the minority dedicated to the issue, a desultory debate, without conviction. It was a topic of the times, as often as not, subordinated to speculations of who would win the next circumferential foot race, or the novel bulkhead paintings on this or that ship, or even more seriously, just exactly what was *the* proper way to conduct this or that ritual. But at the opposite ends of this indifference, the Atoners and Rejectors glared at each other with increasing hostility. The Rejectors, as they called themselves, were a boisterous, strident group. They reveled in the weapon's effectiveness and saw in it a deliverance from the morbid atonement that had dominated man's history. It was guilt over the accident accompanying the perfection of the drive that they rejected; the weapon they welcomed with enthusiasm. The Atoners, conversely, believed that the guilt had been immeasurably expanded—not only was the weapon's use to be proscribed, but there were even some who suggested that its secret be divulged to the aliens. It was man's lot, they believed, to be persecuted, for only through such persecution could eventual salvation be achieved.

The *Gyrfaulcon*, her crew enlarged by the addition of a company of specialists, had again left the conclave to continue perfecting the weapon even farther out in the intergalactic void, hoping thereby to find the means by which it could be controlled. This left the *Petrel*'s crew, particularly Ferenc, Belltone, and Po Lin, as the only eyewitnesses of the experience. They were much in demand in this regard, and despite the ubiquitous museums, they had to retell their impressions over and over again. Though most of the conclave ignored them, it was not surprising that the trio attracted Rejectors and Atoners. The Rejectors, who had taken to wearing a distinguishing gold emblem and, in some cases, gold body paint, adopted the flamboyant Belltone as a symbol, which adulation he was quick to accept, while the Atoners, garbed in muddy blues, gathered around Earthmother Po Lin and cried with her, sharing her sorrow. And Ferenc, despite the widening ideological gulf that separated his friends, tried to find a middle ground, but it was an increasingly futile position. There was justice on both sides, but they seemed irreconcilable.

Ferenc managed to keep them together for several days. Days during which polarization of the opposing parties increased, days in which Belltone, his ego stroked to capacity, became increasingly insufferable and impolite to Po Lin, who in retaliation made cryptic remarks about his youthful misadventures, which prompted even more defensive hostility on his part. Days during which Rejectors and Atoners confronted each other in anger, in brawls, and eventually, although by accident, in death. Belltone left first, surrounded by a raucous group of Rejectors. He turned back toward his two friends, made his magnificent bow, and said, "Good-bye, Ferenc Sourface. Good-bye, Po Lin Earthfarter."

"Good-bye, Shipsmasher," she shouted after him, and then speaking to Ferenc, "He's a good boy at heart, despite his faults." She closed her eyes in resignation and set her mouth. "He'll turn out all right. I'm sure of that."

She continued with Ferenc for several more days and then left also. "Those Atoner friends of mine are too rigid even for me. I don't see helping the aliens abuse us. They do well enough without our help. I'm going to talk some sense into them."

Ferenc thereafter wandered alone. Increasingly he heard Belltone's words from gilded faces, while Po Lin's wail countered them from blued lips. Only his words seemed to have been lost.

———————————————————

He continued wandering from hull to hull, making new friends or finding a lover for a few days, but he avoided the discussion of the weapon; not difficult to do because the debate had abated. The Rejectors were no longer conspicuous, and the Atoners, while still haranguing at the corridor junctions, had lost their previous verve. Ferenc was helping to repair a badly damaged, newly arrived ship, which for convenience had been placed near the low-gravity center of the conclave. Work had progressed satisfactorily, up to the point where the heavy structural repairs had begun. There were simply not enough welding lasers to go around. He was suited up, on the outside of the hull, installing a new plate, pointing the laser's white-hot beam at a seam a few feet away, when the unit quit, this time worn out beyond repair. No further trickery could cajole it into functioning. There were no spare parts on the ship, and if he was to continue with the task, it would have to be either at some other worker's expense or with a new laser. It was sensible, therefore, that he go to the outer ring to find some spares.

The first several ships on the outer ring had no spare welders. They had been borrowed, he was told, by another ship, "in that direction." The shortage, he learned, was endemic and the crews always pointed the same way—a direction which eventually led him back toward the low-gravity center. His quest for the wandering welders ended in a dead-end corridor, at an air lock. Further progress was barred by a trio, all of whom had lasers clipped to their work belts. "I'm Ferenc Petrelborn," he announced. "We're fixing a ship on the other side and have run out of welding lasers and spare parts. They seem to have drifted to here. Could you let us have a few?"

"That's not possible," the first one answered.

"Why not?" Ferenc was astounded at the bad manners. "This ship appears to be sound. Are there such extensive repairs on this hull that all the spare welders of the conclave are needed in her?"

"You might say so," the second agreed.

"Then why are you here when you're needed inside?"

"Are you a Rejector or an Atoner?" the first asked, ignoring Ferenc's question.

"Neither. I'm just a crewmate looking for a spare welder. What has that to do with it?"

"Everything. If you're an Atoner, go out to the first circumferential ring and clockwise to the first spoke and back down. If you're a Rejector, go counterclockwise to the first spoke and then down. If you want to go in, you have to do it by one of those air locks. Otherwise, you can't go in!"

"Why not?" Ferenc asked.

"Because," the second one said, "they're fighting in there."

"Who? Who's fighting?"

"The Rejectors and the Atoners."

"Over the weapon?"

"No—that doesn't seem to be the issue any more. I don't really know what they're fighting about."

"Is that where the welders are? They're using them to fight with?"

"No," the first said. "They're not allowed to have weapons like that—maybe only a few. Only referees like us have lasers."

"What for?"

"To keep them inside—to keep the fighting from spreading."

"Is no one allowed to leave, then?"

"Sure. The referees, or anybody else inside who thinks they've had enough. If they quit, they come out through here. That's the referees' main job—to help those who want to leave—also to keep the fight inside."

"Say!" The third one looked at Ferenc closely. "Aren't you Ferenc Petrelborn?"

"So I said."

"Weren't you teamed up with an Atoner and a Rejector a while back?"

"I suppose that's right."

"Well, your buddies are inside. Or so I've heard."

"On opposite sides?"

"Is Blue opposite Gold?"

"I can't imagine them fighting—especially each other. I want to go in and talk them out of it."

"There's no way to do that—unless of course—"

"Yes?"

"Unless you volunteered to be a referee. Then you could get your friends out and a welder to boot. I'll give you mine if you want. I was getting tired of this anyway. You just have to promise that you'll stay at it for at least two weeks."

"And what do I do?"

"Just enforce the rules. Protect and help anyone who wants to leave. Keep the fighting inside. Don't let them damage the ship. And keep the life supports at safe levels."

"Is that it?"

"That's it. I don't think it'll last more than another week or so. It was getting pretty rough in there from what I heard, and there seem to be fewer recruits going in. No doubt you'll have no trouble convincing your friends to leave with you. Are you game?"

"All right."

"Good!" the former referee agreed. He gave Ferenc the welder and the necklace that was his badge of office and allowed the new peacemaker to enter the air lock.

Ferenc shivered despite the uncomfortable and unfamiliar clothing he wore. It was a spacesuit, hastily adapted by judicious slashes and ties to more or less fit. He huddled in a deep alcove overlooking a large chamber, where other noncombatants were cleaning up the debris of the latest battle. They were, like himself, neither gold nor blue, but arrayed in whatever makeshift clothing they could find. Some of them appeared to enjoy the grisly work of carting torn and bloody corpses to the converters.

It was cold because the Rejectors had captured the life controls. And the referees were not strong enough to recapture it and enforce the rules. The stricture against damage to the ship did not prevent damage to its inhabitants. The gold area was being maintained at normal temperature; it was this battle zone and the blue area that were being frozen out. The Atoners, Ferenc thought wryly, would have little need for their distinguishing body paints before long.

The enforced lull caused by the cleanup crew gave Ferenc time to ruminate on the events of the past weeks. He had spent several days training and meeting with the other referees, most of whom were now dead. He had been lucky. His co-referee, Jarel, had learned how to handle the laser as a weapon better than he, but it had not saved him yesterday, when both teams had turned on them in protest over an enforcement of the rules. The first week had been reasonable, almost civilized. Combatants had attempted to capture their opponents without harming them. Once they were captured, all they had to do to be released was to swear not to return. The Atoners kept their word, but the Rejectors merely left by one air lock and returned by another.

Yet, except for this bit of chicanery, it had been more like a rough game of tag than a war. Then, as one side or the other had found itself momentarily at a disadvantage, there had been an increasing reliance on the weapons and an increased reluctance to abide by the rules. There were not enough welders to go around, so consumable supplies had ingeniously yielded swords, crossbows, and slings. One sorry attempt at poison gas had almost wiped them all out as the noxious stuff had saturated the air purifiers, teaching all over again the fickleness of certain weapons.

The present state of all-out combat, trying anything that referees could not prevent, could not continue much longer. Ferenc had been keeping track of new recruits and casualties. The casualty rate was not much higher than the recruiting rate, and it appeared from the ineptness of the new recruits that both parties had dispensed with training. Neither had reserves left. It would soon have to end.

The temperature was rising again. That meant that the Rejectors would be moving in to consolidate their gains. Ferenc stayed in the alcove and waited. The Rejectors, thirty of them, walked confidently into the chamber. Ferenc recognized the woman who was their leader, Magda. She posted guards facing the entrances to the chamber and sat down to examine some ship plans that a subordinate had hastily unrolled. The plans showed in outline the areas held by both parties, the contested areas, and the areas reserved by noncombatants such as Ferenc. She discussed tactics with her lieutenants, listening occasionally, but mostly talking. She was confident and spirited and frenetic. "They must capitulate in hours. This ship is ours. We shall hold it and recruit a full crew from the rest of the conclave. Then we can—"

She was interrupted by a guard who had spotted Ferenc. She turned to him and waved him down. "It doesn't matter if he hears. Come down," she called. "It's Ferenc Petrelborn, isn't it?" Ferenc accepted her invitation. "You've been a fair referee," she said as he approached, "and from your continued presence in this conflict, quicker than most. You have proved yourself as well as any of us. I want you for the next phase of our operation."

Ferenc, considering the past days, could not imagine how the conflict could be further escalated. Yet he was curious and, not wishing to stifle Magda's expansive mood, he encouraged her disclosure. "What might that be?" he asked.

"You are a reflective individual, not easily swayed, guided more by reason than emotions. You want answers. I shall give you those answers and offer you an opportunity to participate in the next phase of my plan.

Indeed, the next step in man's evolution. This conflict has shown that there are two types of humans—pacific and predatory. Those who chose not to participate in this conflict or those cowards who left are clearly pacific, while those who survive, such as you and me, are the best of the predators. Yes, Ferenc, you too are a predator. How many times have you killed since you've been here? Six? Twenty? No matter. It's at least five that I know of, and that's two more than most of my guards here. This is not a conflict for the possession of a ship that none of us really needs. Nor is it over the so-called morality of the weapon, because that's been settled, no matter what those naive Atoners want to believe. It's a lesson in survival. That's how I always saw it. A weeding out of the unfit. A step in the evolution of man. Man has always fought with himself, ever since he became master of his environment and had no worthy natural enemies except himself. Who can deny that man's greatest achievements were in some way tied up with warfare?"

"But we left that all behind us, thousands of years ago, when we were still Earthbound."

"What are a few thousand years compared to millions of years of human evolution? A mere hiatus in a steady progression of increasingly more intelligent and more aggressive mankind. True, faced with disaster, racial survival overrode the need for conflict. It was, however, only a momentary truce. Here—what you see all around you—that's man's real nature." Ferenc was about to interrupt her again but was impatiently waved into silence by Magda. "Man is subject to the same evolutionary pressures that are on other animals. Only two kinds of beings survive—those that are low on the ecological chain and those that are high. The high types are aggressive. The lower, whether plants or animals, are passive. Man himself is destined to evolve into two types—the majority into the lower forms of passive man, and the select minority into the more highly developed, racially superior predatory man. Less than one in a hundred has the inclination

175

to aspire to this higher form of life, less than one in a thousand has the opportunity, and less than one in a million has the ability. This conflict is that opportunity. With our victory here assured, we can begin the next phase of evolution."

"And what might that be?"

"First we will recruit here at the conclave and weed out those who are unfit by continuing the conflict in a controlled form. A sort of test—a survival test. The survivors will become members of a new ship, the *Destiny*, a ship that will roam the galaxy and build our strength until eventually we dominate mankind."

"I don't understand what you mean by dominate; there's enough for a ship and its crew to do merely to survive. What can a few dozen crewmen do to dominate mankind?"

"Fool! A ship contains life supports for thousands. Do you think I mean an existence in the cryovaults? I mean continuous life for all the crew, not the pseudo-life of frozen sleep that the rest of mankind is destined to."

"That's silly," Ferenc said sharply. "A ship would consume all its resources in a few years if the crew were all awake. It could never keep itself in supplies."

"You've missed the whole point. The *Destiny* will furbish itself from other ships."

"But what ship would give its substance willingly to such a waste?"

"You are brave but dense, Ferenc. I said man the predator. The predator who preys on lower forms of man. The ones lower on the ecological chain. Ninety-nine and nine-tenths percent of mankind will go through the business of refurbishing, or making planetfalls. The *Destiny* will never planetfall. We will take what we need from other ships. Those who successfully resist us are of us, and their survivors will join us. Those who fail are a lower form of man and not part of the grand evolution except as our cattle!"

"Eventually you'll run out of ships to plunder," Ferenc said.

"Not so. Man has been on the increase despite the holocaust. Besides, we do not intend to let the lower forms of man die out. That would be foolish. We shall genetically select them, increase them, improve their passivity, guide them to suitable planets. We...will protect them from the aliens. I calculate that mankind, both higher and lower, will have to increase a thousandfold before we can take over the galaxy and depend only on the aliens for our supplies. Man will have to be increased a thousandfold. A hundred thousand ships like the *Destiny*."

"And then what?"

"And then"—Magda seemed to be carried away by her inspired vision—"mankind, the spaceborne dominant race of the galaxy, will be ready to achieve the even higher destiny of conquering the other galaxies and eventually the universe. I will not see it. I will not see it. I will not see it. It is sufficient to know that in my genetic stock was laid the foundations of the highest form of sentient being. There are no genetic defects in me. I will be the leader, the mother, of a new race of man. The mother of a new race. The free-living race of space. The mother..."

Magda continued, ever more taken up with herself and ever more out of touch with her surroundings. She was lost in dreams of the future, and Ferenc's occasional barbs went unnoticed.

He decided to return to the alcove. The guards ignored him; they were listening, enraptured by the gibberish being spouted by the golden woman. An hour later, through which he had dozed, the guards were still being hypnotized by her ceaseless monologue. Ferenc took out the laser to check and service it. He observed Magda by sighting her through the green rod. How easy, he thought, how tempting to end this insanity now. He put away the weapon. It was time to leave the mad ship.

Magda had finally stopped. She sat exhausted in a ring of admirers. One by one the guards regained their senses and drifted back to their posts.

A gold-clad warrior rushed in and reported to Magda, "We caught the traitor and a spy who was trying to infiltrate our position—the traitor was helping her!" Magda stirred and acknowledged the message. She rose, absently smoothed her hair, and with the gesture the vacant look was replaced by her more usual one of hard determination. The guards arrived, pushing a reluctant and loudly cursing pair of prisoners at the points of makeshift swords.

"If it isn't the gilded bitch of destiny herself!" Po Lin hooted to her companion, a faded, bedraggled version of Belltone. It was the first time Ferenc had seen his friends since he had joined the conflict. He wanted to go down and speak to them, but his position as an impartial referee would not allow it. The best he could do now was to observe and intercede only if the prisoner's rights were violated.

"How many Atoners are left?" Magda asked Po Lin, ignoring her previous insult.

Po Lin refused to answer.

"You're senile." Magda turned to Belltone. "And you, Belltone, I'm disappointed in you—consorting with the enemy, deserting—you'll have to be disciplined for that." She turned to the guards. "Take him to the rear for punishment, and"—she pointed to Po Lin—"kill that one. She's long overdue for recycling."

"Stop!" Ferenc shouted. "They have the right to leave unharmed if they want to."

Magda looked at Ferenc, challenging him. "Kill her," she insisted quietly.

The guard hesitated; it was clear to him that Ferenc had him in his sights. Magda glared at Ferenc again and then at the guard. "Kill the old baggage!"

The guard raised his sword, but Ferenc shot him through the temple. Po Lin and Belltone ran for the ladder to Ferenc's alcove while he provided covering fire. Magda and those of her lieutenants who had lasers began a fusillade toward Ferenc, while others, equipped only with crossbows, loosed bolt upon bolt after the running pair. The poor construction of the crossbows

178

and the minimal training of the archers assured Po Lin and Belltone of their safety. The lethal weapons were being concentrated on Ferenc, who, crouched in the alcove, was able to pin down most of the opposing forces. The Rejectors took cover behind doors and machinery. Ferenc had all of them located and kept a continual fire with his superior weapon from position to position at random, diverting only to aim at the occasional glint that showed that someone was about to attempt a shot either at him or at his friends. Po Lin and Belltone gained the safety of the alcove after a frenzied climb up the ladder.

"Return my prisoners!" Magda ordered.

"They're not your prisoners if they want to leave. Those are the rules."

"Those are not *my* rules. The only rule that matters is the new man. They are not fit. They will be recycled, and so will you. They can leave only if they can fight their way out. Those are *my* rules." And so saying, she loosed another shot at the alcove.

There was a ventilator grille on the ceiling, but it was too small for them to escape through it. By crouching at the rear of the alcove, they were comparatively safe. An enemy had to stand in full view in order to hit them. A few tried lobbing shots with the crossbows, but the shafts merely tumbled in from the peak of their trajectory, causing no worse than minor bruises. It was a standoff. The trio had positional advantage. Their opponents had time and numbers, both of which would eventually work against their quarry.

For the moment there was nothing the trio could do. Ferenc reasoned that if they waited in the safety of the alcove, there would eventually be a distraction below, such as an Atoner attack, that would provide an opportunity for escape. So they sat at the rear of the alcove and told one another what they had been doing since they had last met, but their presence in the conflict was a subject avoided by all of them. At last, having exhausted the small talk, the subject of the conflict and their parts in it sat palpably between them, squatting in the center of their little circle, no longer to be ignored.

"For my part," Belltone said, "I'm here because of circumstance, ego, and idiocy—and Mad Magda."

"Magda?" Po Lin asked, incredulous.

"Before this fighting," Belltone explained, "we were lovers. She's quite something, I tell you—"

"If your taste runs to overblown fat cows," Po Lin interjected.

"That's muscle," Belltone said defensively. "Anyway, I was in with a Rejector crowd, sort of the company minstrel. Magda looked at me and said that we were to be lovers. She's hypnotic—and that was that."

"That explains her anger with you," Po Lin said. "Shipwreck, there were always holes in your personality. You ran out on her. You just don't know how to treat women."

"Just wait until we get out of this, old slut, and I'll show you what kept me as her pet all these weeks."

"Weeks, is it? More likely minutes by your usual exaggerations."

"But didn't you see where it was leading?" Ferenc asked.

"I was enjoying the lady's rough caresses. She's quite aggressive, as you can imagine, and that suited me at the time. I composed ballads, proposed excursions, and provided entertainment to a willing, appreciative audience. It was fun—at least until last week when she gave me a weapon and told me to take my place with the rest of the troops. She had no more time for sex. Then I discovered what was really going on."

Ferenc listened without saying a word, evaluating his friend's confession. He broke the awkward silence that followed by announcing his judgment.

"You knew all along. It was there for you to see, but it was more comforting to ignore it. Look at her now, Belltone. Was she really so different a few weeks ago? Wasn't she really saying the same kinds of things, if only you had listened?"

Belltone did not answer, but Po Lin came to his

rescue. "It was a game at first. A rough game, I admit, but merely a game."

"With deadly weapons?" Ferenc asked.

"Not at first, but it escalated. That was Magda's fault. She forced this conflict on the Atoners."

"How could she force that bunch of mewling, self-pitying—" Belltone demanded.

"You can push people so far, Belltone, and then they have to react," Po Lin said. "The Rejectors were roughing us up. Stopping our speakers. Things like that. We started to defend ourselves, and eventually the militant members took over the Atoner leadership. When Magda proposed the conflict as a way of resolving our differences, the leadership accepted—enthusiastically, I may say."

"And you, Po Lin—you followed them?"

"No, Ferenc Petrelborn—this old woman doesn't follow. I went with them into the conflict because they were young and needed guidance. I left yesterday, when it was clear to me that they wanted the fighting for the sake of the fighting and not for any principles. But, Ferenc Petrelborn, you sit here with us and judge us, your friends. Yet you're the one most in need of judgment. I've killed no one and I will not kill. I doubt that Belltone has either." Belltone nodded. "But you, Ferenc Petrelborn, you're the arch killer of this conflict, and yet you take upon yourself the right to judge. Can you justify yourself?" she asked bitterly.

"I would like to say that I came to this conflict to find a welder," Ferenc said after a long silence. "I would like to say that I came looking for you two with the intention of getting you out, that it just happened and that I didn't really know where it was leading. But none of that would be true. I knew what the welders were being used for and what a referee's job was to be—if not at first, then after the first few days. And if I had tried, surely I could have found you long before and we could have left before now. But I didn't really try. When I killed for the first time, it was with great reluctance. An Atoner group was trying to disable the

181

life-support controls for a Rejector area. I caught them at it and told them to stop. They refused. The confrontation escalated, and there was nothing to do but to shoot at the leader—not to kill but to disable. Then he attacked me—and it was self-defense. It stopped them cold. We took time to go through the funerary ritual as we put her body into the converter. But the words were hollow."

"You stayed then," Po Lin said with new insight. "You stayed after that, because you enjoyed the killing!"

"There was a thrill to it at first, and also revulsion. And then I understood. I understood from looking at myself and all the others that this conflict was inevitable. If not over this issue, then some other issue—whether cataclysmic or trifling doesn't matter. The conflict was an inevitable consequence of the conclave. Think of what has happened. This conclave is not to discover how we are to survive. The fact that it was at all possible, that we have the resources to keep so many persons awake for so long is a clear proof of our survival. There are more humans awake here, consuming more resources, than the rest of the fleet. And look what happens. We're released from the oppression of a common enemy so we make our own enemies instead."

"We've had four thousand years without wars," Belltone said.

"No, friend, merely four thousand years without the opportunity."

"But the colonies. Who ever heard of a colony with war?"

"That's right. Who ever heard of a colony with war? Are you sure, Belltone, that all the colonies were destroyed by the aliens? I'm no longer certain. Not now. Not any more."

"So what do you intend to do?" Po Lin asked.

"First, survive and bring this particular conflict to an end."

"You imply there will be others?" Belltone asked.

"I'm certain of it. And that's the reason I will stay here at the conclave."

"And judge," Po Lin said. "And judge your fellow humans. A right that no person has. You're as bad as Magda!"

Ferenc shook his head. "I hope not, Earthmother. We have had no wars and no judges for four thousand years. The aliens gave us conflict enough and judgment enough. Now, with the weapon to protect us from the aliens, and our freedom, and our material surpluses, we will need judges again. As for being as bad as Magda, if she were sane, she would probably be better at it than I. It's the Magdas who will have to be judged, and the Belltones, Po Lins, and Ferencs. And why not me? Is anybody qualified? Does anybody have the right?"

"It's a rhetorical question, Ferenc," Belltone said. "We won't get out of this alive. And if we do, the conclave will be over. The ring will be broken up and there'll be nothing here for you to judge but some uncollected, useless debris."

Ferenc disagreed. "No, the conclave will remain. Ships will come and go. The ring will continually shrink and then expand again, and there will always be a conclave. There will be other weapons to agonize over, and from time to time there will be factions so strong in their convictions that they'll believe that only force will suit the accomplishment of their ends. Let them come to the conclave and discuss it, or fight it out if that's what they need. And let the rest, the sensible part of humanity, learn from it."

They were awakened by a volley of crossbow shafts, indicating that their adversary had not lost interest in them. The barrage continued from time to time, with waning intensity and gradually shifting direction. Ferenc concluded from this that they were up to something new. He motioned to Po Lin and Belltone to stay at the rear of the alcove while he went forward to reconnoiter. He reached the edge of the ladder and put his ear to the floor to listen. He heard nothing. He cautiously extended a fingertip to the ladder's handrail while with his other hand he held his weapon ready. He felt slight tremors that indicated that someone was slowly climbing the ladder. He shinnied back to the rear and whispered to Belltone, "Move up with me and hold my feet. When I wiggle my toes, push me forward, but be ready to drag me back when I yell."

Half crawling, half pushed by Belltone, he went forward again. Again he felt the handrail. There was no doubt of it now. He adjusted the laser to maximum strength, the tip of his left index finger on the handrail. The movement stopped. He could hear shallow breathing a foot below him. A change in the vibrations made him tense. The muzzle of a laser suddenly appeared over the edge of the floor, and just as suddenly Ferenc snatched the weapon and threw it to the rear of the alcove. He gave Belltone the signal. Belltone shoved him forward, using Ferenc's head as a battering ram. The surprised Rejector, who had jumped up after her weapon, was thrown back to the floor below. Ferenc washed the foot of the ladder with the furious beam of his weapon. In less than two seconds he shouted to Belltone, who promptly dragged him back, on his face, to the safety of the rear of the alcove.

Ferenc's nose was bleeding profusely from the collision with the edge of the alcove's lip. Belltone crawled forward while Ferenc sat in the rear, his head tilted back, trying to stop the bleeding. Belltone, in the meanwhile, used the tip of a crossbow bolt as a screwdriver on the flange that held the ladder to the alcove's floor. He forced the head of the crossbow bolt under one of the flanges. The slight gap thus created between the other flange and the floor now rattled audibly each time a wounded Rejector below thrashed against the ladder.

Ferenc removed his bulky suit and tried to use the Rejector's laser to seal the slashes he had made in it.

184

The plastic melted and charred but would not seal properly. Po Lin, without knowing his purpose, took over the job. She heated the point of a crossbow bolt, which, when drawn along the seam, did an admirable job of sealing the material. It took a few tries before the suit was airtight again. The hood and face plate, which Ferenc had worn pushed back, were now sealed into position, giving the general semblance of a head. He opened a fingertip, and the three took turns blowing the figure up, with occasional pauses to discover a previously undetected leak. There were now four figures in the alcove.

"Ferenc!" Magda called, with a hint of warmth bordering on friendliness, "I've underestimated you. If you agree to join me, I'll guarantee your safety."

"What about the others?"

"They'll be allowed to leave the conflict as you requested."

"How about me if I don't want to join you?"

"I hope to persuade you otherwise. But if you insist, you may also leave."

"What assurances will you give us?"

"We'll withdraw, in open sight without weapons."

"We'll think about it," Ferenc said. He turned to his companions. "How many were there by your count?" They discussed the probable number and concluded that there were between eighteen and twenty-three persons left standing in the room below. With seven wounded lying by the ladder and several guards in the outlying chambers that Po Lin and Belltone knew of, there were at most thirty-five Rejectors left.

"All right," Ferenc shouted. "Move back to the opposite wall, facing away, hands up—call out when you're ready!"

Moments later Magda replied that they had done as he asked. Ferenc, lying on his belly near the front of the alcove, did a few quick push-ups and accounted for twenty Rejectors with their backs to the alcove. He motioned to his friends to stand the dummy up. Together, they pushed it toward the front of the alcove. "We're coming out now. Keep your hands up!"

The dummy was barely half exposed when the first Rejector fired. They pitched it out of the alcove and it took off, gyrating wildly in the light gravity, under the random thrusts of half a dozen punctures. Other snipers broke cover to fire at the threatening apparition. Ferenc and Belltone, now at the front of the alcove, gunned down the preoccupied snipers and then continued firing at the backs of the upright figures at the opposite wall of the chamber, wounding several more.

The trio returned to the safety of the alcove's rear as their enemy kept up a futile barrage of attempted ricochet shots. The firing stopped: the lasers because they needed recharging, and the crossbows because the archers had run out of bolts. By now a large supply of spent bolts had accumulated in the alcove. Ferenc, Po Lin, and Belltone gathered them into bundles of ten, tips pointing in the same direction. Each took a handful, with several spare bundles alongside of them. They waited until Ferenc judged from the sounds that there were several Rejectors retrieving ammunition at the base of the ladder. On signal, the three pitched the bolts out of the entrance from the safety of the rear. What had not been possible from the ground proved damaging when done from above: the balanced arrows curved outward and accelerated slowly downward in the low gravity. The rain of missiles was so intense that the Rejectors below could not duck them all. Minor wounds were inflicted, some from tripping in an attempt to avoid the bolts, others from the demoralization caused by the vicious defense. Another quick reconnaissance showed that the Rejectors had taken cover again and were no longer attempting to replenish their ammunition from the rich cache that lay near the foot of the ladder.

The hours passed slowly. The trio took turns in standing watch and sleeping. There were no more parleys. It would have appeared that they were being ignored by the Rejectors, except that every reconnaissance was met with a well-placed shot—each time from a different direction, and occasionally a crossfire. The Rejectors were cautious now and not likely to be fooled again. Belltone was sitting on the side of the alcove, beneath the ventilator opening. He heard a sound and fired up into the grille, but not before the assassin had loosed a fatal shot. The assassin, his hand burned to a stump, screamed as he backed out of the way of Ferenc's furious retaliation. The laser had cauterized the flesh so that there was no bleeding from the remains of Belltone's head or from the ventilator grille above. Ferenc kept shooting at the grille until it fell off, and then reached in and continued the execution of the sniper, who had not yet managed to reach the safety of a bend.

They took Belltone's body and laid it out at the rear of the alcove. They knelt on either side of their friend and sang the funeral song. At first the Rejectors below hooted with joy when they realized that one of their tenacious opponents had been killed. But as the depth of Ferenc's and Po Lin's grief emerged, sundry Rejectors left their posts to gather fallen comrades and to give them a just departure also. Despite Magda's angry commands to continue the fight, her subordinates created an impromptu truce.

A Rejector called out to them, "Where is Piet?"

"Do you mean the one who came after us in the air duct?" Ferenc asked.

"The same."

"He's dead."

"May we get his body?"

"Yes," Po Lin answered. "Will you take Belltone's also?"

"Yes."

Shuffling was soon heard in the duct; Ferenc investigated. Two unarmed Rejectors were dragging Piet's corpse out. Shortly thereafter a bruised and bloodied Rejector poked his head above the alcove's lip. "I've come for the body," he explained. They pulled it forward, now in open view and not fearful of another am-

187

bush. Magda stood in the center of the hall, glaring and powerless. A lieutenant had temporarily disarmed her. "Let them lie with the stink!" she screamed as the body of her former lover was lowered. The Rejector looked at Ferenc apologetically.

"Will you continue with this now?" Ferenc asked.

The Rejector looked at Ferenc, at the corpse, and at Magda, and then again at Ferenc. "Yes."

"But why? Can't you see where she's taking you?"

"I see, Ferenc Petrelborn. And I know it's madness. But she's the leader . . . and . . ." He stopped because no further explanation was possible.

Rejectors below were hauling corpses to the chamber's entrance, where a neutral cleanup crew had materialized. Through all this, Magda stood in the center, exhorting her subordinates to the attack, without effect. Ferenc was sure that the conflict had now come to an end. They would no longer take Magda's orders. The last corpse had been removed, and the few Rejectors who remained were drifting toward the exits—all but Magda, who continued to stand in the center, bewildered, and the faithful lieutenant.

A wounded Rejector who had just left rushed back into the hall, pursued by a dozen blue warriors. Magda seized her weapon from the surprised lieutenant and shouted, "To me! To me!" The deserters turned and rallied to a determined counterattack. The chamber was a furious melee of blue and gold figures too preoccupied to notice the fugitives in the alcove. Ferenc and Po Lin scampered down the ladder and obtained refuge behind a wrecked control console. They moved furtively from cover to cover toward the nearest exit—a target for both Rejectors and Atoners.

The sounds of the battle stopped as they reached the exit. It was quiet except for the aftersound—the moans of the dying and wounded. Magda alone remained standing, waving a heavy bar about her head. "I have won! The ship is gold! I have won!"

"What have you won, Magda?" Ferenc asked.

"What have you won?" he asked again as he raised the weapon and sighted it on her.

"I have won the ship." She recognized Ferenc, ignored his weapon, and, apparently having forgotten her determination to kill him only a short time before, she said, "Join me, Ferenc. We have won. The ship is ours. It belongs to us, the survivors, the superior parents of the higher race of man."

"What have you won?" He waved his arms about, pointing to the carnage. She looked briefly at the interlocked remains of blue and gold bodies at her feet, and, seeming not to see them, continued her monologue to the receding backs of Ferenc and Po Lin.

"I will recruit more volunteers and test them myself. I will seal the ship and guard it. In a month—in two at the most—we shall have a full crew. There will be others, more than enough. We shall forge powerful new weapons. In six months we shall have a full crew. Others will join *me*, the leader. The mother. We will not be alone—others who can stand my test will join me. There will be a full crew...."

The conclave was around him—a rotating, undulating, multicolored pearl bracelet of ships ten miles in diameter. Along the ring there were gaps where dumbbell ships were being reassembled prior to being splayed out on their escape cables. Along other tethers of random lengths lay the kits, ships that had not yet been cut loose, ships that were joining for the first time, re-entry gliders, and shuttles, still providing an outer ring of diamonds to the setting. The soft light of the galactic hub reflected and re-reflected on the ships and the severed segments of former inner corridors. Ferenc watched as the *Petrel* cast off—a spinning dumbbell at the end of a five-mile tether. The catch was opened and the ship dwindled, soon visible only by the glint of the galaxy's light on the hull—and then she disappeared.

Ferenc, at last, had the last verse of his poem, the missing refrain:

> *The manifest destiny of the human race,*
> *To live in space, to live in space.*

12

Sarpedon

The stream was dry, and he was thirsty. He concentrated. There *was* water below—Sarpedon had seen it the last time he had come through, but Melthacton could not find it. There *was* water below, so he might as well dig for it—it would be easier than trying to get the stream flowing again. Besides, Demophon, the nosy, selfish cripple up the road, was probably drying it up for spite. He would not beg Demophon, so dig he must. Sarpedon had taught him how to avoid the digging by finding the subterranean fissures, expanding them slightly so that the water would come up, but he had not mastered that trick yet—besides, digging took less effort. He sat on a rock and stared at a clear space a few feet away. He concentrated, and soon a little dust devil began to whirl in the center of the spot. With more effort, the dust began to fly faster and faster until a fountain of fine dust, rocks, and debris spouted from the ever-deepening hole. The dust was annoying and coated his face, so he created a breeze to divert it, but the effort cost him the digging. He could do one or the other but not both—dig a hole with dust in his face, or no dust and no dig. After half an hour, choking and spluttering, his face and cloak completely soiled, he gave it up. Certain that there was no one around to see him, he willed a handful of clear, pure, cool water and sipped luxuriously. Several more handfuls and his face and his palms were clean again, and his thirst sated. He looked at the hole, a yard in diameter and ten feet deep, shrugged, and urinated into it; it was a gesture and a justification.

He left the soiled spot, angry with Sarpedon. Sarpedon had the power and could have freed the water, but no, Sarpedon wouldn't do that. Sarpedon had brought the water up from thousands of feet below, but would not bring it up the last few yards on principle—pfaah on Sarpedon and his principles—he wasn't there to stop Melthacton from creating the water, anyway.

It was time to return to the village—without water. The others could thirst or create as they wished. He worked at it hard enough in accordance with Sarpedon's commands, and it was all Sarpedon's fault. He walked in a straight line, ignoring the worn path from the streambed to the village. Why go the long way? he thought. He was angry, and he absentmindedly blasted shrubs and small trees that stood in his way. Once, a furry rodent crossed his path, and he pinned it, lifted it high into the air, tumbling it as it rose while slowly roasting it from the inside. It was screaming now, so he lifted it several thousand feet and annihilated it. It was a forbidden thing, and the priest would have been angry, but the reduced mass did compensate for the created water. Sarpedon the priest could have his Balance. A few more annihilated shrubs compensated fully for the water, by which time Melthacton had reached the village.

"Good evening, Elder," the gateman said as he approached.

"You needn't be obsequious with me," he snapped in response. "There is no water yet. Go complain to the priest if you wish. It's his fault." Disgruntled, he returned to his hut in the center of the village, let down the door, prayed for energy and a pox on the priests, elevated the carbohydrate content of his bloodstream, and went to sleep.

The next day the villagers came to him for judgment. Melthacton took his place on the dais in the center square with the other elders and opened the proceedings.

"We are here to be judged and be forgiven. Together now."

"We are here to be judged and be forgiven," they repeated.

"For the sins of creation and annihilation. Together."

"For the sins of creation and annihilation."

"For the sins of anger and the sins of envy."

"For the sins of anger and the sins of envy."

"For the sins of . . ."

Melthacton droned the ritual mechanistically. Although not a priest, it was second nature to him. It was priest's work, but as usual there was no priest here. Damn Sarpedon, he had promised an acolyte last winter. It was all an elder could do to keep the climate bearable. The monthly visitation by the priest wasn't enough. Look at them, he thought, they indeed have all those sins to be forgiven. Not a dirty face in the lot, and the village without water all these days. They all created food and water and didn't bother annihilating a compensating mass—oh, no, annihilation took too much effort. That much they wouldn't do. He'd have to figure out how much they were creating and try to destroy enough things so that the priests wouldn't catch on; probably have to ask for help from the other elders—fat lot of help they'd be; some of them could barely create, never mind annihilate.

"For the sins of rancor and the sins of pride. Together."

He was hungry again, and again he elevated the carbohydrate level in his bloodstream by some judicious synthesis. Look at them! They overdo it all the time. He searched out the worst offenders and modulated their digestive hormones so that they would really feel the pangs of the morning fast.

"For the sins of gluttony and the sins of spite."

"For the sins of gluttony and the sins of spite," the crowd repeated.

"For the sins of smugness and the sins of hypocrisy."

"For the sins . . ."

It was no easy job being an elder. You had Talent, and the priests picked you, and that was that. You had to watch yourself all the time so that the priest wouldn't catch you. He was ten times tougher on an elder than on the lesser Talented. Other youths of his age already had wives and were having children, but no, not Melthacton. Melthacton had to wait for a genetically suitable mate—a young female elder from some other village. Or an old bag of a widow like that bitch from Kolum, the village fifty miles south. She had shamed him and laughed at him for his youth and inexperience. He stood it for three days and returned to the village, without a wife. Demophon had a nice woman, though. If only he could tip him over a bit— blood pressure or immune system—it was all Demophon could do to keep himself alive, much less minister to a village. A little more time, a little more Talent, and he could do it without the priest's being able to detect it. Perhaps a brain clot. He needed more practice to get by Demophon's defenses. Time and patience. Time and patience. "For these sins forgive us. Together."

"For these sins forgive us."

"Your sins are forgiven in the name of the Holy Balance. Go and be cleansed; create no more. Will those of you who have a creation to confess come up to the dais to be judged and absolved."

The elders of lesser Talent took care of the little creations. It was only the guilt-ridden and the gross creators who sought out Melthacton. Always the sweaty jobs for him. Skinny Kega as usual was the first, confessing massive creations of boulders and other useless items, all of it imagined. As usual, Melthacton had to annihilate some air with a loud pop to maintain a sem-

194

blance of sanity in the old man. They created; he annihilated, judging their lies and trying to maintain the Balance. A stern lecture on the immorality of created foods and the superiority of natural growths. It was dull and thankless and took most of the morning.

With the completion of the sin judgments, the other elders were free to do as they wished, but Melthacton had to stay to arbitrate petty disputes, levy fines, and reward informers. Evening had come when he finished the work. There was only one supplicant left, a stranger to the village who had arrived the previous night. Melthacton impatiently asked what he was doing in these parts.

"I've come from the plateau village, by the lake north of here. I'm going to the town to find the priest."

"Have you no sender in your village?"

"No, Elder. We do not even have an elder or any lesser Talents."

"How do you live, then?"

"Game is plentiful. There are fish in the lake."

"Are you here to be absolved of your sins?"

"We cannot make the great sins, Elder. We have no Talent."

"Why are you here then? Why do you need a priest?"

"We've seen strange things on the plateau, Elder. Things that the priest should know about."

"Foolish man! If there is strangeness he will know about it without your telling him. What kind of strangeness?"

"It comes from the sky."

Melthacton was interested now. That was supposed to be a legend—oh, yes! How did it go—on the Day of Anger? "Protect us from the scourge from the sky. Avenge us from the scourge . . ." Something like that. The man was probably balmy, but if there was some truth to it, Melthacton could possibly use it to advantage. If it was real and he could claim the discovery, it might convince the priest that he had enough Talent to be accepted as an acolyte. Or maybe the priest could claim the discovery for his own purposes and reward

195

Melthacton for letting *him* take the credit. Anything was possible. It was worth pursuing.

"Have you told anyone else about this?"

"I passed through the other village yesterday morning—the one with the crippled elder? But he wouldn't talk to me until today. I decided not to wait and pushed on to here. No one else knows except the people in my village."

"How many days' travel is it from here?"

"Four days, Elder. Four days up and three back. The escarpment is hard to climb."

Sarpedon was not due to return for ten days. It would be time enough to go to the man's village and investigate. He probed the man as deeply as he could and could find no trace of lying. Whatever there was up on the escarpment, the man believed in it. "It is not yet a matter for the priest," Melthacton pronounced. "You are to say nothing about this to anyone. We will go to your village in the morning."

"Welcome, young Melthacton," the crippled elder greeted him expansively. "What brings you to Demophon's poor village?"

"I'm going to arbitrate a family matter," he lied, "at Agsta village on the plateau, on behalf of my cousin Esus, here. We also have a few things to discuss between us, if you can spare the time."

Esus was directed to the common hut, while Melthacton accompanied the hobbling Demophon to his house. They maintained polite social chatter as a cover, Demophon trying to determine the real reason for the visit, and Melthacton trying to find some weakness in Demophon's psychic armor. Demophon was sure that Melthacton was lying, but he could not penetrate the younger man's defenses. He had probed Esus also, but found the memory either wiped out or suppressed. Melthacton had done it, that was obvious; it was a clear sin, and Demophon was sure he would be able to use the fact to his advantage.

Demophon's woman was as attractive as ever. A cautious inquiry showed her to be not averse to Melthacton's advances—if he could overthrow her husband. She was not pleased with the idea of being married to a cripple, who, Melthacton gathered from her hints, was deficient in more than his limbs.

"You said," the cripple reminded him after they had finished the meal, "that there were things to talk about."

"Yes," Melthacton replied. "It's about the stream. It's dried up below your village."

"It has merely gone underground, young Elder. A man of energy could bring it back easily enough."

"It's not a matter of ability, Elder, but justice. It is for the one that diverted the stream to restore it to its proper place."

"Demophon does not waste time submerging streams for pleasure. It is a natural thing. I would be pleased to help you return it if you cannot do it yourself."

"I insist that it's a matter of justice, not nature. I have sensed it!"

"Oh, yes, I was," the cripple admitted, "extracting copper from a vein about a thousand feet down. This could have caused a disturbance which resulted in the stream's going underground. But that was accidental. It is a nature matter, you see, and not a justice matter. I still extend my help."

"I don't need your help. But I can't return the stream without destroying the evidence of your tampering. It is a justice matter, and the priest will decide when he comes."

They had reached an impasse, so the conversation continued in a lighter and more polite vein as a cover for their mutual probings. It was past midnight when the cripple began to weaken, giving Melthacton an opportunity to examine his defenses. He had not intended to act yet. His Talent was still too weak. But the tired older man had slipped, giving Melthacton an oppor-

197

tunity to create a small embolism—it might as well be now. He waded in and disturbed the clotting mechanism in one of the lesser cranial arteries—weaken him a bit first and then act outright. He was concentrating on building the clot when a sharp pain hit him in the chest. Breaking off, he found that he was undergoing a massive heart attack—the chemical balance in the nerves was totally askew and one heart valve was torn almost loose. It took all his effort to ward off the attack, reverse the chemistry, and patch things up enough to continue living. The old bastard had trapped him, sucked him in for the fun of it.

Demophon turned to his wife, who had been, with her limited perception but not without interest, following the contest: "Our young friend has had an attack of indigestion. He needs rest."

Pale and shaken, Melthacton allowed the woman to lead him to a couch in the guest room. She was laughing at him; he could sense that. It took hours to repair the damage and to erect new defenses; he had underestimated the cripple.

Outwardly urbane but inwardly seething at the humiliation, Melthacton took polite leave of Demophon the following morning with the uncomprehending Esus in tow. He could still sense Demophon's laughter well beyond the gates. Furious now, he lashed out in a savage thrust that severed the nerve that controlled the older man's colon. The cripple had not expected such an inconsequential and spiteful attack and had been taken by surprise. He quietly annihilated the mess with hardly a break in his inward laughter.

Esus, his memory restored, led the way up the escarpment and onto the plateau above. The huge lake that drained to the west in a series of waterfalls was barely visible at this distance. There were mountain peaks to the east; their melting snows fed the numerous streams and rivulets that fed the lake. It was a lush area, one in which non-Talents could live in comfort. Far to the north and high in the sky he saw a curious cloud, perfectly straight and very thin. Esus saw him looking at it and said that the strangers were making it. Melthacton could not sense that far, so it still remained a mystery to him.

During the two days it took to reach the village, Melthacton saw more of the strange clouds. They appeared to point toward a spot on the far side of the lake. The clouds formed quickly, starting from nothing and extending in a long finger, only to stop abruptly. Melthacton noticed that shortly after the clouds had stopped growing he could hear the sound of thunder far above, but there was no storm. They would have to go to the other side of the lake. "How long will it take to get there?" he asked Esus, who replied that the trip would take two days on foot or one by boat.

They reached the hamlet in the late afternoon. Although tired and grimy from the hard journey, Melthacton performed the absolution ritual. Afterward he gathered the "elders" and requested a boat. They objected because all their serviceable boats would be in use the next day, the fishing day. Angry over their refusal, which Melthacton reasoned was caused more by fright than by need, he filled their cooking pots with created protein and announced that they would be taking him to the other side of the lake in the morning. They were uneasy about eating the created food, so he had to waste still more time absolving them of this sin, pointing out that the special circumstances justified the creation. After he had dramatically annihilated the greater part of the communal privy, the villagers, now more frightened of Melthacton than of the strangeness on the other side of the lake, agreed to take him.

There was a brisk wind, which, having originated at the other end of the lake, had beaten the water into choppy waves to which the small, round-bottomed boat responded with sickening regularity. Melthacton fought the sickness, induced partly by the choppiness but more by the residual stench of decaying fish, which the fisherman had, without notable success, tried to eradicate. The bile seemed to well up, again and again, in synchrony with the rocking of the boat; he ended that by annihilating his breakfast, only to discover the greater discomfort of dry heaves. He cleansed the boat at a considerable expense of mental energy, but that did nothing for the rhythmic tilting of the horizon. He tried levitating, so that at least he was stationary with respect to the water, but now he had to suffer the independent rocking of the boat beneath him and its continuous sliding out from under him. He gave it up, resigned to misery, and sat facing the stern, hoping for a quick end to life or to the trip, whichever might come first.

They beached the boat. Melthacton jumped ashore, thankful for the end of the torture. He had momentarily forgotten the strangeness that had brought him there and was surprised that none of the villagers had left the boat. He turned back, no longer the miserable landlubber, and exhorted them to join him. A few timidly left the safety of the boat and followed him. Halfway up the small lip of the lake, the thunder came again, the first of the day, much louder and nearer than ever before. The villagers ran back to the boat, afraid to accompany him farther. He probed them and found that more threats would be useless; they would not go. He commanded them, at the risk of a priest's wrath, to remain by the shore until he returned.

The terrain leveled out into a flat plain beyond the lake's lip. He climbed the low rise to reconnoiter the place. There was activity below. The fields were scarred, laid bare to the earth, in a long, flat strip. There were strangers below and strange machines, which were pushing back the dirt, filling depressions, and cutting down the hillocks. At the nearer end of the strip he could see another wonder—a smoking, birdlike, blunt thing, which emitted a combined whine and growl. The growling stopped, followed shortly thereafter by the disappearance of the whine. The thing had been dragged down the strip. Melthacton could tell because of a fresh gouge in the earth that terminated at its tail. He could hear voices but could not make out what they were saying. He tried to probe them, but got no response at all. He was sure he was in range.

He continued observing them cautiously as he approached. The thing had been dragged off the strip now by one of the machines, and the gouge was being filled in by another. He could see the people distinctly now; they were not of his world. Their features were arranged in a different way, and their limbs had the wrong proportions, and they were small, very small, as little as children.

He was close now, and he had a headache. The sun, he thought. He probed again, and again got a blank, but his headache worsened despite the remedial blocks he had set up. He was about to launch a strong probe when the thunder came again. There was a fresh white streak in the sky that he had not noticed. The thundering increased, coming from the far end of the strip. The sun flashed, momentarily reflected from the huge birdcraft that was now landing, the sound louder than ever. It hit the strip, bounced, and gouged its way down, coming to rest where the other aircraft had previously been. They had come from the sky, as in the legend. Melthacton launched his strongest probe and was almost destroyed by the fury of the response. Staggering, blinded, his skull seeming to split, he ran back in the direction he had come. The little ones below, unmindful of his presence, continued in their purposeful activity.

He retreated to the lake's lip and restored his composure. His vision had cleared, and his headache was gone. He was afraid, but he launched another strong probe, this time weaker, but still strong enough to give him a new headache. The boatmen were in a daze. With no defenses, even at this distance, they had been sorely discomfited by the backlash. They rowed back to the village, quiet and grim.

"This isn't some ill-conceived acolyte's joke?" the angry priest muttered.

"Our most sensitive Talents discerned it in a linkup, holy Sarpedon. There are also confirmations coming in from other priests. Surely you must have sensed it yourself, Holiness?" replied the senior postulant, who was on his knees before the priest.

"Yes. Yes. Of course I sensed it myself, but I had to test you. It's quite serious and must be attended to immediately. Can the other priests be reached with clarity?"

"No, Holiness. The confirmations are too vague for that—they're mostly emotions, not facts. If a clear message is needed, we'll have to send runners."

"All right, Felapton. Get up. And thank you for the warning. Um—write out this message—to be delivered immediately:

"To my holy brothers in the faith, blah, blah, blah, chief priest of the town, city, whatnot of blah, blah, blah, conserver of creation and dispenser of justice, blah, blah, blah, et cetera, et cetera:

"Know that we have discovered indications of a possible invasion by the legendary hosts—no, change that—I could be made to look like a fool. Know that phenomena of a previously unknown nature have been detected in the vicinity of Lake Agsta. At present it is suspected that these are manifestations of grossly blasphemous utilizations of Talent. I am proceeding to Agsta Hamlet to investigate and to dispense justice on the offenders. In the name of Balance, righteousness, and the Ultimate Creator, I entreat you to maintain maximum watchfulness should this turn out to be even more serious. The evidence will be described to you by the bearer, to whom you should relay corroborating facts, if any. Thank you, et cetera.

"You might make it more diplomatic, Felapton, and perhaps include an appropriate personalized note. Send it to Brothers Tsaphon, Gwydion, Wakodon, and, of course, the bishop. Write it over for the bishop, will you? The proper amount of humility and obeisance. Don't use any Talents for messengers, except for the bishop. Send—uh—Daxhbogon to the bishop. He doesn't have much Talent and he does grovel well, doesn't he?"

"He grovels most excellently, Holiness."

"Good. Good. I want the ten best Talents and yourself to accompany me to Agsta first thing tomorrow."

"Permit me, Holiness, but you are not due to visit the northern villages for another two days. Leaving early would mean missing a judgment day in town. You also have appointments and the final examination for the acolytes. It will grievously disturb the schedule."

"The junior acolytes can handle the judgments. The supplicants can wait until we return. And, I fear, the final examination may be held in the field. Don't waste any more time—there's too much to do."

"Yes, Holiness. Uh—uh—there is one more thing about the preparations—what provisions should we take?" Felapton asked uncertainly. He could not suggest outright that a body of Talents set out on a holy mission with the intention of sinning by the deliberate use of created supplies. On the other hand, if the party, which with all its attendants would number at least thirty, was to leave the next day, there would be no time to prepare supplies. Felapton had phrased the question ambiguously in order to leave the priest some maneuvering room. The priest understood his intent and returned an equally vague but nevertheless clear answer.

"Let each man obtain provisions en route by the most effective means," which meant, "Let each man synthesize his own needs and those of his slaves, but don't let me catch you at it or know about it."

203

"I understand, Holiness."

"You always do, Felapton. You will make a good priest someday." And Sarpedon thought, You would have long ago except that you have ability, Talent, and loyalty, none of which I can afford to lose. Besides, Sarpedon knew that the arrangements suited Felapton, who would rather be the senior postulant and right hand of a powerful priest than to be himself a minor priest in some backwater village. When Sarpedon became the new bishop, it would be time enough to elevate Felapton to the priesthood as chief priest over the town; the town. The town as usual was a mess. The evening Talents had not yet gone out to annihilate the sewage which even now ran along the gutters, adding its stench to that of the accumulated garbage. It was a fact of nature that creation was so much easier than annihilation—enough so that despite the concentration of Talent in the priesthood and the elders, they appeared to be slipping behind. He looked across the square from the window of his chamber to the decaying buildings—easier to recreate than to repair—and why bother, since they were empty anyway? If only we could accumulate enough annihilation credits to clear out a few more buildings and widen the square as his predecessor had done! But the garbage and the filth had to come first, leaving nothing over for aesthetics.

As bishop he would outlaw the use of Talent altogether. Elevate it from a mere sin to blasphemy (except in the service of the Balance, of which he would be minister), thin out the town. Force them to be more dependent on grown food. Why, he had seen a few town folk so lazy as to have let their teeth rot out—synthesizing everything in their own bloodstream, they couldn't eat now if they wanted to. Go back to the essentials of the religion. It would be a long night. Longer by minutes, the records showed, than it had been a few centuries ago, so much additional mass had the planet accumulated. And a long day also, and warm. It was always warm, or hot; it had been cooler when he was young.

Melthacton pressed on to his village. He avoided Demophon's place, for there was no time for another bout with the sly cripple. He had mixed feelings when he came to the stream. It was running again, and he was glad of that, but Demophon's hand was all over it, and he was furious over the planned humiliation. Exhausted, barely able to walk after his exertions of the past days, he stumbled along the path home where he could commandeer a litter to carry him to the town.

The village was just in sight when the gates opened to reveal a procession en route to the escarpment. Felapton, swinging his ceremonial mace, was followed by Sarpedon, who was being carried on a litter by four slaves. Sarpedon was levitating, as much to show his power as to ease the slave's load. Melthacton, in a last burst, raced up to the priest and prostrated himself. "Welcome, Holiness, in the name of the Balance—" he began.

"Skip the ritual greetings," the priest interrupted. "You've just come from the north in a great hurry. From Agsta?"

"Yes, Holiness."

The priest motioned to the litter bearers to let him down. He examined the young elder and adjusted his endocrine system to alleviate, at least temporarily, his exhaustion. A night's rest and he would be fully recovered. "We are going to Agsta, and I would have you return there with me. We may need all the available Talent. Tell me what you found up there."

Melthacton related the entire episode, except for his bout with Demophon. Felapton was still leading the procession, and under the priest's direction the rest of the troop had fallen back so that Sarpedon could question the elder privately. When Melthacton had described the strange ships, the crew, and the other activities, the priest called to Felapton to arrange for runners to be sent back to town so that the latest developments could be relayed to the other priests and the bishop.

It was late in the afternoon when they reached Demophon's village. The cripple, who had been forewarned, met them at the gate and offered his obeisance and hospitality. Sarpedon sensed the hostility between the two elders, and upon seeing Demophon's wife, he understood what was behind it. The young elder needed a woman of Talent. The cripple had one who was attractive enough to excite even the priest, and Balance knows a priest had an unlimited choice of Talented women. Damn the genetic accident that so often linked Talents with sterility—and doubly damn the rule that forbade a high Talent from marrying a lesser Talent. He hoped the rancor between the elders would not jeopardize their mission. He intended to take both of them along.

The priest dispensed with the ceremonials of the procession the following morning by giving the litter to Demophon. He continued partial levitation and did what he could to reduce the exhaustion of the group. They pushed on in a forced march, making the three-day trip in two days. The villagers, though frightened, had continued observing events on the other side of the lake. They reported increased activity, more landing, more equipment, and more aliens, whose population now exceeded that of Agsta. Sarpedon wasted no time at Agsta and was rowed across early the next day in the first boat. The rest of the group was relayed across throughout the morning.

He crested the rise, and from the same cover that Melthacton had used, he stared at an incredible sight. What had been described to him as a strip of cleared earth had now been replaced by a uniform smooth slab of white stone. It was not possible, even by creation, and yet at the near end of the huge strip there were even now strange carts that moved in a phalanx, like farmers harvesting grain; they gobbled up the dirt in front of them and deposited the white stone in their wake. The slab was thick, thicker than any sensible need for a road or for the foundations of a building. It was madness and without any purpose that he could discern.

Felapton joined him. "Is it the scourge?" he asked.

"It can be nothing else," the priest said. "Send another runner to the bishop. I'm afraid this is too much for one town priest and a few dozen Talents."

"Have they been here before?"

"No, Felapton. But the warnings of their coming have been with us from the beginnings of our history. It is part of a priest's initiation. It is a stricture even more important than the Balance. In fact, what we shall do now is the one thing contrary to the Balance that is entirely free from sin. It is the greatest blessing of all."

"I'm confused by the contradictions, Holiness."

"Be at ease, Felapton, the bishop will utter dispensation when he comes, as will the Archate."

"They're coming here?"

"Undoubtedly. Unless they think me a complete fool."

"It will take weeks for them to get here. What do we do in the meantime?"

"Wait, watch, probe."

With this, he began a sensitive probe of the aliens. He could feel nothing but a strong distaste for the process. He increased the intensity and got the expected headache. He further increased his efforts, despite the pain. He fixed on one of the nearer aliens and concentrated on him, holding the intensity of the probe at the threshold of his own ability to endure pain. He was tiring and getting nowhere. In frustration, he loosed a sharp blast, which was returned to him, magnified, rendering him almost unconscious. When his vision cleared, he saw Felapton lying next to him. He revived the unconscious aide, and together they stumbled to the lakeshore, where groggy men were recovering from the alien's counterattack.

The porters arrived in the evening, arranged by the ever-thoughtful Felapton. Demophon, also not one to endure the field in discomfort, had set up tents and facilities for himself and his small entourage. Melthacton had not had time to arrange a baggage train for himself, so he had to share a tent with the acolytes— it was humiliating.

Sarpedon issued strict orders that no one disturb the aliens until the bishop and Archate arrived. Recovered from the previous day's painful experience, rested and well fed, he decided to continue his observations alone. There had been no more landings since the priest had arrived. The craft that had landed before and the machines they had disgorged were ranged neatly alongside the near end of the strip. The purposeful activity had stopped. The little aliens were lounging about, squatting together in small circles, playing games and otherwise relaxing. He tried another probe and found that his own discomfort was proportional to his effort. He attempted to communicate with them but got nothing in return.

At noon, with the sun directly overhead, he caught a glimpse of one of the clouds that had been described to him. There was no thunder. The cloud elongated quickly before it disappeared. He had been tracking its tip and could just see the craft that had made the track. Following it down, with occasional assistance from reflected sunlight, he kept it in sight until it disappeared over the horizon beyond the far end of the strip. He continued to look in that direction. Within a minute he saw a spot crest a far hill and blossom into something immense. The sound of rushing air reached him. The new craft was monstrous—a mountain hurling itself at incredible speed against the smooth stone of the strip. It hit the ground, producing a series of shrieks, bounced up, hit again, and continued to grow as it approached, more slowly now. It came to rest at the near end, wheels smoking, nose glowing, and dropping charred material on the immaculate strip. It tinkled and crackled as it cooled.

Despite the height of his lookout point, he was level with the top of the craft. It had a small window on each side of a minuscule projection that spoiled the otherwise smooth lines of the thing. He could see an alien through the window. The alien turned and waved to *him*. The big ship lumbered off the strip, moving under its own power, and was parked alongside the now dwarfed craft that had preceded it. Its nose was pointed toward him. Ramps were let down and hatches opened. More machines came down the ramps, accompanied by even more aliens. He counted three hundred of them now, and who knew how many were within the ship? They set to work immediately, enlarging the strip, using larger versions of the machines that had created it originally. Buildings, which had a discomforting look of permanence, began to go up on the other side of the strip. Another hour passed, and another monster craft had landed.

By nightfall six of the monsters had come to the ground, disgorging a population of tiny aliens greater than that of the town. The stone pouring continued through the night, and another strip, narrower this time, was laid alongside the original. Sarpedon wondered if this was merely the preface to the construction of an even greater field of stone intended to service craft of such immensity as to dwarf the newcomers in the same proportions that the monsters dwarfed their predecessors.

They used artificial lights as bright as the sun to illuminate the scene to the level of daylight. Some kind of continuously created energy, he thought. His own camp by the lakeshore had grown as well. A makeshift arrangement of tents and huts, half of Agsta's boats and population now fishing for the camp, advance parties sent out by the other priests—a motley, disorganized, purposeless rabble compared to the aliens on the other side.

The next day he looked down upon a small city of aliens. There was no more building by the strip, but the machines were now pushing a road toward the hills at the rate a person could walk. The road was straight and level, ignoring the dips and rises by filling the former and annihilating the latter. More Talent, more blasphemy, although the aliens did not seem to have as much trouble with the Talent as they did. It occurred to him that with the awesome display of energy control that he was witnessing these aliens might be impossible to destroy. But the legends were clear. Clearer and more specific than any other ancient writings. They were, in some way he had not yet discovered, pitfully vulnerable. They were destroyers, but they could be destroyed with impunity—if only he could find out how. He resolved then to go down among them.

Sarpedon left his omnipresent assistant on the hill to observe and stand by if needed. He went down to the aliens. They were small, like children, and only half his height. They were squat, and their joints moved in unfamiliar places and through strange angles. The faces were almost normal, if you ignored the large eyes, the tiny, probably nonfunctional nostrils. Most disturbing was the mouth. The fleshy lips hid a cavernous (in the proportions of the tiny face) red maw, lined with a row of teeth, top and bottom, that would have been a credit to the fiercest of the planet's long-departed predators. They had aggressive hands with claws that were unseemly in an intelligent race. He took the fleshy protuberances on the sides of their heads to be some kind of ears, similar to those of a small rodent's. They were mammalian, no doubt about that, despite the unfamiliar arrangement (the shameless nakedness of the females allowed such observations); the two organs in question made up in size for what they lacked in numbers.

They wore few clothes but were profusely decorated. He doubted that such a diversity of skin coloration and pattern was natural. Males and females worked at interchangeable tasks, worked subordinate to each other with no concern for the importance of the specialized roles ordained to each sex.

He walked among them, and they ignored him. They

knew he was there, for if he stepped in their way, they moved aside for him. Some made openhanded gestures, directed at him; he did not understand their meaning. These were accompanied by speech and threatening facial gestures involving bared teeth. He was allowed to wander in the complex without restraint—except once, when he stood by a large machine and was hurriedly urged aside, avoiding what would have been personal destruction if he had persisted. He returned to the camp more puzzled than ever. Whatever their purpose, they did not seem to intend to harm him personally—if he did not use Talent—in fact, and more galling, they seemed intent on ignoring him.

They did not ignore him on the third day of his wandering among them. He came down the hill, crossed the strip, and was greeted by a trio of the little aliens, who indicated by signs that they wanted him to follow them. He was led to a room without windows or furniture, except for two seats—one large and one small. He was told to sit in the larger seat. He had been led through a series of doors, all of which had been closed behind him. The little alien left him—he had allowed himself to be trapped. He was on the verge of panic and could not suppress a defensive probe; nothing happened. No response, no pain. He tried creation. It was normal. Mystified, he found that in this room his Talents worked normally and others were nullified.

A door opened and an alien entered. He could not be sure of its sex, since, as he had noted earlier with interest, both males and females had breasts, although they were much smaller and possibly vestigial in the males. This one was old, very old. He was sure of it. He could tell by the slow, dignified walk and by the care with which it positioned itself in the opposite chair. The head fur was long and white, and, he assumed from the small breasts and the fact that this one was considerably taller than the others, that it was a leader or some notable in a position of authority. He addressed it telepathically. The response was immediate and unmistakably female, yet it had a clarity

211

that he had previously experienced only in a great Talent such as the bishop's.

"You'll find," she told him, "that your abilities are normal. I am here to welcome you and to explain that which needs explanation."

"Are you a leader?" he asked. The thought of a female in such a role was as incredible as it was distasteful, but everything else about these aliens was strange, so why not female leaders?

"No," she said, "I'm no leader. I'm just an old woman with nothing better to do. The others have neither the time nor the inclination to talk to you."

"I want to talk to a leader!" the priest insisted.

"You'll have to make do with me, I'm afraid. There are no leaders such as you want. It's me, or if you want to wait a bit, one of the children."

Sarpedon was furious at the insult. He probed the old woman, attempting to pierce the center of her psyche, but there was nothing there. He calmed down and methodically tested his powers. They were intact. He examined her. She was frail and defenseless, and she did nothing to counter his probes.

At last she stopped his examination. "Are you quite through? It's not very comfortable, you know, even though I have been through it before. It's no fun having an alien mucking about in your head!"

"Who are you?" he asked. "What do you want?"

"We come from space," she said. "We're here to get food and supplies. We'll leave when we're through."

"But you're destroying the Balance. Blaspheming by your wanton creations!"

"Ah," she said, "the Balance. It's always something like that, isn't it? 'The Balance,' or 'Equality,' or the 'Holy Equipoise,' or something nonsensical like that. Now don't get all excited. It's important to you, as well it should be. But we aren't going to upset your energy Balance—we can't. We don't create or annihilate—and by the time we figured out how to do those tricks we found out that it wasn't a very good idea in the first place."

"You only *use* energy?" It was more of an accusation than a question.

"Something like that. In fact, we don't have any of your abilities. We're not even telepathic."

Sarpedon understood now. "You are *man!*"

"Yes."

He lashed out with the most destructive psychic blast he could generate, simultaneously attempting to annihilate the entire room and especially the female obscenity in front of him. Nothing happened.

"You can't harm us that way, you know," she said, "but don't try that sort of thing outside this room. It would probably kill you and your friends. I have to warn you about that so you can warn the others."

Sarpedon was angry at the multiple humiliation of being treated like a child, by a woman, who thought that Talent was inconsequential. "We destroyed you in the past," he boasted, "and will again."

"Not you, Holy Sarpedon. Not you and not your race. In your legends and myths, but not in reality. We have never harmed your race, and except in self-defense we never shall. You have no reason to hate us, nor we you. Your hatred comes from a telepathic message that your race received thousands of years ago. A signal that continues to reverberate around the galaxy. A signal that was re-enforced when you went through your space-faring stage and visited with other telepathic races. A dimly received, ill-understood, and wasteful message—its reasons and meanings and origins are unknown to you." She told him of man's history and of the holocaust in which they had lived, of being hunted and destroyed, of not being able to evade the myths and dark legends. Sarpedon, with increased knowledge and understanding, began to believe that it was as these aliens said—that they intended no harm. However, he was still suspicious.

"If it is you say, why are you not afraid of us now? How did you dare to land here?"

"You can't harm us now. There isn't enough Talent on the entire planet to be more than an annoyance.

213

When you were at your height, we would not have dared. Both of us would have died. In your senescence it doesn't matter."

"But why now?"

"This is a convenient planet for us. We need supplies. When we last came here, you were too strong. That was about four or five hundred years ago. You could still have reached other races such as yours and caused thereby wholesale destruction of this world and others. It wasn't worth it to us. This time we are in need, you are impotent, and we are here."

"There is still much Talent here," he said.

"Give it up, Sarpedon. How much Talent? Three hundred years ago you had many cities and a population of hundreds of millions. Now only a hundred thousand, most of whom have no Talent except the useless one of creation. Talent, as you have undoubtedly found out, as so many other races have learned before you, is genetically self-destructive. Breeding for it is breeding for sterility and racial senescence. In three hundred years your Talent will be gone. In three hundred and fifty the pitiful few who remain will revert to total barbarism. In five hundred or a thousand years you'll be extinct. Your races are short-lived—brilliant as shooting stars you rise from stone age to the peak of civilization and back down again in a few thousand years, and it's all tied up to the Talent."

"How long?" he asked incredulously.

"I'm not really sure," she said, "but we live long enough for some of us—me, for instance—to have seen it happen personally. If you don't want to take an old woman's word for it, you might be interested in the records of your own history. You're headed for extinction."

"And there is nothing to be done for it?"

"Could you give up creating energy? Could you start using it instead? Could you willingly breed for fertility and vitality instead of Talent? Could you build a technology and risk the ostracism of your fellow races? If

214

you could do that, all of that, eventually you would become another kind of Man if you survived."

"Has it ever happened?"

"Perhaps. We don't know for sure."

"Can you help us to change?"

"Yes, but we don't."

"I don't understand."

"It's a question of respecting the right of a fellow being to engage in whatever self-destructive foolishness he wishes, so long as it doesn't interfere with others. We don't interfere with other races except to protect ourselves. If one of us wants to be recycled, whether young or old, no one will stop him. Death is an ultimate right and the ultimate (if stupid) act of free will." She pointed vaguely overhead. "I've got a lot of shipmates who think that I should be recycled—should have been years ago. But not one of them would shove me into a converter against my will—unless, of course, I couldn't get about any more. If I represent no danger to my ship and consume no more than my just due, then I may live without interference. So it is between you and us. We will not harm you or allow you to harm us, but neither will we interfere with your own destiny, happy or sad, whatever it may be."

"And if we changed and didn't die?"

"We would destroy the traces of our base here immediately and quit this planet forever. But your races never change. They never have." With this pronouncement she terminated the interview. The doors were opened again and Sarpedon was led back into the brilliant sunshine, ignored by the aliens once again.

Sarpedon did not go back to the aliens' complex. He stayed in his tent brooding, confiding only in Felapton what he had learned. The Talent was sterility linked. They had been given a choice between Talent and fertility and had chosen Talent. Yet the aliens said that it could be reversed, and from his own knowledge he knew it to be so. He did not precisely know what had set the races against Man—she had not told him, nor would she—but he was sure that they would have to face similar ostracism and risk. It was, in his estimation, better than extinction, and to that end he dedicated himself. He told the other priests of his experience and tried to convince them of what he had learned. Neither priests nor bishops accepted his position, and each one in turn went down to the aliens, but none of them was invited into the small room. Without personal corroboration, and because they were suspicious of the aliens' ability to nullify their Talent, the priests reserved judgment, awaiting the arrival of the Archate. They believed only the fact that the aliens were Man, of the legend.

The Archate arrived, resplendent in his trappings, surrounded by a concentration of Talent equal to that which already crowded the camp. He established himself at the center and held numerous conferences with the bishops, spending as much time on routine clerical matters as on the issue that had brought him there. He was a political Archate rather than one of great Talent and could not forgo the opportunity to entrench himself further in his position. He wasted no time with mere priests, except for Sarpedon, whom he questioned for a day. They referred to a transcript of his experiences with the aliens that had been pieced from what he had been saying to the other priests and bishops before the Archate had arrived. When he was through, he was allowed to read the manuscript. It was free of bias, consistent, and, on the whole, it was a more eloquent presentation of his case than he could have made himself. At the end of the interview he was told to drop all his defenses so that a team of experts could probe him in depth. Their examination confirmed the truth of his beliefs, and they could find no evidence of tampering by the aliens.

"Do you confirm this manuscript as your position?" the Archate asked as a matter of form.

"It is, Holiness."

"Have you anything to add, to say to me, that you have withheld from your brothers?"

"No, Holiness, it is complete."

"Have you suppressed anything in your memory or your mind?"

"I am open, Holiness."

"You are dismissed then."

The next day the Archate with his entourage went down the hill to visit the aliens. It was a large group and would have disrupted the aliens' activities if they had not been escorted. The first road, to the mountains, was out of sight, and in the foothills more buildings could be seen. A large pipe had been laid to the lake. It terminated in a half-submerged structure, its function as mysterious as the rest. The building activity had now stopped, and the aliens appeared to be using the facilities for their intended purpose. The Archate sought and found the building where Sarpedon's education had taken place. He shouted to the aliens telepathically, demanding a confirmation and an explanation. The aliens responded by leading him into the room, where he sat for hours, feeling foolish, while no alien came to give him what had been granted to a town priest. He returned angrily to his quarters by the lake and called a meeting of all Talents.

"This is Man of legend," he told them. "They offer us a choice of joining in their blasphemies or dying. Perhaps it is as they say. However, we have always been able to destroy their evil in the past, and I do not doubt our ability to do so now. They have spoken with only one person, a priest of lesser Talent, little fame, but much ambition. His story has been confirmed as absolute truth by all methods known to us, but their powers are not inconsequential. I do not doubt that they have the ability to twist the truth or to implant seeming truth in the mind of one weak priest—why else would they have refused to communicate with anyone else? Why else except that falsehood cannot be consistent and they cannot take the risk of lying in such depth to more than one of us? They have weapons,

217

powerful weapons, and can cause us great discomfort and possibly death. But the records are clear and their actions confirm them, and this Man is vulnerable. They are bluffing. This is the greatest confluence of Talent ever assembled—they cannot prevail over us. Evil is, and is to be destroyed. Rest now, conserve your powers for tomorrow."

Sarpedon remained in the center of the camp after the others had returned to their tents. He went to the Archate's quarters for a final attempt to convince him of the inherent folly of his plan. He was met by an adjunct bishop, the Archate's secretary. "You have presented your case many times before," he told Sarpedon. "The Archate left explicit instructions concerning you. There is nothing more you can say."

Sarpedon turned away and walked up the lip of the lake and down to the aliens, who were busy as ever and unconcerned. They seemed to be making no preparations for the coming battle. He found the building and sat outside its door in hope of a final conversation. An alien recognized him at dawn and hurried off. He returned with the old woman, who caused the door to be opened. Sarpedon was led back to the room. They took their places as before.

"What do you want?" she asked, obviously annoyed.

"Only that you tell the Archate, the others, what you have told me. They intend to destroy you."

"We know what they will attempt. It's the tragedy of races such as yours. As for telling the others, we have said it once, to one well equipped by the standards of his society to relate it to others and convince them if possible."

"But I am not the best for this task. A bishop would have been more effective, or the Archate himself."

"I'm just one old woman, and I tire easily. The rest of us have neither the time nor the interest to talk with you. You would have me repeat everything to the Archate and expect him to be convinced of the truth. All I would be convincing him of was our ability to manipulate your minds. The trouble is, Sarpedon, that they don't disbelieve you. They do believe you and that's the reason they will act the way they will. If we can't convince them with the truth, what can we convince them with?"

"A demonstration?"

"Haven't we been doing that since we got here? If the backlash of your own Talent isn't a demonstration, what is?"

"Must they be destroyed?"

"If not today, then tomorrow. Look at their choices—the true choices. To change themselves into the image of something they hate—us—or die trying to destroy us. For them, it's a choice between death in one form or in another. Say we minimize the power of the backlash, and your entire priesthood gets off with a splitting headache. And tomorrow they try again without success. Then they decide to scoff at the nullification of Talent, and they create conventional weapons and attack with them, with no effect, for the most part, except that some of us and some of you die. So we quit this planet, destroy all traces of our coming, and the priesthood declares a victory. The jubilation is great, and it reaches out to other worlds—the legend is confirmed by your death throes, because that's what it is. And in a few hundred more years there are no more priests or bishops or Archates, only savages with Talent, and soon they too are gone. So you see, Sarpedon, today or five hundred years from now, it matters little to us—only the waste is to be mourned."

"You could convince them—you could change their minds."

"That would be interference. We don't interfere with other races' destiny."

"But you have interfered. Your coming here *is* interference. The legend, whatever its reason, is interference. You are responsible. Don't you care what happens to us?"

She considered his accusation and his question and weighed them against aeons of suffering at the hands

219

of races such as his, and she replied, "No. Not really." With that, she stood abruptly, strode out the door, leaving a grieving Sarpedon locked in behind her.

Melthacton girded himself for the attack, constructing such defenses as he was able. He stood, not far from Demophon and his woman. The Archate and the bishops stood on a platform overlooking the aliens' city. The Archate raised his hands to give the signal. The hands came down and Melthacton hurled his full psychic strength, not at the aliens, but at the cripple, who immediately collapsed. He had just enough time to recognize his success before his defenses were demolished by a coruscating, white, searing pain that turned his brain and much of his body back into basic proteins.

Sarpedon remained locked in the room for hours. The room had shielded him from the blind fury of the priesthood's attack, but not from his knowledge of the aliens' retaliation. He sat for hours more, grieving, and at last the ancient woman came and wordlessly released him from imprisonment and sanctuary. She led him outdoors, into the still bright light of the setting sun. A thin thread of smoke curled up from the platform on the hill. She stood next to him, looking at it. He dropped to his knees in grief, and for the first time she touched him—a thin, wrinkled hand smoothing back the thatch of coarse fur on his head. He rose and walked to the hill. Sarpedon threaded his way past the corpses. The charred remains of the Archate were recognizable only by the glint of the fused metallic portions of his vestments. They were all dead; all dead, even Felapton, who had waited for him on the hill.

There was no one left alive in the camp to row him back to Agsta. There would be no one to accompany him on the long trek to the city where he would now take up the Archate's work. A city denuded of Talent. He rowed across the lake, not yet daring to levitate, and not wanting to. He saw a great ship rise majestically to the stars on a plume of controlled thunder and an inconceivable display of energy. He thought about the aliens, the little evil ones, our nemeses between the stars. They had protected *him*—Sarpedon. He was alive and going back to the city, he thought as he watched the rocket go out of sight. He had been saved, he had survived. "They cared. They cared. At least they cared a little."

ABOUT THE AUTHOR

Ethan I. Shedley was born in Brussels and raised in the United States. He was educated at City College of New York and received his M.S. and Ph.D. from the University of Pennsylvania, majoring in physics, engineering, and computer science. He lives with his wife and two children in eastern Pennsylvania.

NEW FROM POPULAR LIBRARY

CLASSIC BESTSELLERS
from FAWCETT BOOKS

☐ **PROBLEMS**   24360 $2.95
    by John Updike

☐ **THE WIND**   04579 $2.25
    by Dorothy Scarborough

☐ **THE FAMILY MOSKAT**   24066 $2.95
    by Isaac Bashevis Singer

☐ **THE GHOST WRITER**   24322 $2.75
    by Philip Roth

☐ **ALL QUIET ON THE WESTERN FRONT**   23808 $2.50
    by Erich Maria Remarque

☐ **TO KILL A MOCKINGBIRD**   08376 $2.50
    by Harper Lee

☐ **SHOW BOAT**   23191 $1.95
    by Edna Ferber

☐ **THEM**   23944 $2.50
    by Joyce Carol Oates

☐ **THE FLOUNDER**   24180 $2.95
    by Gunter Grass

☐ **THE CHOSEN**   24200 $2.25
    by Chaim Potok

☐ **THE SOURCE**   23859 $2.95
    by James A. Michener

Buy them at your local bookstore or use this handy coupon for ordering.

COLUMBIA BOOK SERVICE (a CBS Publications Co.)
32275 Mally Road, P.O. Box FB, Madison Heights, MI 48071

Please send me the books I have checked above. Orders for less than 5 books must include 75¢ for the first book and 25¢ for each additional book to cover postage and handling. Orders for 5 books or more postage is FREE. Send check or money order only.

Cost $_____   Name _____

Sales tax*_____   Address _____

Postage_____   City _____

Total $_____   State _____ Zip _____

The government requires us to collect sales tax in all states except AK, DE, MT, NH and OR.

This offer expires 1 November 81   8130